Pranic, Pregnant, and Petrified

Karen Ranney

CHAPTER ONE

Bouncy Marcie here

"What do you mean can fangs show up on an ultrasound? Is this a joke?"

The woman on the phone did not sound happy.

"How did you get this number? This is a private line for fledging vampires. Who are you?"

I was left speechless by the nurse's rage.

"If you call here again I'll report this number to the authorities!"

Phones didn't make a resounding click anymore, but I could almost hear it as she hung up on me.

I thought it was a perfectly good question, plus it would make the situation so much easier. If the baby I was carrying was the child of a vampire, surely he'd have fangs. Wouldn't they show up on an ultrasound?

Since I didn't have anybody else to ask, I'd dug out the orientation materials I was given when I woke up in the VRC - the Vampire Resuscitation Center - and called the Nurse Helpline.

Some help she was.

In my human days - and I still cringe when talking about myself as human in the past tense - I was sitting in the ophthalmologist's office one afternoon. An older woman sitting beside me suddenly asked if I was married.

"No, I'm not."

I was expecting a speech on the sanctity of marriage, my age and the fact I was probably always going to be single, and other lectures. Instead, she only nodded.

"Do you have any children?"

I shook my head.

"Fantastic!" She grabbed my arm and squeezed. "You young people are planning your lives a lot better than we did."

Like hell.

Before I moved in with Bill, a relationship that only lasted for a few years and ended like a balloon with a slow leak, I'd already had a few relationships. I didn't hold a grudge when it was over. I didn't cling to something I knew wasn't going to work. I put the guy mentally on an ice floe. It wasn't always his fault we didn't mesh. Sometimes, you can like someone but hate them in a relationship. It's oil and water. Once out of the relationship, you're surprised by how nice he is. I'm sure that would apply to Bill, but I haven't seen him since I moved out of the house we shared. If two people are assiduously trying to avoid each other, it's easy to do in a city the size of San Antonio.

For someone who hasn't had all that many relationships, I've been on a roll lately. I'd been "with" Dan, a hunky, handsome former Ranger, and Maddock, a master vampire, the scourge of the earth, the most loathsome creature to be found in the universe. The former was most definitely consensual. The latter wasn't.

Frankly, I was out of my depth. My former life as a commercial insurance adjuster had not prepared me for turning into a vampire, learning I was a special kind of vampire called a Pranic vampire, further discovering I was a special, special kind of Pranic vampire which meant that I was on the level of a goddess.

Oh, and I'm pregnant.

Ergo, the call to the Fledging Vampires Nurse Help Line.

Twenty four hours had passed since I learned I was pregnant. I'd gone from being fecund to gravid in the blink of an eye.

Twice in the last two hours Dan had knocked on my door. The first message he'd left on my phone had been an angry one, but that had been yesterday evening. The subsequent messages had been a little more mellow, segueing to worried. I think someone in the kitchen told him I was okay since I'd ordered food. I hadn't offed myself or anything. I hadn't disappeared in a puff of vampire smoke. Since I could walk in the sun, I doubted that was going to be a problem. Since I was semi-immortal, how would I off myself, if I ever got to that point?

What would make me get to that point?

Carrying a child certainly wasn't it.

When I was human - there was that cringe again - I felt human. I acted human. I didn't suck blood and when my fangs did come down, I ended up with an ache in my jaw and a headache for two days. Anyway, BF - before fangdom - I'd wanted, very much, to have a child. Now I wasn't going to do anything to jeopardize this pregnancy.

In the intervening hours I'd barricaded myself in my room, figuratively speaking, and refused to answer the intercom, my phone, or the knocks on the door. The only time I'd escaped from my self-imposed prison was to take Charlie out twice.

Charlie has the bladder of a racehorse.

I begged kibble from the kitchen and they delivered it on a tray in a chrome dish along with my order: four slices of cheesecake, a pot of excellent coffee, and some chicken noodle soup. I was nursing my wounds.

I don't know how many people were employed here at the castle Cluckey's Fried Chicken built, but I bet it was more than twenty. Every single one of them seemed to have my comfort in mind. I've never seen one of the staff frown or look depressed or angry. Maybe I should ask one of them what their secret was and could I please have some.

I wasn't without company. I had Ophelia to talk to. Unfortunately, she had a tendency to wander in and out of Charlie at will. We would be talking along and all of a sudden I'd look over and Charlie would be fast asleep, his tail twitching spasmodically. I'd asked her once about the separation of powers. She said there were times when the dog was more dominant and times when the human spirit was. Evidently, when Charlie was tired, Opie had no choice but to go along with him.

Charlie was the golden retriever I've adopted, in a manner of speaking. He has an owner, a cruel man who will never see Charlie again if I have anything to say about it. Charlie also has a resident ghost. Her name is Ophelia, and she was a vet vampire my mother ran over, thinking she was me.

The more complicated my life gets, the more *boring* sounds better and better. Yet I had a feeling the minute I started bitching about my life, something else would happen to mess it up even further.

At the moment, I just wanted to be left alone. Not forever or even for a week. Just a day or two, until I got my bearings. I felt like one of those inflatable toys you got as a child. It had a clown's face and was weighted at the bottom. You punched it; it fell down but immediately bounced back up.

Bouncy Marcie, that's what I needed to be. Unfortunately, some of the punches had been pretty rough lately.

I had to tell someone about being pregnant, but I didn't know who. My grandmother was the first person who popped into my mind, followed by a thought I'd had only a few days earlier. Was Nonnie the reason I'd had two miscarriages in the past? After all, I was the product of a vampire and a witch. I shouldn't have lived. I imagine she didn't want me to procreate, either.

I hadn't exactly been polite to her last night, and I was still smarting from the guilt. She might not have been honest with me from the very beginning. She might have lied and given me spells, but I couldn't forget that she was my grandmother. I've been reared to respect my elders. So I would respect her, but I sure as hell wasn't going to trust her.

I had the feeling when I saw her last night at the round table discussion that my grandmother would willingly sacrifice me if it meant ensuring the safety and health of her coven.

Last night, when I'd gotten the news that I was going to be Marcie the Mommy, I'd bailed out of the witch meeting. Now I couldn't help but wonder what the consensus had been.

I looked down at Charlie who was eying the plastic bag of dog biscuits with a ravenous gleam in his eye. I trotted over to the table, peeled open the bag and tossed him one. He grabbed it out of the air like a land shark.

"I'm pregnant," I said.

Charlie coughed as he swallowed. It was such an odd sound that it made me wonder if I was going to have to give him the Heimlich maneuver. I was more equipped to give mouth to mouth, because I'd seen a video on a pet site. You don't actually put your mouth on the dog's mouth. You cup your hands around his nose and blow into it.

"What?" Opie asked.

Charlie had evidently been able to swallow on his own.

"What do you mean, you're pregnant?"

"Enciente, preggers, with a bun in the oven, expecting, in the family way, or with child."

I had, for a little while, amused myself by trying to remember all the various euphemisms for being pregnant.

"How did that happen?"

"Well," I said. "First you have a girl egg. Then you have a boy sperm."

Charlie growled at me. "I know that. I mean, who? How?"

I came and sat on the chaise. Charlie jumped up on the end, staring at me. He really did have a pretty face. He had the intelligent eyes of a golden retriever. Right now, though, they were incredulous, but that was Opie.

"No wonder Maddock wanted you. He evidently knew you could get pregnant."

That was a teensy bit offensive. He could have wanted me because I was pretty or sexy or exuded a certain *je ne sais quois*. Oh, who was I kidding? Opie was right.

"So, are you going to tell him?"

Now this part was delicate. I didn't like looking like the slut du jour, frankly, but I was hoping, praying, wishing, and crossing every appendage with the ability to be crossed, that Maddock wasn't the father.

"He might not be the baby daddy, if you'll pardon the expression."

One of Charlie's eyebrows arched toward his ear.

"I had an interlude," I said.

That word was an obvious effort on my part to class up what had happened in the gun range, on the concrete floor, without an ounce of shame in my body.

"An interlude?"

I nodded.

"With whom, or do I have to ask? Dan the Divine."

"What?"

"Hey, I might be a dog, but I have a woman's memories."

7

That admission made the whole intact male dog/female ghost vet thing even weirder, if that were possible.

"So he's the father?"

"I don't know."

Both eyebrows arched, making Charlie's forehead a mass of horizontal wrinkles. He looked like a shar-pei.

"Don't look at me like that. You can't tell me you didn't have any interludes in your life."

I wasn't sure if I was talking to the vet or the dog.

"You need to tell him."

"Which one?" I asked.

Charlie tilted his head, looking confused.

"I know, right? I'd tell Dan, but he might not be the father and I don't want to tell him right now if he isn't. And even if he isn't, I'm not about to tell Maddock. He wants to chain me to a bed somewhere and make me a baby factory."

Charlie didn't say a word, only looked at the bag of dog biscuits again.

"I need to find out who the father is," I said. "Before I tell anyone."

I got up, got Charlie another dog biscuit and watched as he curled up on the floor beside the chaise. I guess the heart to heart talk with Opie was over. I couldn't blame her. I'd want to disappear into dogdom, too.

CHAPTER TWO

Lists, lists, nothing but lists

I grabbed the Kindle on the table and scanned my library, annoyed when nothing felt right. None of the free books I'd downloaded or books by my favorite authors interested me. Nothing tripped my trigger.

I didn't want to read about love, unrequited or otherwise. I didn't want to read a mystery. My life was mysterious enough, thank you very much. Nothing in the adventure genre sounded promising, either. I mean, if you're being stalked by a vampire, human rights groups, and your mother, any other adventure kind of pales, don't you think?

I switched off my Kindle with a sound of disgust and turned on the TV, only to have the same problem. There wasn't anything I felt like watching. I could always use the tablet on the table and surf the net, but my recent Google searches had taught me that okay, the Internet doesn't know everything and a lot of what it does know I don't want to learn.

Charlie let out a bark, a sound so hollow and loud that I nearly jumped off the chaise. He stood beside me, the fur along his spine sticking up, his feathery tail show ring straight. His nose was pointed in the direction of the closed curtains.

Oh hell, if Maddock was doing the suction cup thingy again, I was going to have to zap him one more time. How long does it take until the man learned a lesson?

Maybe the rabies virus was having an impact on his brain.

One could only hope.

Charlie let out a long stream of barks, something he'd never before done.

I got off the chaise and dared myself to walk toward the window. If I were like some of the heroines in the books I've read, I would be a formidable opponent. I'd stride toward the window and fearlessly jerk back the curtain. My hands would be fisted on my hips. My bosom would be thrust out and my legs would be spread in a Wonder Woman stance.

Instead, I tiptoed to the curtains and peeked out where they met in the middle, hoping I didn't see glowing red eyes and bright white fangs. I didn't put anything past the master vampire. Maybe he could reach in through the glass itself.

I did see lights, but not orange and not belonging to a vampire. A black drone slowly zigzagged in front of the bedroom window. I knew the castle had a lot of technological gadgets, but I would bet the drones were new, thanks to Il Duce.

Dan was not only sexy and handsome, but he was a smart cookie, too.

He was also protective and I was coming to appreciate that trait more and more, especially after learning I had another group out to get me. Not only was a master vampire trying to make me his brood mare, but the witches weren't all that happy about my existence. Now add the OTHER - Organization of True Humans for Equal Rights. They had the idea that a great evolution was coming and the Brethren would all merge to create a super being. They didn't want humans left out of the equation. Ideally, they wanted humans to have all the powers of witches and vampires with none of the drawbacks.

That's where little ol' me comes in. Everyone wanted to experiment with me. A vial of blood here, a vial of blood there, and suddenly I'm as dry as a three thousand year old mummy. No pun intended, given my gestational state.

That wasn't the only group out to get me. The Militia of God, The Council of Human Creationism, and the National Association for the Advancement of Humans didn't care about my blood. They just wanted to wipe me off the face of the earth. I was distinguished by being among the equal opportunity hated.

"It's okay," I told Charlie. "It's friendly. You don't have to worry."

He snuffled a little, but went back to his place beside the chaise.

My phone wasn't on the table where I could have sworn I left it, but the effort to find it was suddenly beyond me. I wanted to discover what had happened at the witch pow wow, but I really didn't want to talk to Dan yet. He had a way of looking at me that made me want to bare my soul and tell him everything. I couldn't tell him everything, not right now.

When I was human, my life was uncomplicated. I knew exactly what I wanted in life.

I wanted to be the first woman VP of the Southwest Region. I wanted to be respected, admired, even be a mentor and model for younger women in my division. I wanted people to whisper about me as I walked down the corridor of headquarters. I wanted to hear people say things like: "There goes Marcie Montgomery, she's such a powerhouse. Did you hear what her percentage of closed claims were last quarter? My God, she blew everybody out of the water."

I wanted a house. Maybe a pet, a cat who would meow at me when I got home and only be calm once he heard the can opener. Or a dog like Charlie who wasn't haunted but otherwise exactly the same.

In the dark depths of my soul where the most important wishes and wants were held like treasures, I wanted more than that. I wanted a husband who adored me. I wanted someone who liked me, who thought I was sexy, that I was his Playboy centerfold, the culmination of all his dreams and desires. He would do silly things that he never thought he would ever do, like sending me flowers because it was Tuesday, or leaving me notes on the refrigerator like, "Be home soon, honey. Doug wanted me to come over and see his man cave. But wait until I come home and show you mine."

Then, a little deeper into my subterranean soul, excavated and revealed only under threat of death to all those I loved, was the desperate wish for children. I didn't care if they were girls or boys. I didn't care if I had one or two or five. I wanted squabbles and shouting and arguments about Sally staring at me, and Bobby taking my diary, of seeing if toothbrushes were really wet, and giving lectures of how soap is your friend. I wanted to sit on the side of the bed and hear my child's prayers, look up and see my husband leaning against the door jamb and know the perfect joy of love in a dozen manifestations.

I wanted to have crying jags occasionally, especially when I doubted myself. I wanted to be angry at my husband for something silly and nonsensical. I wanted to be confused and certain, wise and stupid. I wanted all life had to offer and to gulp it down in greedy, gluttonous swallows.

I wanted to love, to feel my heart open so wide the emotion burst out of my chest. I wanted it to shine on people I never knew. I wanted strangers to turn, look at me and say to themselves: "There's a happy woman."

That was my life, all mapped out in my imagination. And it never, ever came close to happening. I could whine about that for the rest of my life or deal with what I had. I decided to whine a little first before getting all adult.

Being an adult was not all it was cracked up to be, frankly.

I sat staring at the wall for long enough that the little voice inside my head started kicking at some of the brain cells. I had to *do* something, but I didn't know what to do.

I've always had a habit of making lists to help me cope, to help me plan, and make some organized, rational sense of my life. I went to the desk, plunked myself down with both forearms on the desk, hands clasped under my chin. I stared at the wall in front of me again. Nothing like getting inspiration from drywall.

Finally, I grabbed the pad of paper and a pen and wrote: *Things I Know* at the top.

1. I am a Pranic vampire, considered a goddess in ancient lore.

2. I can do lots of nifty things other vampires can't do.

3. I suspect I can do a lot more nifty things and I need to figure out what they are.

4. I haven't the slightest idea who my friends are, but I have a damn good idea who the enemies are.

5. I am pregnant. In addition to protecting myself, I now have a child to guard with my life.

6. If my child was born with fangs, breast feeding was out.

Okay, as a beginning list, it wasn't bad. In fact, I was ahead of my game. A month ago I didn't know I was a goddess, for example. I didn't know I could do the little zapping things that I could do. All I had to do was concentrate on something and direct my hands toward the offending article/creature, and he got a jolt of energy from me. I was sort of a walking taser.

I tore off two more sheets of paper and wrote *Friends* on one and *Enemies* on the other.

How sad was it that it was easier to start with the *Enemies* list?

Maddock topped the list, of course, followed by my mother. That wasn't as depressing as it seemed on the surface. I had years to get used to the idea of Demi not feeling all Madonna-like around me.

I added the OTHER and all the quasi-religious groups. Right now, unfortunately, I had to add the witches to the *Enemies* list, at least until I heard from their representatives.

Depressed, I reached for the *Friends* list and put Ophelia/Charlie on it.

Then I added Dan, because after all was said and done, I have never suffered because of him or his actions. In fact, he had protected me from the very beginning. Why, I don't know. Maybe it was his good guy training as a Ranger. Maybe he just didn't like my odds: Marcie vs the rest of the world.

If it turned out that he was strictly human, didn't want anything, and was just as he appeared, then he got my vote for being the most selfless, kind, compassionate, empathetic, sexy, nice guy I've ever known. In fact, Dan might be the nicest guy in the world.

Mike and I had a weird relationship. He was still mad that I'd slipped out when he was supposed to guard me, which meant Dan had been furious with him. But I'd done a little matchmaking and he was dating Kenisha when he wasn't fighting for his life. I added him to my *Friends* list.

I didn't know where to put Kenisha, so I grabbed a third sheet of paper and wrote *Maybe* on the top and added Kenisha's name to that list. She was a vampire, so she was subject to the Council's rules. Um, so was I, since I was technically a vampire, but I'd gone so far afoul of their dictates that I'd probably be burned at the stake - in daylight - if they ever figured out everything I'd done, like giving Niccolo Maddock a dose of rabies.

If he'd only start foaming at the mouth, I'd be one happy goddess.

I wrote Nonnie's name to the *Maybe* list, too. The jury was still out about the witches, and as much as I wanted to think that my grandmother would put her coven aside for my welfare, I wasn't sure that was true.

There, my allies and enemies on three sheets of paper. The paucity of the allies list concerned me, especially since I was going to need lots of people in my corner fast.

I pressed my hand over my abdomen in a gesture of protectiveness I suspected that every pregnant woman has made at one time or another. I didn't know what this child was, hybrid of vampire and goddess, or leaning toward human with witch blood.

Double witch blood, come to think of it, since my grandmother was a witch and Dan's mother and sister were witches.

Double, double, toil and lots o'trouble.

I needed information about everything.

What did a baby vampire look like? What were the laws, especially custody laws, about vampire babies? I would be willing to bet that the Council, who ruled over vampires, didn't have a damn thing in their Green Book about custody of vampire children.

If I were lucky, the child would be Dan's. But the way my luck was going lately, I wasn't going to bet on anything.

I couldn't stay in my room with only taking potty breaks for Charlie. First of all, it wasn't fair to my dog. Secondly, I owed Dan an explanation. Plus, I needed to find out what the witches were planning on doing. You didn't mess around with witches and I'd left a meeting called for my benefit. There was sure to be some bad feelings, so I needed to smooth ruffled feathers.

I had to know more about vampires. I'd only attended one session in my orientation class and that just wasn't enough. I'd met with my instructor, a woman I called Eagle Lady because of her unfortunate resemblance to said bird, but she'd turned out to be a snake in the grass, which is probably giving snakes a bad name. She'd gone to Maddock with personal information I'd given her.

I could always go to Kenisha, hoping she didn't spread my curiosity around, but Kenisha was still sitting vigil over Mike. That's another thing on my list, to check on Mike. Even hiding myself away in my room for a day didn't mean that I'd forgotten what Maddock had done to my bodyguard.

As a goddess, there was remarkably little I could do. I had no talent in healing. The only thing special about me, other than the zappy thing, was that I suspected I had some ability in astral projection, which sounds all New Age and woo woo. In other words, my consciousness could be somewhere my body wasn't.

The first time it had happened I'd been here in this room and felt witches around me. I'd imagined myself on a river and the whole situation had felt so real I wouldn't have been surprised to find mud squishing between my toes.

I really had to practice that and anything else that might help keep me safe.

"Is it getting time for dinner?" Opie asked, stretching, revealing Charlie's manhood in all its glory.

I couldn't help but smile at both of them.

Then it hit me. I'd been overlooking a perfect source of vampire information.

CHAPTER THREE

They're not dead: they're just un-alive

Granted, Opie had only attended one orientation session, just like me. Getting murdered kind of puts the kibosh on further education. But she'd deliberately become a vampire. To do that she had to pass some kind of psychological examination in addition to being interviewed by a couple of vampire committees. Surely she had to learn a lot about the *Frater Cruentus*, Il Duce's favorite name for vampires.

Her reason, as she'd told me the night she died, was that she hadn't wanted to grow old and ugly. I don't think she gave any thought to growing old and furry.

"How about some liver?" I asked, certain the kitchen must have chicken liver floating around. God knows they had everything else. "If I can get you some liver, will you answer a few questions for me?"

Charlie rolled over on his stomach and regarded me with unabashed lust in his eyes.

"Liver?"

I wasn't certain who was asking me the question, Opie or Charlie. I decided to make it a half-and-half proposition and answer them both.

"Liver. No onions, since they're bad for dogs."

"Liver pate with crudities?"

"I presume you're talking carrots and celery sticks and little toasted bread things."

Charlie's head bobbed.

"Crudities it is," I said.

"I would answer your questions anyway, Marcie. You know that. But I'm particularly fond of liver pate."

I smiled. I would've given her liver even if she didn't answer any questions. I think we were bonding, Charlie and Opie and me. A triumvirate of the truly weird.

"By the way, we need to go see the vet today about your stitches."

Charlie looked away, put his head on his paws, and sighed gustily.

I decided to go ahead with the questions before canine petulance overwhelmed ghostly cooperation.

I wasn't all that prepared, to be honest. I needed to know a lot of things, some of which involved vampire politics. In the meantime, I was going to stick to the basics. As I've mentioned before, what I knew about vampires (other than the experience with my stepfather, Paul) had been mostly condensed through popular culture, books and movies. Most of those myths about the undead were wrong.

So, let's start at the beginning, shall we?

"Are you afraid of garlic?"

"Everyone can tell if you've eaten garlic. Even the next day. And if you've eaten a lot, it seems to seep out of your pores. But afraid of it, no."

I remembered my first experience of garlic and blood. Il Duce told me that they used garlic to mask the taste of blood for the newly fledged vampires. Otherwise, it was too much. Blood was, if you'll pardon the expression, an acquired taste. Thank the Lord and all the archangels that I didn't have to acquire it.

"What about mirrors? Could you see yourself in the mirror before the, um, incident?"

"I could," she said. "And if I must say, I was quite good-looking."

Charlie's tail shook, feathered out, then lay on the floor, almost like Opie was throwing her hair over her shoulder.

"How much does Charlie realize about you?" I asked, curious. "Does he have a consciousness? Does he mind you being there?"

If what I thought was true, I'd never known Charlie without Opie around. The first night I'd met him I'd been running for my life on the school grounds of the Vampire Training Academy. Opie had already been dead by then and found herself possessing a golden retriever.

"I don't think he minds, and yes, he's most definitely here. He quite likes you. And Dan." She made the strangest sound, almost like a purr. "I quite like Dan, too."

I would have to warn Dan not to let Charlie hump his leg. It wouldn't be what he thought it was.

Opie came and sat on the chaise and propped her chin on my knee.

"To truly understand what a vampire is," she said, "is to forget everything you thought you knew."

I had already figured most of that out myself, but I remained silent.

"A vampire is a vampire because he's contracted a mutation, one passed on from one vampire to another. It causes your organs to go into stasis." She looked at me. "You know what stasis is don't you?"

I nodded.

She answered as if I hadn't responded. "Medically, it's defined as stagnation, but it means more than that with vampires. It's basically when the cells exist in a state of suspended animation."

Charlie addressed himself to an itch on his leg, then let Opie return to the lecture.

"Vampires aren't like zombies." Charlie shook his entire body as if he were wet.

I was going to have to address the zombie question, but not right this moment.

"Is drinking blood one of those myth things?" I remembered the first time I'd gotten a case of O Positive from Fed Ex. My stomach still turned at the memory.

She shook her head. "The mutation is a delicate balancing act. Vampires drink blood to keep more cells from dying off, and replacing those few that might have died. The new blood takes on the mutation, but never changes the state of the host. A vampire could replace his entire blood volume and never go back to being human."

She scratched again before returning to the subject. "More vampires die each year from cell destruction than any other kind of death," she said.

I'd never heard that before.

"That's why they take such care with their health. A common cold can kill a vampire. He has no immune system. If he doesn't replace the red blood cells that die, he's toast."

"So, if you've got a cold, that means you have to feed more often?"

She nodded. "That's just with a cold. If they get any other kind of diseases, especially blood born things like anemia or leukemia, they almost always die."

"Then why are they so afraid of the sun?"

She gave me a very human exasperated look from warm brown doggy eyes.

"Everything a vampire does is to protect himself. One of the reasons they don't go out in the sun is that the skin cannot regenerate. A human being gets a sunburn. The skin peels, new skin replaces the old. Once a vampire gets a burn, the skin is dead and it's never coming back. It's like being skinless. They don't actually turn to dust like popular culture states. They just evaporate without skin to protect themselves. The same thing with the rest of a vampire's organs. They have to be preserved and protected just as they are, because if they're damaged in any way, there's no such thing as a liver transplant or a spleen removal. In actuality, vampires are very delicate creatures."

I was trying to wrap my head around Il Duce being a delicate creature and couldn't quite make it.

"And you wanted to be a vampire?" I ask, amazed.

She nodded. "Stasis means that nothing changes. You are what you are at the moment you acquire the mutation. You never get older."

I had a question, but she answered it before I got a chance to ask.

"Vampires aren't stronger than other creatures, even human beings. They've created this whole mythology to protect themselves."

"Maddock can fly," I said. Okay, maybe he couldn't fly, but he could levitate pretty damn well. I'd been on the other side of the glass on the second story. He'd hovered.

She didn't look surprised.

"Very old vampires can sometimes acquire other skills and traits, some of them from creatures they might have ingested."

Thank heavens I hadn't eaten anything. I was feeling just the teensiest bit queasy.

"You mean like bats and things?"

"Maybe. Or it could be that they've simply mutated themselves, the older they get. Younger vampires don't have those traits."

I hadn't had them, either. In the first three days I'd been a perfectly normal vampire and if that isn't an oxymoron, I don't know what is. But in the first two weeks, when my body was supposed to have been adjusting to stasis, I was going over to the taco side. I'd eaten my way through the menus of every fast food place near my house, not to mention the ice cream and cookie aisles of the grocery store.

"What about the ability to compel?" I asked.

"That's something odd. The brain is affected by stasis, but not in the way you would think. In a human, brain cells don't regenerate except in the hippocampus. In a vampire, the cells don't regenerate, but they don't die, either. Vampires can do things mentally that humans can't do, and compulsion is one of them."

"I can compel," I said. "Only humans, though. But I can't stand the taste of blood. And walking in the sun isn't a problem."

Opie did a Charlie/dog shrug, which meant that one shoulder lifted and then dropped.

"You're different from other vampires," Opie was saying. "You aren't walking the line, like they do, between death and life. Your organs are working. You don't need blood to continue to replace those cells that have died. You're manufacturing them on your own. In other words, you haven't entered stasis."

"Does that mean I won't be immortal?"

"Most vampires aren't immortal," she said. "They can live for hundreds of years if they're careful, if they monitor themselves. Most simply get tired of all the trouble and deliberately infect themselves with something."

"What do you mean, if they monitor themselves?"

"Have you ever seen a blood glucose monitor?" she asked. "The kind that people with diabetes use to measure their blood sugar?"

I nodded.

"There's one for vampires. It's called a cell viability monitor, a CVM."

"And it was developed by MEDOC, wasn't it?" I asked. That's probably how Maddock had made his millions, if not billions.

She looked surprised at the question, but nodded.

"When the CVM indicates that cells are dying at an advanced rate, the vampire feeds."

"To keep the balance," I said. "Between life and death."

She nodded again.

"They aren't the undead, are they? They're the Un-alive."

If a dog could smile, Charlie managed it.

"I injected Maddock with something," I said. I couldn't remember if she'd been there when I'd used the hypodermic or just after.

Her big brown retriever eyes watched me with interest. She didn't ask and, for a moment, I thought about not telling her. Only for a moment, though. She was the closest thing I had to a friend, either in the guise of a ghost or a dog.

"Rabies," I said.

She didn't even blink. She just stared at me as if I were a rabbit and she was spotting me for her pal, the hunter.

"Rabies?" she finally said.

I nodded. "It seemed like a good idea at the time. The incubation period is long enough that the Council wouldn't connect me to his illness. He'd go mad before he figured out what was happening, so it would be too late to survive."

She nodded. Opie had been a vet before she'd become a ghost, so she knew a lot more about rabies than I did. But I sure as hell didn't expect what she said next.

"You realize, of course, that he'll infect everyone he feeds from."

It was my turn to stare. "What?"

She sighed, more human than dog. "Remember, a vampire's cells are in stasis. So is every organ in his body. He doesn't acquire disease as much as he's simply a vessel for it. Think of a Coptic jar, one of those Egyptian funereal jars that hold a mummy's organs. That's what a vampire is."

"Typhoid Mary," I said.

"In this case, Rabid Randy."

"Holy crap, what have I done?" I said.

If Maddock thought he was sick, he'd feed more often. The more often he fed, the more people he'd infect. I'd created a plague.

Not to mention what he'd done to Mike.

Dear God, I'd killed Mike.

CHAPTER FOUR

They're not all kitchen staff

Charlie blinked at me and for a moment, all I saw was dog. He jumped off the chaise, and began to walk in a circle, nose to the carpet.

"Oh, oh."

The conversation about vampires was about to be pushed aside for bodily needs.

I rushed Charlie down the main stairs and out the front door. He ran ahead, barking once to announce his joy before looking back at me, tongue lolling. Then he promptly squatted near one of the topiary bushes and, with a quick, apologetic look in my direction, defecated an amount that would have made a Clydesdale proud.

I wish I could have Charlie's single-minded pursuit of what he wanted.

If he wanted to go sniff butt, nothing in the world was going to stop him. If the object of his nose ardor sat down, Charlie simply waited him out. When the reluctant dog finally stood, Charlie dived beneath the tail and took a big whiff.

If he wanted to investigate something interesting on the ground, he did so. He didn't look around and ask for permission. It could be a snail or a frog or a dead bird. Charlie pounced on it with no apology, embarrassment, and complete curiosity.

If something itched, Charlie scratched. If it smelled good and it belonged to him, he checked it out. Sometimes he licked it, just because he could.

He never looked around to see if the world was watching. Never once did he ask approval.

I wanted to be more like my ghost ridden dog.

"You know I don't have anything to clean that up," I said, searching my pockets.

I didn't want to leave Charlie out here by himself while I went back inside the castle to get something to pick up his present. Frankly, I didn't want to be out here by myself at dusk, either. The threat of Maddock hung around every corner once the sun set. I didn't feel right leaving Charlie's present on the front yard, either, especially when I turned to find Dan standing there.

Not exactly what I would call an auspicious meeting.

He was wearing a yellow shirt again. He looked good in yellow and blue and green or any damn color he wore. He had three styles of dress: jeans, tailored slacks, and suits. Jeans meant he was staying in the castle. Tailored slacks: appointments outside the castle. Suits: important meetings such as attending the board meetings of Cluckey's, the company his grandfather had founded. But, then, Arthur Peterson had also founded the OTHER.

Mike's condition had made an impact. There were dark circles beneath Dan's eyes. He hadn't shaved, either, yet the shadow of beard somehow added to his attractiveness. Maybe I go for the bad boy look. His hair wasn't combed, but the biggest difference in the Dan I knew before and the one who stood there now was in his eyes.

"Do you have one of those baggie dispensers around here?" I asked. "You know, for doggie stuff."

His face was stone, his eyes as expressionless as a corpse. "I'll call someone from the kennel to take care of it. You and I need to talk."

I shook my head. "Charlie's my responsibility," I said. "I'll do it."

He pulled out his phone, pushed a number and said something I couldn't hear. In less time than it took me to tease my hair (I sometimes liked the Texas big hair look), a fresh faced young man in a blue shirt and black pants appeared at the front door with a roll of plastic bags.

"Yes sir?"

Dan pointed to me and the young man proffered the roll of bags as if it were a crown. While they both watched, I took the bags, thrust my hand into one to reverse it, and grabbed the Clydesdale mound. I tied a knot in the bag and stood there feeling as stupid as I've felt in a long time.

"Would you like me to take that, ma'am?" the young man asked.

The stone god still hadn't moved.

"Yes, please," I said, handing the warm bag to him.

"And Charlie?"

The moment of reckoning had come. Having Opie listen might be helpful, but I nodded.

"I promised him liver," I said. "Chicken liver. Pate, if you have it. You know, with celery and spices and those little crackers."

The young man didn't say anything, but he did glance at Dan who deigned to nod, just once.

The stone god moves.

A moment later Dan and I were alone at the front door of the castle. I turned and entered, brushing past him and walking to the bathroom down the hall. After I washed my hands, he was still standing there.

His face hadn't changed.

"How is Mike?"

"I'm not going to talk about Mike right now."

Okay, then.

Was I going to be marched off to the dungeon? And don't tell me Arthur's Folly lacked a dungeon. I didn't believe it. Arthur Peterson was a crazy old coot who built weird shit and not all of it was contained in this castle.

I was not, frankly, in the mood to be chastised or lectured. I was feeling too emotional for my peace of mind. I didn't like getting teary eyed, especially when I couldn't help it. Maybe I had just a teensy weensy bit of a chip on my shoulder. I sent a look in Dan's direction just to warn him about my mood.

"Can we take a walk? I've never seen the inner courtyard."

He gave me a quick once over, then nodded, leading the way to one of the elevators.

I haven't seen a lot of Arthur's Folly, the name the locals called the castle where I was a semi-guest. I insisted on paying rent, but that was laughable. I was probably paying a tenth of what my suite and all the amenities were worth.

"Are you cold? A front's supposed to come in tonight."

As a topic of conversation, the weather wasn't a bad place to start. The castle was located outside of San Antonio, in the foothills of the Texas Hill Country. We got the worst of the weather that never made it to the city, like freezing temperatures and occasional snow. Still, it was only November, which meant that summer hadn't quite departed the area.

I used to try to tell my friends who weren't from here that summer lasted ten months. Fall - about a week, winter - three weeks, tops, and spring the rest of the time. The Hill Country had more of a winter and sometimes it got downright cold, so if a front was coming through, it was time to get out my coat, mittens, and ankle warmers. People from Chicago laughed like hell at South Texans the first winter they lived here. After their blood thinned, though, they froze along with the rest of us.

"How's Charlie doing?" he asked.

We'd segued from the weather to my dog. Dan was really good at this stone god turned cocktail party maven persona. Me? I pretty much sucked at small talk.

I had to address what might have happened to Mike and I didn't know how to push past Dan's wall.

Instead, I answered his question. "Fine. I've been putting that ointment on his neck and it seems to be healing well."

Charlie's dick of an owner had chained him with a barbed choke collar and he'd escaped, which was the reason I was determined that the idiot would never see Charlie again. People who abused the helpless, whether they were human or animal, earned my endless disgust.

"The vet would probably like to see him again."

That wasn't a hardship since the vet was located on the second floor of the castle.

"I was planning on taking him," I said.

He nodded. I nodded. So far, so good.

We entered the elevator, but instead of pushing one of the visible buttons, Dan slid a panel aside. S-1, S-2, and S-3 appeared.

"You have sub-levels?"

He nodded. "S-1 is where you go to access the courtyard."

"And the others?"

I wondered if he was going to answer me and he surprised me when he did so. "The armory and other areas. S-3 is a food storage facility and the entrance to the cistern."

Dan was prepared for a siege.

When the elevator stopped and the doors opened, I was surprised again.

I've never been around the uber rich. One of my friends in college was a member of the Dalton Ranch family. Their wealth was in land, thousands of acres in the Rio Grande valley. They drove nice cars and had nice houses, but most of all they didn't sweat the small stuff. If something happened to one of their cars or houses, they simply got it fixed or bought a new one. Their kids went to Ivy League colleges without their parents going into debt. They all had pools. They didn't have to juggle money and I remember thinking that their lifestyle must be nice.

But the uber rich were different. They didn't worry about money, either, but they also made money do fantastic things. Like developing a spaceship to take tourists to outer space. Or constructing the world's tallest building. Or creating a castle in the middle of the Texas Hill Country that was part medieval world and part Disneyland.

I walked side by side with Dan through the arched door. I stopped in the middle of the path and looked up at the wall of brick in front of me, then turned to look at the back wall. The castle was much bigger than I'd thought. The square the four wings created made for a huge courtyard, one with mature Texas red oak trees, a creek with several arched bridges, and rolling topography created to look like you were on a meadow covered with Texas wildflowers on one side, and a metropolitan street on the other.

Above us, the Texas night sky was brilliant with stars. I saw the drones circling the perimeter of the courtyard, their blinking lights the only sign they were patrolling for vampires and other nocturnal creatures.

We began to walk, taking one of the graveled paths. We passed two gazebos, each one filled with laughing people, several of whom waved to us. Dan smiled and waved back.

I didn't know who all the people were and couldn't think of a way to ask without sounding rude. I sometimes think I was raised with too many manners. Mannerly Marcie, that's me. I find it difficult to hang up on recorded messages. I also had an Amazon Echo and found myself telling Alexa, "Thank you." She answered with "No problem," which was, to me, borderline rude. If you were going to have a robotic device in your home, it damn well better be polite. Right now she was in storage. I wondered if I was going to get lectured when I finally plugged her back in.

"We have three shifts," Dan said.

"So, they're all employees?"

He nodded.

"Round the clock service?" I asked. "If I want Rum Raisin ice cream in the middle of the night, somebody's waiting for my order?"

"They're not all kitchen staff. We have a large IT department, plus personnel monitoring the cistern, the food supply, and other aspects of the castle."

He led me to a bench placed along the path and we sat.

"What is it that you do here?" I asked.

"What do you mean?"

"Do you run Cluckey's from here? Or the OTHER?"

"I don't have anything to do with the day to day operations of the company. And I only make appearances at board meetings of the OTHER to defray suspicion."

His answer didn't satisfy me, but hopefully I kept my expression bland.

Here's the deal: I know a lot about business. It's been my concentration ever since leaving college. I'm not all that up to speed on major corporations like Coca-Cola or Pepsico, but I do know about small and medium sized businesses. I know about payrolls. I know about net worth and projections.

Dan was running the equivalent of a medium sized business here at the castle. In order to be able to afford all those employees, either the chicken empire was really profitable or he was involved in some other operation. My bet was on the latter. He'd mentioned that he had people looking for his sister. Were they involved in some sort of group, say an anti-vampire organization?

"How many people do you employ here?" I asked.

He only smiled, which was a clue.

I once had to take a seminar on Emotional Intelligence. The higher up the food chain I got at my insurance company, the more meetings and seminars I attended. The more meetings and seminars I attended, the less I got done during the day. The less I got done during the day, the more work I had to do at home.

Managers are grumpy because they have no personal time, their marriages are on the rocks, and they're exhausted. No, that's not what I learned at the seminar on Emotional Intelligence.

What I learned at the EI seminar is that there are some people who just don't have a clue. Trust me, I could have taught the course.

People who have emotional intelligence have that certain something we're never taught, I guess because we think everybody has it. It's going to a party and knowing when your host would really like you to get the hell out now. Or sitting in your boss's office and getting an invisible signal that the meeting's up. Or knowing how to read people, realizing when their tolerance has been reached.

Surprisingly, EI seems to be a dying trait, at least in the people I interviewed for open positions.

Some people didn't have the sense God gave a gnat. They were the last ones to pick up on signals. Or they didn't understand that what they said was callous or cruel. Sometimes, they were the first to be offended. Every slight had to be responded to, every slightly jarring remark was a slur or an offense.

Most of my managerial time was spent adjudicating arguments between co-workers. Or Kindergarten Central as I sometimes called it.

I was really good at picking up clues, just like the one Dan was giving me. He was smiling. He looked calm and relaxed, but he was focusing on the bushes in front of us and not looking at me.

He wasn't about to tell me the secrets of Arthur's Folly, but he would be very, very polite about his silence.

CHAPTER FIVE

Eager beaver Marcie

"The witches were there to see you, Marcie. To talk to you. To make a decision about you."

"I know." I looked over to see him frowning at me. "I really do know, Dan. I had to leave because of circumstances beyond my control."

Boy, that wasn't an understatement, either.

"What circumstances?"

"When I can tell you, you'll be among the first to know. I promise. But I can't talk about it right now."

"Marcie, how can I help you if I don't know what's going on?"

That was a fair question and one I didn't know how to answer.

If I was one of the heroines in the books I love to read, I would only incidentally be a vampire. I would have another job, saving the world or catching a monster or battling magic. Only once in a while when I be bothered with my true persona. Unfortunately, I was living in the real world and I didn't have another job other than being me.

I had to find a job. I had to save the world or catch a monster. I wasn't so interested in catching Maddock as I was stopping him. Saving the world would take a little more time to think about.

"Tell me what happened at the meeting, especially when I left. Do we need to call another powwow? Do I need to send out email notes of apology?"

He studied me for another long moment and I smiled over at him. Okay, maybe it wasn't a come hither smile and maybe I wasn't looking my best, but it seemed to do the trick.

"The witches think we're heading toward war," Dan said, startling me.

"War?"

He nodded.

"A full blown internecine war. There've been skirmishes from time to time in the past, but nothing involving humans."

"The OTHER," I said. "The OTHER will make sure that humans are involved, won't they?" I was getting goose bumps, and it wasn't from the cool breeze.

He nodded again.

Lights were cunningly placed beneath the bushes at regular intervals. They softly illuminated the path but they weren't glaring.

I knew we were safe here in the darkness because of the drones. They were soundless, but I could see their lights high above us, along the roof line. I wondered if they had special detectors for vampires. If so, what would that entail? It certainly wouldn't be heat sensors because vampires were, by their very nature, cold-blooded. Motion detectors? Il Duce was one of the fastest creatures I had ever seen. Did vampires give off a scent?

I decided to ask Dan.

"They have a different bio impedance," he said.

I remained silent rather than demonstrate my ignorance.

He smiled, reached for my hand, and drew a square on the back of it with his finger.

"If I put a small electrode on your skin and applied an alternating current to it, your skin would react a certain way. The way you respond would be different from the way I do."

"So the drones send out an electrical current?" I asked.

"In a way. It's a probe. We've found that vampires don't have the same bio impedance range as humans."

"And you have those detectors mounted on the fence around the castle, too, don't you?"

It was only a guess, but he nodded.

"Do you have anything similar to detect witches?"

"No."

There was something more to that answer, something I wasn't getting, but I let it go for now. We had a lot of those aborted conversations, things we should have discussed, but didn't. On my part I don't know if it was embarrassment or my choice to avoid humiliation or simply not wanting to know everything. Sometimes, too much information was simply too much information.

"So, are all the witches are gunning for me?"

I had been unpardonably rude last night, but if I had to do it over again, I would have done the same thing. I don't see how I could've sat there with the knowledge I'd just been given and attempted anything like a cordial conversation.

Let's pretend, shall we? Strip the drama from my life, the fact that I was a vampire and all the other stuff, and pretend that I was just a normal woman. As a normal woman I couldn't help but wonder if other pregnant women felt the way I did. I didn't want to share the knowledge that I had this little person inside me yet. I wanted to keep the information mine. I wanted to revel in the mystery of becoming a mother, the sheer wonder of being pregnant, of creating a life.

Besides, my condition made me even more dangerous to people around me. If Maddock knew, he would move heaven and earth to get to me.

I was hoping that Dan had super duper Ranger sperm armed with little bayonets between their teeth and hand grenades on their wiggly little tails. That image was immediately replaced by one of a fanged sperm, dressed in a microscopic black tux.

Please, let me have been impregnated by a human.

I was being paranoid for two.

"They were upset when you left. You know how important the meeting was, Marcie."

"I know."

"But you're not going to tell me why?"

"I can't tell you," I said. "Not right now."

I didn't want thirteen witches to see me scream or descend into maniacal laughter. Heaven only knows what would have happened then.

But I wasn't going to lie to Dan. First of all, I didn't lie well. I couldn't remember all the various permutations of the lie I'd begun. It was just easier to tell the truth. But in this case, I wanted a few more days.

He was studying me in that way he had. I would bet that he knew my exact pulse rate and what my blood pressure was, not to mention my temperature. He probably knew how many times I blinked in a minute and what my tells were.

Finally, he nodded. Just one nod.

In that instant, what I felt for Dan Travis became deeper and resonated more than anything I'd ever felt for another man. With that single gesture, he accepted my word. He accepted me, weird Marcie, a little warped, certainly confused and most definitely working on terrified. He didn't demand that I explain. He didn't make me promise. He simply accepted what I said and I loved him for it.

The reason I was blinking back tears was no doubt due to the rush of hormones throughout my body. Pranic vampire or not, I was pregnant. I was going to be emotional. I had been very teary eyed when I was pregnant as a human. I burst into tears at any commercial that featured babies, animals, smiling men, and pretty music. And the SPCA commercial? I cried for fifteen minutes. I was, as Bill said on more than one occasion, a blubbering basket case. Of course, this was the man who got all choked up when the Dallas Cowboys lost the playoffs. He put his bobble head doll in a place of honor for next season and warned me to be careful dusting it.

"Are you all right?" Dan asked. "You're crying."

I mustered up a smile, which must have looked odd, but all he did as extend an arm around my shoulders and pull me close.

"I told the witches it was an emergency," he said when I pulled away and wiped my tears with my hands. "I pretended I knew what the hell was going on."

I put one hand on his thigh. Hormones, again. Or maybe just the fact that I was a woman and he was a handsome, sexy man. I might be weepy, but I wasn't dead. Oops, I was.

"I explained the situation with the OTHER," he said.

"Did they believe you?"

He glanced over at me, frowning. "Why wouldn't they?"

"Your grandfather being the founder and all."

"You might say my mother vouched for me."

For a moment I'd forgotten that his mother was a powerful witch.

"Did your grandfather ever allow your mother to come to the castle?"

"No," he said.

I didn't know Janet, but I would be willing to guess that the first time she'd come to Arthur's Folly was on the day of Arthur Peterson's death. She probably came to dance a little jig. Or maybe scatter his ashes in a witchy kind of way.

"So she's always known about the OTHER," I said.

He nodded.

"That couldn't have made her happy."

"No, it didn't. She thought my grandfather was a dangerous man."

I glanced at him. "How did you feel about him?"

He stared straight ahead at the bushes in front of us. "It's complicated," he said.

"The people we love don't have to be perfect," I said, knowing how conflicted he must feel. I felt the same way about Nonnie. "Loving your grandfather doesn't mean you're like him," I said, wanting to comfort him in some fashion, ease the burden of the guilt he must have felt for loving Arthur Peterson.

"I'm not sure I loved him," he said, surprising me. "I admired him for his determination and ambition. He started with nothing and he built an empire. I respected his business acumen. I appreciated that he loved my grandmother so much. But when he hated, he hated like no one else I've ever seen. He never got over my father dying."

Dan had already told me that his grandfather had blamed his mother because she'd somehow survived the car accident that had killed his father. Maybe that's when he went off the rails, because he formed the OTHER not long after that.

"Did he really think that magic saved your mother?"

He glanced over at me. "Magic is the province of witches," he said, shrugging.

"None of the other Brethren have magical abilities?"

"You don't know very much about the Brethren, do you?"

I was beginning to think I didn't know much about anything, but I kept that revelation to myself.

"That's why witches aren't that happy about you," he said, startling me again. "You're a hybrid. You probably have some talent for magic."

"Like hell," I said. I turned on the bench and stared at him. "Okay, the only thing I can do is that zappy thing, but that's the goddess in me."

"You sure?"

I didn't have an answer for that.

"They want to test you."

"What?"

"The witches want to test you, to determine your magical abilities."

"I don't have any magical abilities," I said, but it wasn't as forceful a declaration as it might have been.

My grandmother had never talked to me about witchcraft. Neither had my mother. Until I'd become a vampire, I hadn't realized that Nonnie was a witch and my mother didn't have any skill in the art.

Did I? And if I did, what did that mean?

"Are they making that part of the agreement to be on our side? If I test negative on the witchy meter, are they saying they don't want anything to do with me? Or if I test positive, that they'll protect me because I have some magical abilities?"

"It isn't part of the deal," he said. "They just want to know."

"That doesn't sound right," I said. "Look, I've never been around a group of witches, a convening of witches, whatever you call a mass sighting of witches until last night, but one thing I do know is that nobody ever wants to know anything just because. There's an agenda there and I want to know what it is. What kind of test is it? One of those Salem trials thing? If I drown, I'm not a witch? If I float, I am?"

His laughter startled me into smiling.

"No," he said, shaking his head. "I think it's in the realm of seeing if you can make things disappear, cast spells, have any reaction when placed next to crystals, that sort of thing."

That still didn't sound right, but I decided not to argue the point. After all, Dan had probably gotten the information from his mother and one didn't come between a man and his mother, especially if one had designs on the man.

Well, not right now, but maybe in the future.

"They're sending another delegation here tomorrow," he said. "Do you have any plans, any last minute meetings, anything that will interfere with attending?"

I shook my head. I wasn't expecting another phone call from my gynecologist, if that's what he was asking. Still, I wasn't sure another meeting right now was a good idea. I didn't know how *in tune* witches were, especially Nonnie, but I didn't want one of them figuring out I was pregnant. Not yet, not before I'd taken steps to protect my child.

Don't ask me what those were. I hadn't a clue, only that I had to do something.

"Does it have to be tomorrow?" I asked.

He looked at me. I bit my lip, glanced away, absolutely enthralled by the sight of a snail making his way home. Where had he been all day? Out with the snail guys? Had they been watching worm football?

"Is there a reason why it shouldn't be?" His tone was even, but there was an edge to it.

I didn't know much about the Rangers, but I'll bet only a certain type of man got into the Army program. I had the feeling that, in addition to the rigorous physical requirements I'd heard about, an applicant had to pass other kind of tests as well. Things like: can you outstare your opponent, remain silent in that cobra stalking kind of way, transform your expression to resemble a stone mask? Pass, pass, pass.

I looked back at him. "If I said yes, but I couldn't tell you, would you trust me?"

That was asking a lot, even for Dan and he was one of the most generous people I'd ever known.

He finally looked away, giving me the feeling I'd just been released by an invisible lariat.

I think I've watched too many old episodes of Wonder Woman.

"You want me to trust you, but you can't trust me."

It didn't have anything to do with trust, but everything to do with not wanting to reveal my pregnancy right now. My knowledge was only twenty-four hours old. Short of calling the Vampire Help Line, I hadn't come up with any concrete ways to tell who might be the father.

If Dan was the father, that was one thing. But Maddock being the baby daddy?

Being pregnant with a vampire's child would change the dynamic in a whole bunch of ways I hadn't even figured out yet. The witches sure as hell wouldn't be pleased. Maybe someone would target me for, well, extinction, for lack of a better term. I didn't just have myself to look after, I had another creature, one who might just be gnawing through the umbilical cord as I sat there worrying.

Let's face it, harboring a woman who was bearing the first ever vampire baby might be too much for even Dan to handle. The whole vampire world would descend on Arthur's Folly. I don't care how fragile Opie said they were, I'd be willing to bet a whole bunch of vampires would be right up there in the mega-scary department.

Even the idea made me nauseous.

"You're going to have to give me something, Marcie. Agree to some date."

"Give me a week."

A week would give me time to talk to Dr. Fernandez. Maybe he'd have some ideas of some tests I could have. I wasn't about to call Dr. Stallings again, not after she'd betrayed me to Maddock.

He nodded. "A week."

"One more thing," I said.

He didn't look like he was feeling all that magnanimous and I couldn't blame him. I'd asked and asked for stuff and hadn't given him anything in return. No information and only a teensy bit of honesty.

"What?"

"Does it have to be all the witches again? Can't it be a smaller group, say your mother and my grandmother?"

He stood, looking down at me. "I'll ask. Don't be surprised if they say no. I've got some calls to make. Can you find your way back?"

For the first time since I'd met Dan we were parting in, if not anger, then certainly irritation. I'd made him mad before, a few times on purpose. But I'd never had the feeling like I did now that it was serious, as in a crevasse between us, one the size of the Grand Canyon.

I stood as well. "I know you don't want to talk about Mike, but you have to tell me something."

"He's not good," he said. "We've moved him to one of the sub-level rooms."

Either I was dense or he wasn't telling me enough.

"Why?"

"They don't have any windows."

I'd been in the clinic/hospital rooms myself. The room I'd occupied had been just like any normal metropolitan hospital with an emphasis on state of the art. The window had overlooked the garden Arthur Peterson had planted for his wife. The sun had been bright on my bed, waking me.

"You think he's going to become a vampire," I said.

He didn't answer me. I had already pushed him as far as I dared.

"I've got to go," he said, polite to the last. He might be super pissed, but he was always a gentleman.

I watched him leave, wanting to call him back. Wanting to tell him things I couldn't say. Wanting him to hug me. A kiss might be nice, too.

I needed to sleep now. Really sleep and pretend, just for a little while, that everything was perfectly normal and I needed to get to work in the morning. I'd wake with my alarm, get on the treadmill, make my coffee, then shower. I'd be in the office before anyone else, even my boss. Eager beaver Marcie, destined for great things.

I left the courtyard before I started laughing like a loon.

CHAPTER SIX

I didn't need anyone to tell me he was dying

I left the courtyard and headed for the elevator. I didn't go to the kennel to pick up Charlie, because dogs weren't allowed in hospital rooms.

Dan said that Mike was in one of the subterranean rooms. I don't know what I expected in level S-2, but it wasn't the bright, wide corridor and dozens of people passing by, most of them smiling, all of them looking as if they had a place to go and a reason to be there.

The castle wasn't just a private home of the uber uber rich. Something else was going on here and I would have stopped someone and asked if I thought I'd get an answer. People at Arthur's Folly were loyal and tight lipped. I couldn't criticize Dan all that much since I was being Marcie Mum myself.

The main corridor branched off into several smaller corridors to the left and right, each marked, thank heavens. I passed the Eco Lab, the cafeteria, Human Resources, Training, and something called R&R. I didn't know if that stood for Rest and Relaxation or Research and Reversal.

I'd have to ask Dan. Would he tell me? He hadn't been all that forthcoming about Mike and he'd probably be angry that I was here. I knew, logically, that it wasn't my fault Mike had been injured. Maddock was the one who'd sucked on him like Mike was a straw. But Mike had accompanied me on my visit to the gynecologist, a wasted trip as it turns out. If I'd only known I was pregnant before going, Mike wouldn't have been injured and I wouldn't have had to see Maddock again. And been scared out of my skull.

I decided to ask someone if there was a hospital wing, but I caught sight of a woman in a white coat in the farthest corridor from the elevators. I strode forward with confidence, a trick I'd learned when facing down railroad personnel or co-insurers. It was *never let 'em see you sweat* bravado that worked most of the time. If nothing else, it made me focus on the attitude I was exuding so that I faked it well.

The white coated woman was wearing heels so high I wondered at her penchant for masochism. By the end of the day her arches would probably be killing her, not to mention her big toes. I had to admit, though, that they made her legs look great.

She was leaning against the counter of a five sided nurse's station. A series of monitors were on the work surfaces. No doubt they were all the neatest and newest gadgets. The nurse, however, wasn't there. Three open doors on the left side of the corridor revealed state of the art hospital rooms. The door closest to the station was closed and it made me wonder if Mike was in there. Or behind one of the four closed doors to the right.

Eight hospital rooms? I thought the setup on the first floor was all the medical facilities at the castle. Hadn't Dan said that his grandfather's clinic, the one where he experimented on witches and vampires, wasn't located at the castle. Had I remembered that wrong?

Just what the hell was going on at Arthur's Folly?

The doctor turned and I found myself wanting to stop and stare. I've always thought that Asian women were beautiful. Jemima Fong, MD - her name was embroidered in blue thread on the right side of her coat - was truly gorgeous.

Why was it that some women seemed to have it all? They were intelligent, talented, and spectacular.

Her eyes were a shade of blue tinged with green, making me wonder if she was wearing colored contacts. Her black hair was scraped back into a bun, revealing a perfect oval of a pale face with expressive black brows and a pink mouth formed in a solemn expression.

I had the feeling that she'd given a lot of bad news to a lot of people.

Hopefully, I wouldn't be the next one.

"Hi. I'm looking for Mike," I said.

It wasn't until that moment that I realized I didn't remember Mike's last name.

"Miss Montgomery," she said, nodding at me while she tucked a pen into her pocket. "He can't have visitors."

How did she know my name? I decided to be daring and ask her.

"Everyone knows your Mr. Travis's guest."

I set that aside to mull over later.

"Are you sure I can't see him?"

"Yes," she said, surprising me with a gentle smile. "We've restricted visitors to five minutes with family."

Dr. Fong was a triple threat - beautiful, educated, and kind.

"But Ms. Hamblin is here. Would you like to speak with her?"

"Ms. Hamblin?"

She only nodded, leaving me no clue who she was talking about. I guessed that it was Kenisha and made a mental note to find out everyone's last name. What about Meng and Felipe, the other two Fledglings in my orientation class? For that matter, what was Opie's last name?

Jeesh, where had I been?

She pointed me to a room opposite the station. I walked over there, but hesitated before opening the door.

"How is he?" I asked, looking back at her. "Can you at least tell me that?"

Again, I got that gentle smile. "I can't comment on his condition."

"Because I'm not a relative?" Had Kenisha qualified as family? Evidently, or she wouldn't be here.

"Because I've been given orders not to comment on his condition."

Dan had evidently put a gag order on the staff. I didn't know what that meant, but I suspected it wasn't good.

I hadn't considered that I might be making Maddock a carrier when I injected him with the rabies virus. I never realized it would come home to haunt me like it was right now. Dan knew, of course. Mike probably did too, if he was conscious enough to make that connection. If Mike survived as a human, would they be able to stop the virus?

The guilt was getting heavy.

I pushed the door in slowly. I'd guessed right. Kenisha sat on a pretty blue couch against the far wall, staring down at her hands draped on her lap.

I walked into the room and closed the door softly behind me.

When I was growing up, I was prickly about certain things: my mother having been married three times with in-between boyfriends numbering in the dozens. Being on the edge of poor most of the time. Cantaloupe boobs that were about two sizes too big for the rest of me. Never having a hint of a father around.

On Father's Day I pretended that the man I knew as my father would stop and think about me for a little while. He'd lift his beer in honor of my carrying his blood, being his kin, and then salute his balls for having done all the work. Of course, my real father had been nothing but dust since my birth, but I didn't know that at the time.

Now? Chalk it up to all those seminars I had to attend, but I didn't get my knickers in a twist about very much. Or maybe, and this was a thought that had just begun to make it to my conscious mind, I didn't get upset because I hadn't cared.

Take Bill, for example. If I'd found out Bill had been cheating on me, I'd ask him to move out. Or I'd schedule the movers myself, find a nice place, and get on with my life.

If Dan and I were a couple - and I'd played around with that idea in my imagination for a few hours - and I'd discovered he'd had sex with another woman, I'd spend a little time sharpening my fangs, take a few Tylenol for the pain in my jaw, and let him have it. Or just spare myself the discomfort and grab a meat cleaver.

I didn't know for sure, but I suspected Kenisha was at the meat cleaver stage with Mike. Any woman who looked as wrung out as she did wasn't feeling just "friendly" about a guy.

She looked like a warrior woman sitting vigil over her warrior, except that he was probably across the hall and her visits were timed for five minutes every hour.

The guilt started expanding until it nearly choked me.

I'd always kept a wide berth around Kenisha because she basically scared me. She was one of those women who wouldn't hesitate to get in your face. I was more of the demure, back down, back away, bow low type of confronter.

Maybe my avoidance had something to do with sensing that Kenisha was super sensitive about behavior most people wouldn't notice. I didn't know if that sensitivity was because she was black, a woman, or a cop. It could be one or any combination of the three.

I walked to the other side of the couch and sat. For a few moments I didn't say anything and neither did she. She hadn't even glanced in my direction. I wondered if she was as exhausted as she looked. Her lips were pale. Even her color seemed off, as if she'd been drained.

She was evidently sleeping here, a deduction I made from the cot on the other side of the room. Did they put a Do Not Disturb - Vampire Within sign on the door?

She was dressed in a dark blue tank top and black slacks. Her sneakers were the only touch of color with their pink stripe on dark blue.

This was going to be a bitch of a conversation. Kenisha had never made a secret of the fact that she didn't like me. She still blamed me for Opie's death and, to be honest, I could see where she was coming from.

I debated making a break for it and returning to my room, but I couldn't do that. I had information people needed to know.

"Mike told me he wouldn't date a vampire," I said.

For a long moment she didn't answer me. Finally, she spoke. "He said the same thing to me. On our first date."

I nodded, staring down at my fingers, wondering if I had the courage to say what I needed to say. Seeing the obvious grief in her eyes was hard. There were lines on her face that hadn't been there when I'd seen her last. She looked like she'd aged a decade since Mike had been injured.

I don't think I'll ever forget how Maddock looked curved over Mike, devouring him. Mike hadn't stood a chance against the master vampire. If it hadn't been for Charlie/Opie coming to the rescue, Mike would probably be dead right now, instead of dying by inches.

"He got hurt protecting me," I said, letting some of the guilt out to play.

She looked over at me, her dilated pupils startling me.

"When was the last time you ate?" I asked.

Surely the castle could come up with some blood for a vampire. Was there a delivery service? I wouldn't be the least bit surprised. Maybe Task Rabbit had some kind of auxiliary service like 1-800 GOT-BLUD.

She didn't answer me, only shook her head. That meant she hadn't eaten tonight.

I went to the intercom by the door, and buzzed the kitchen. The very last thing the castle needed was a hungry, grief-stricken vampire on the premises.

"We have a vampire guest," I said. "Is there anything to feed her?"

Given the state of my stomach, I really didn't want to mention the word blood or even think about it. Thank heavens for the people Dan employed.

"Certainly, Miss Montgomery," the pleasant voiced woman said. "We'll send a tray down now."

If I didn't miss my guess, they'd provide some epicurean vampire delight. I didn't even want to think what that might be.

After returning to the couch, I studied Kenisha. It wasn't just that she hadn't eaten tonight. There was a look of hopelessness in her eyes, one that made me want to wrap my arms around her and tell her Mike was going to be all right. I didn't. First of all, we had never had a close relationship. Secondly, I had the feeling that if I made a move toward Kenisha she'd deck me.

"How is he?"

"Dying."

Okay, that was confusing. Why was she grieving that Mike might become a vampire? Wouldn't that be a marriage made in heaven? I mean, they were dating. They liked each other. He was happy. She was happy. What was wrong?

When I said as much, her eyes blazed in that *I want to kill you* way.

"He's dying. What part if he's dying don't you get?"

Well, technically, she was dead. Or what I had decided was un-alive. Status quo, stasis, that sort of thing.

"He was drained. He can't transform."

This was new. I had the feeling that Kenisha was probably going to bite my head off, but I just didn't have the patience to wait until I saw Opie.

"You mean, you can be drained to the point that you can't transform into a vampire?"

There was that look again.

That meant Maddock had done it on purpose. Why? To prove a point? Or just because he was one mean son of a bitch, which was really an awful thing to say about his mother.

Something had to be done and I could do it. That wasn't false confidence, or fake it until you make it speak. That was the certainty of a Dirugu.

I am goddess, hear me roar.

"Where's Dr. Fernandez?"

If she gave me that look one more time, I was going to be the one to deck her, grief or no grief.

"He's with Mike."

She finally pointed across the hall.

I stood. She reached out and grabbed my arm.

"What are you going to do?"

"I have to talk to the doctor," I said.

"Why?"

Just then there was a knock on the door. I pulled away from Kenisha, grateful for the reprieve. I didn't want to tell her about the rabies bit. Kenisha had been sent by the Council to ask me about some personal facts which meant that she and the vampire governing board were close.

In other words, I didn't trust her. I had the feeling she would go straight to the Council with anything I told her. I wanted to save Mike, but my baby came first.

I opened the door to admit one of the uniformed staff. Were they prepared for any eventuality? It appeared like they were because there was a crystal decanter filled with something red - I still couldn't think *blood* without gagging - a goblet, and a vase with one red rose.

Slipping out of the room, I made my way to the one closed door on the other side of the corridor. Dr. Fong was nowhere in sight, thank heavens. I had a feeling she was a really good gatekeeper.

I tapped on the door. Dr. Fernandez opened it himself. Behind him was an entire hospital suite all laid out like intensive care. I hated intensive care. It scared me. It was mortality with a capital M. Of course, I didn't have to worry about that now, but the room still bothered me, especially with Mike laying there looking like an empty shell.

Mike's coffee complexion was grayish and there were two IVs connected to him, one with blood, the other a clear liquid. I've never been one for hospital shows and I avoid real hospitals, so I didn't know what all the machines were for. No doubt measuring his blood pressure and brain waves and breathing.

After one look at Mike, I didn't need Kenisha to tell me he was dying.

CHAPTER SEVEN

Physician, heal thy bedside manner

I turned back to Dr. Fernandez who was frowning at me. Evidently, I wasn't in his good graces. Did he remember that I'd compelled him to forget me? I might just compel him again if I needed to. In fact, if I discussed my pregnancy with him, I had every intention of making him forget. Right now I didn't think anyone was very trustworthy.

"What do you want, Miss Montgomery?" he asked, in a voice that left little doubt that he was not a fan of mine.

That was fine with me. I'd never liked doctors and my recent brush with them hadn't changed my opinion.

He glanced down at the paper in his hand, then reached up automatically to push up his Buddy Holly style glasses. I hadn't remembered him wearing glasses before, but then I hadn't been paying all that much attention, either.

Just think, he could become a vampire and never have any problem with his vision.

Was that real, though? According to what Opie said, vampirism was only a blood mutation caused by a virus. You don't become prettier. You don't magically become the winner of the Next Top Model. But vampires, as a whole, were an attractive species. You didn't see any vampires wearing glasses or hearing aids. I'd wondered, earlier, why there weren't any vampire amputees. Was it because vampires were prejudiced about turning anyone who wasn't, well, perfect? Was that why the punishment for making unauthorized vampires was death?

Were vampires trying to create a master race like the Nazis? They couldn't procreate, so maybe they had a set of standards everyone had to meet. What would they have done if someone truly ugly - if you'll pardon the un-politically correct label - had wanted to be turned? Would they have refused them?

Did they know that the OTHER was all about a master race, too?

This was just getting weirder and weirder.

"I came to find out how Mike was doing," I said, pushing the other thoughts aside.

"I can't tell you," he said.

I restrained myself from rolling my eyes. "Yes, I know. You've been told not to say anything."

"I can't tell you anything about my patients. There are rules and I'm not about to violate patient confidentiality. Even if I were not governed by rules, it would be my moral duty to keep Mr. Palmer's records confidential."

Well, at least I'd learned Mike's last name.

"You can't let him die, Dr. Fernandez. Being a vampire is better than being dead, don't you think?"

He gave me a look I interpreted as incredulous. Okay, I'd had some problems with being a vampire, but as long as I was conscious, for lack of a better term, I could still love, achieve some goals, and experience life even if it was on my terms.

"I have nothing to tell you, Ms. Montgomery."

"If he got a transfusion from a vampire, would he survive?"

"I can't discuss Mr. Palmer with you."

He was being, and I'm trying to be tactful here, a hard ass. A flicker in his eyes told me he knew he was being intransigent (there's the English major thing again) and wasn't going to change.

Segue here: I'm not an angel. Could a vampire be an angel? Anyway, I have flaws. I work on them every day. I'm hoping to be a nearly perfect person when I die in a couple hundred years. It will probably take that long to achieve perfection. However, I was so tempted to push aside the Marcie Improvement Project and just let him have it. I'd compel him to take off all his clothes, enter the courtyard and strut around like he was a rooster, complete with sound effects. In fact, the mental vision of doing that was so enthralling I almost did.

I didn't need him. I'm sure Dr. Fong had just as much expertise. Perhaps she was even more educated. I could prevail upon her to help me with my pregnancy, too.

Except for one thing: I knew I could compel Dr. Fernandez because I'd done it before. I didn't know if I could compel Dr. Fong. I needed a doctor who was subject to a whispered command here and there. Something about being extremely discreet about the information they shared.

However, Dan's edict seemed to be working just as well as a vampire's compulsion. Way to go, Dan.

There was another thing to consider. If I did the naked rooster thing, someone would tell Dan. *Mr. Travis* wouldn't be happy.

I backed off, closed my eyes and opened them again, staring at Mike as if I could infuse him with some of my own health.

Regardless of the way he'd left me, I needed to go see Dan. I knew the art of negotiation, however. I'd practiced it for years in my job. In order to get information from him, I'd have to give up something.

Unfortunately, I knew exactly what it had to be.

I shook my head as I left the hospital room.

I was so screwed.

CHAPTER EIGHT

Zingers, zingers everywhere

I was wearing my soft, fluffy, and warm burnt orange UT sweatshirt and my favorite well washed jeans when I asked directions to Dan's office. I was comfy. It was important to always be comfortable when entering battle, and I was more than sure that Dan and I were going to war.

Frankly, I hadn't expected Dan to still be working. It was almost nine, which meant that he kept weird hours. Why? To deal with the paranormal community? Or because he was involved in tracking down vampires? My second surprise was that his office was on the first floor, in an area I hadn't yet explored. Office is a misnomer. It was more a corporate suite entered through large glass doors. The mahogany reception desk in the shape of a horseshoe reminded me of an old and venerable law firm. Instead of gold letters on the door, however, there was nothing to reveal the name of Dan's enterprise.

A sweet young thing with bright red hair looked up, gave me a gamin smile and instantly triggered a thought: were there such things as leprechauns?

"Good evening, Miss Montgomery."

What the hell had Dan done, circulated a flyer with my picture on it?

"Would it be possible to see Mr. Travis?" I asked, all prim and proper.

If she was going to call me Miss Montgomery, I certainly wasn't going to turn around and ask to speak to Dan-ee-poo. I didn't say anything about not having an appointment, though. That would have been just a little too pretentious. Like living in a castle. Or having my own suite.

"I'll let him know you're here," the sweet young thing said, smiling up at me so brightly I felt about a hundred and twenty.

Was I ever that young? I don't think so. Nor did my eyes ever shine with that much innocence. I was, as they say, an old soul even as a child.

She pushed a few buttons, spoke sotto voce into her headset. When she finished, she looked up at me and smiled again.

"It will be just a few minutes. Can I get you anything?"

"No," I said. "I'm fine."

I wandered away from the reception desk and stood in front of a four foot square photo of downtown San Antonio. Although we had the population to qualify as the seventh largest city in the country, we were also spread out over a large geographical area. Downtown and the River Walk was well developed because tourism was a driving force in the city. Still, the skyline was similar to a dozen other metropolitan areas. The only distinctive landmark was the Tower of the Americas, erected during Hemisfair in 1968.

I heard her heels on the terrazzo tile before I turned and saw her. A smack, slap that said: watch out, get out of my way, don't mess with me. I tensed even before I turned.

I don't judge people on sight. Granted, my training as an adjuster had me making decisions quickly, but I'd learned that it was foolish to do that with people. Human beings surprised you. The guy who looked like he was homeless was worth three million dollars and the woman driving the Porsche was up to her neck in debt.

In those thirty seconds or so when our eyes met, I blew it. I forgot everything I learned about not making snap judgments.

The woman who stood in front of me, her mouth already moving, was a grade A, card carrying, certifiable, pin-wearing bitch. I knew it. I just couldn't tell you *how* I knew it.

Her black suit clung to every curve, the pencil skirt hitting her at the knee and revealing legs that, as they say, went on forever. The clickety clacking shoes were black, high, and enhanced her damn legs.

I took in her figure in about five seconds, leaving me plenty of time to study her face. Like the receptionist, she had red hair, but hers had been toned down to a deep auburn. Her cheekbones were high, her cheeks hollow, and her mouth permanently pursed in a fish kiss/selfie portrait. Her eyebrows were black and dramatic, set on top of heavily lashed green eyes glittering at me like emerald chips.

Some women were beautiful. Some were attractive. Some were just okay, but they had something about them that made you think they were prettier than they were. This woman, unfortunately, was not only beautiful, but she had that extra something.

I hated her on sight.

"Miss Montgomery?" she asked, in a voice that sounded like bells on a summer solstice morn. I would have preferred that she had a screech or at least brought calling the cows into the barn to mind.

"I'm Diane Trenton, Mr. Travis's assistant."

No secretarial post for her. No, she probably made more than twice what I had as middle management.

She also smelled good. If she had been another woman, I would have complimented her on the scent and asked the name.

Adult that I was, ahem, I remained silent. I don't think I've ever been as jealous of anyone in my life or as suddenly.

"Dan sends his apologies," she continued. "He's on a conference call. Can I get you something while you're waiting?"

A few days ago, I could have eaten my way through the castle. Lately, however, I wasn't all that hungry. The idea of some foods made me roll my eyes and put them on the back burner list, which was a shame. A little comfort food wouldn't hurt right now.

"No, thank you," I said, determined to be as polite. Too bad my voice sounded like croaking frogs.

"Well, if you don't mind waiting," she said, her hands fluttering in the air.

Was she French?

"Not at all," I said.

Let's face it, my mission was a damn sight more important than my feelings, girly as they were. I was not jealous. I had overcome jealousy. I was flying high above it. I was in the stratosphere above jealousy.

She didn't lead me to a cozy nook. She didn't escort me to Dan's outer office. She just gave me a pale imitation of a smile, turned on her heel and left without another glance at me or the receptionist.

I caught the sweet young thing's look and smiled. She ducked her head and pretended she hadn't been sending the death ray to the "assistant".

Evidently, the fairy tale castle had a few personnel problems.

I skimmed through all the magazines - each of them recent and none of them giving me a clue what kind of business Dan was in. No Soldier of Fortune, Guns R Us, or Mercenary Digest. I gave up the magazines and spent five minutes marshaling my arguments, plus an equal amount of time trying to quell my anxiety, and a good two minutes contemplating my shoes.

I love sneakers. They beat the heck out of heels as far as I was concerned, but they did zip, nada, squat for your legs. In fact, in my orange sweatshirt and jeans, I was as far from Diane Trenton as a pot belly pig was from a lioness.

Damn the woman.

"Marcie."

I looked up and saw him. The earth didn't move. A crack of thunder and a white zigzag of lightning didn't blind me. But something happened. My stomach moved. I felt it turn over and an attendant rise in my blood pressure. I'd made love to this man. I'd laughed with him and slept beside him. He'd saved me more than once.

I met his eyes, watching as his widened.

What did he see when looking at me?

He reached me, holding out his hand as if I were infirm and needed help standing. In a few months that might be true. Regardless, I put my hand in his and allowed him to pull me up until I stood in front of him.

Had he always been so tall, so masculine? Had he always smelled so good?

"What is it, Marcie?"

I didn't want to say anything in front of the sweet young thing.

"Can we go to your office?"

He nodded, but there was a question in his eyes. At least he wasn't acting cold like he'd been in the courtyard.

We walked down a wide corridor lined with pictures of buildings. I didn't stop to investigate whether they were Cluckey Fried Chicken locations or something else. I should have stopped and looked, but I had other things on my mind, like talking Dan into doing something I bet he didn't want to do.

Dan turned left, led me through a warren of closed doors with names and titles in brass beside the door frame. Nothing looked wrong, like Jeff Smith, Chief of Weirdness or Lance Thomas, Chief Excuses Officer. Everything looked fine, but I've learned in the last few months to delve beneath normal to the oddities below.

Miss Pursed Lips, aka Diane Trenton, sat in her own glass fronted office beside Dan's door. She looked up, did a cursory lip movement and then went back to studying her monitor. How much you wanna bet she pulled up information on me? Maybe I should come back and wake her up after she read it.

Dan halted beside double doors, reached out, turned the handle on the right one before stepping back. I walked inside, hoping that my mouth wasn't dropping open and my eyes weren't buggy.

I've seen quite a few offices, from headquarters of the CEO to the broom closet occupied by the accountant. I've never seen anything like the room I entered. The castle had a medieval, King Arthur and the Round Table kind of theme. I expected it to be replicated in Dan's office.

Instead, it was just the opposite.

Eight monitors on the far wall showed charts and scrolling lists. I know zip about the stock market, but I could certainly tell that they were stocks and that it wasn't just the New York Stock Exchange up there.

A mammoth black glass desk in the shape of an apostrophe sat in front of the wall of monitors. Three monitors, connected together, sat elevated on the fattest part of the desk facing a large leather and stainless steel chair. The arms were fixed with keypads, making me wonder if all Dan had to do was punch a number to get all sorts of things to happen in that room.

In front of the odd shaped desk were two chairs, both black leather and stainless steel. A conference table of the same black glass surrounded by a dozen or so chairs sat on the other side of the room. Above it was a pod of black metal. I wondered if it was a projector, a hologram machine, or a super duper communications system. Two large dark squares at either end of the table probably changed into television screens.

The only thing not high tech was the view from the wall of windows. The tear shaped lake took pride of place, the lights of the gazebo glittering in the blackness.

I crossed over the large oval rug woven with a red pattern on a black and white background.

It took me a minute, but I finally figured out that there was some kind of coating on the window. Either that or a shade that blocked any glare and was invisible outside the castle. I suspected everything about this room was shielded from just about anybody.

Dan had been quiet during my inspection. I turned to face him.

"Just who are you?"

"You know me better than anyone, Marcie. I'm surprised you're asking that."

That was a good move, playing on my embarrassment. I knew him, in the biblical sense, but did I know him in the intellectual - *who are you really* - sense? I didn't think so.

He stood a few feet away from me, arms folded, face impassive.

"Why did you join the Rangers?" I asked.

He frowned at me, but answered anyway. "To serve my country. Because it was a challenge."

That answer didn't take any second guessing since it sounded like the truth.

"What did your grandfather say?"

"He wasn't happy," he said.

"But you didn't care. You did what you thought was right."

He nodded, but there was a waiting and watchful look in his eyes.

I took a seat in front of his desk. I'd always thought Dan was an anachronism, a twenty-first century man who looked at home in this medieval world, but I was wrong. He looked even more comfortable in these high tech surroundings.

Instead of sitting behind his desk, he sat beside me. I almost wanted him to put the acre of glass between us.

"Is there such a thing as a werewolf Congress? Or a shape shifter counsel? Some group that works in an organized fashion? Do the elves have a guild?"

"Each has an organizational hierarchy, yes. Why do you ask?"

"How do you know?" I asked. "If you aren't one of the Brethren, if you aren't a witch or a vampire, how do you know?"

"My archives," he said. "My grandfather collected everything there was to know about the strength, numbers, and cultural aspects of both witches and vampires. I added to them, plus made a copy of all the OTHER's files. If you ever want to read what's there, you're welcome to access the vault."

"What, you haven't digitized it?"

He shook his head. "Our system is as secure as the best IT professionals can make it, but that doesn't mean it's perfect. I've never seen a system that's a hundred percent secure. Some of that information should never become public."

"Can I see it?"

I half expected him to refuse. I didn't think he would whip out a business card. On the back was written: Level S-3, Archive A, followed by a series of letters and numbers. Just key in the combination at the door, then sign in with the archivist.

Archive A? Archivist?

"How many archives do you have?"

"A few," he said.

He did that a lot. He was very generous with information, then he just clammed up. It drove me nuts.

I turned the business card over, half expecting only his name and a phone number. Instead, the card read: Dan Travis, CEO, UI, Inc.

"What's UI?"

"Universal Investigations."

I looked up at him. "You're a private eye?"

He shook his head. "I'm an investigator," he said.

Tomato, to-mah-to.

"And you concentrate on the paranormal, don't you?" I said, guessing.

"Not necessarily."

That wasn't exactly an answer, though, was it?

"What about zombies? Are there such things as zombies?"

Please say no. Please say no. Please say no. There were just so many things I could accept and zombies were two steps beyond that line in the sand.

"I don't know," he said, unsmiling.

I thought about Charlie. I suspected his owner wasn't quite human, but I didn't have any kind of Brethren radar. I used to get headaches when I was around witches, but even those had faded. If I ever got any kind of signal with other species, I didn't know about it.

"Are you sure you're not a shape shifter or werewolf or an elf or fairy?"

He raised his right hand, palm toward me. "I swear on my life, Marcie Montgomery, that I am not any of those things."

"Do you employ any shape shifters, werewolves, elves or fairies?"

"I'm an equal opportunity employer," he said. "As long as you can prove that you don't bring ill will to me or mine, I don't care what you are."

"Do you employ laundry fairies?"

I'd joked in the past about how quickly my laundry was done and in such an expert manner.

"Laundry fairies? No."

"Why don't I ever see anyone collect my dirty clothes or deliver them back to me?"

"There's a panel in your dressing room that's accessible, by code, whenever you're not in the room. It leads to the operational part of the castle. My grandfather believed that servants should neither be seen nor heard."

Did they all commute? Or did some of them fly here, like the fairies? Or did they reside in the flowers that bordered the paths of the courtyard? What did I know about fairies? They may not be the size of my palm with translucent wings. Heck, they could be adult size, with teleportation skills.

"Does everyone live here?" A reasonable question since I hadn't seen an influx of cars to Arthur's Folly every morning.

"No."

He was answering all my questions easily. I decided to press my luck.

"Where are all the employee cars?"

"The entrance to the underground parking is about a half mile away."

Just when I was fumbling with that, he confused me even further.

"When we begin preparing for our siege, we won't have as many employees as we do now. Those who want to continue their employment will have to reside here. Not everyone will make that choice."

"Siege?" That was not a word that came up in normal conversation in the 21st century.

"We're in a fight for the future of humanity, Marcie."

"Isn't that a little dramatic?"

The look he gave me was one hundred percent Dan, one eyebrow arched, a half smile, and a measuring look in his eyes.

"What would you call it? People are trying to experiment with your blood to create a new race."

Well, if you put it that way, he had a point. Maybe he hadn't been dramatic enough. Maybe a little screaming and panicking was called for.

"What about the families of your employees? Have you made arrangements for them, too?"

"Key personnel will have a choice: their families will either be relocated or they will be accommodated here."

"Here? Is Arthur's Folly that big?"

"We can house about fifty families."

Talk about the uber uber rich.

"How long do you expect this siege to go on?"

"Until something is decided."

That wasn't a really reassuring answer.

"Why all the questions, Marcie?"

"I think we should have a meeting," I said. "With representatives from the Brethren. Let them know what's happening."

He didn't say anything.

Here was where I threw down my biggest bargaining chip.

"And I want to have the witches test me as soon as possible."

He took one of my hands and studied it. "Why the change?"

He linked his fingers with mine. I squeezed his hand before pulling mine free. I didn't want to fall under his spell right now. I was keeping a secret from him and it made me feel guilty as hell. The more distance between us, the better because I wanted him, too. And if I couldn't have him, then I wanted a few minutes with him. Companionship, a few laughs, a little bonding, what was wrong with that? My little voice was getting shrill and I silenced it with a mental neck chop.

"Mike is dying," I said.

"I know."

His voice was impassive, the two words uttered in Ranger-speak. Not one scintilla of emotion leaked through, but I was getting better at reading him. The look in his eyes, carefully flat and inscrutable, said what words couldn't. Whenever Dan didn't emote, it meant he was feeling plenty.

"I understand that he was drained down to the point of not being able to become a vampire," I said, plowing ahead, words my bulldozer.

"Yes," he said.

Just that one answer, but something sparked in his eyes.

"Let me give him a transfusion," I said. I was relatively certain that giving some of my blood wouldn't hurt my baby.

"Unless you would rather he die than become a vampire," I added. Or something else. Would Mike become Pranic? Nobody, and I mean nobody, had that answer.

I had to add the rest.

"He might have rabies, so maybe it's good he can't be turned," I said. "I think my blood could heal him."

He stared down at the pristine glass surface of his desk. Was he one of those paperless office people? I didn't see a scrap of paper in the whole place. Several soft pings happened every minute or so. Either Bass Lips was instant messaging him or he was getting emails like crazy. Either could be the case.

"You don't know what a transfusion would do to him. Especially of your blood."

Well, that put me in my place, didn't it? I looked away, clasping my hands together tightly until my knuckles protested. I was not going to reveal my hurt.

"You're one of those who would rather Mike died then become a vampire, is that it?"

"I'm not fond of the species," he said.

Another zinger. He was filled with them today, wasn't he?

God forbid I should be the guest who came for dinner. What's that saying about guests and fish after three days? They both began to smell. Well, I'd been here longer than three days.

"I'm a vampire," I said softly.

He shook his head. "My mother doesn't understand. Mike doesn't understand. Nobody in the castle who knows about my mission understands. I'm not even sure I understand how I feel about you."

I forced myself to look at him.

"You're not like the rest, Marcie." He waved his hand in the air. "Forget about the Pranic stuff. Even as a plain vampire, you weren't like the rest."

My heart was beginning to pick up its pace. I might get to a whole twenty beats a minute if this kept up.

"I'm attracted to you. I'm drawn to you. I feel connected to you, somehow, and I haven't the slightest idea why."

What had I expected, an avowal of love? A decree of undying affection? He sounded as confused as I felt.

"I would say it's lust, but it's more than that. I don't know what the hell it is, but I'm fighting it every step of the way."

"Good to know," I said.

What did he expect me to say? That I'd never been as confused in my life as when he kissed me? That my dreams had been fevered imaginings and I'd wanted him in my bed and in my body for weeks?

Lust, love, attraction, fascination – whatever you wanted to call it – it was out of place right now.

"He's going to die. You know he's going to die."

"Why do you care?"

I was suddenly blazingly angry.

"Because I'm mostly human. Because he's another human being. Because a monster hurt him. Because whatever you think of me, I'm not a monster. At least I don't want to be. And he saved me. He saved my life. If Maddock hadn't gone for him, he would have gone for me. If Maddock had gotten his hands on me, I'd be in a cage in his basement. I can only imagine what my eternity would've been."

"He's been getting a series of transfusions. He's losing it as fast as it goes in."

That might have something to do with the rabies vaccine. Or whatever Maddock had done to drain him down.

"Then you have to let me try," I said.

"You'll have to get it approved by Kenisha," he said.

I stared at him, incredulous. "I can't talk to Kenisha. She'll tell the Council about me."

He shook his head. "I doubt it, especially if it means saving Mike's life."

I threw my hands in the air. "Why are you, suddenly Dear Abby of the vampire set? How do I know that turning me into the Council won't get her some great kind of reward like saving Mike's life?"

"Because I've already gone to them."

"What?" Now that was a shock.

"Their representative verified that if a human is drunk down to the extent Mike is, the chances of saving him are nil."

"Will Maddock be punished for it?"

"No. It was, as they said, 'A regrettable and horrific act, brought about by an excess of passion.'"

"What?"

I know, I know, Marcie Montgomery, brilliant conversationalist.

"Evidently, you spurned him, and Maddock is a man exquisitely sensitive to rejection."

"I spurned him?" My laughter sounded like a cackle. I uttered a word I normally do not say in polite company and, despite the fact that Dan had been a Ranger, I'd never heard him use it, either.

I would apologize later.

"I understand that you're trying to do the honorable thing by Kenisha. I get it," I said. "But is her affection, her love, for Mike strong enough to make her defy the Council?" I really couldn't take the chance that she'd betray me, especially now. "If she goes to them and tells them what I am, are you ready for vampires to storm the castle?"

He didn't say anything to that.

"Look," I said. "I don't know if my blood will save him, but if there's no hope, shouldn't we at least try?"

"Only if Kenisha agrees," he said.

I almost rolled my eyes, but I refrained. I couldn't do anything about the sinking feeling in my stomach, though.

I'd traded a witch test for another conversation with Kenisha. I'd failed Bargaining 101.

CHAPTER NINE

What's one more aberration?

I was delaying. I knew I was delaying, but sometimes procrastination has its advantages. I didn't want to talk to Kenisha, especially as drained as she was. All the way to the kennels, I occupied myself with thinking of the various strategies I might employ. I could throw myself on her mercy, but she had never struck me as a merciful kind of person. Granted, she'd been through a lot. I don't know how warm and fuzzy I would feel about the world if my son had turned me into a vampire and then was killed for doing so. That was another thing I had to take into consideration. If Mike was turned, we had to make sure that Kenisha wasn't held responsible. If the Council thought it was her act, she'd be killed.

In order to get her approval for what I wanted to do, I'd have to count on her feelings for Mike. She had to agree. I didn't want his death on my conscience. I was trying to keep it as clean as possible. I might need a blank slate in the future.

Charlie was out gamboling with the labs when I got to the kennel. They had opened up another part of the yard, something I hadn't seen before: an agility course. Next to it was large shallow pool that I bet the dogs loved in the summer.

Were the labs used as guard dogs? Or were they trained to detect vampires? Just add that to the list of things I didn't know and needed to find out. Right now my list was about fourteen feet long.

As I watched, Charlie ran up the narrow ramp and across what looked like a balance beam before jumping down. He raced over to sit in front of me, tongue lolling, a look of pride on his canine face.

I bent down to pet him and he stiffened.

"You've got Kenisha on you," Opie said.

One of the kennel workers was standing five feet away. Opie had never spoken in front of someone else, especially when the risk of discovery was so great. I don't know what surprised me more, the fact that she was talking or that she/Charlie was now sniffing me from toes to knees.

His/her nose was wet and very, very intrusive.

I backed up, but Charlie followed, nose ready to dive into places his nose had never been.

"Stop it!"

I heard laughter from behind me and I wanted to explain. But what could I possibly say? Look, if it was just my dog, I wouldn't feel so weird about the whole situation. But this is a vet who sniffing me. A ghost vet.

Yeah, that would go over really good.

I backed up, turned around, and started walking away from the kennel. Once we were alone – if you discounted the security cameras that were probably everywhere – I addressed Charlie, but without looking at him.

"What the hell has gotten into you?"

"You have Kenisha on you," Opie said. "K girl."

"What?"

"K girl. Kenisha."

I knew that she and Kenisha had been friends, but she was acting strange.

"We're best buds," Opie said. "At least we were. We met before I was turned," she added. "I took care of her cat."

I was having trouble with the idea of Kenisha having a cat. She was more the German Shepherd type. K girl?

"Best buds? Like you went out partying together?"

"No, Kenisha wasn't a party girl. But we were on the phone a lot. Plus, we went to church together."

Okay, now I really was having an episode of cognitive dissonance.

"Does a vampire go to church?"

It was difficult for a dog to give me a look of disgust, but Charlie somehow managed it.

"Of course a vampire goes to church."

"So, you were friends? Best buds?"

"Yep." Opie said it so emphatically that it came out as a bark.

"Do you trust her?" I asked.

"Trust her?" Charlie's head tilted up to look at me. "Of course I trust her."

"Can I?"

One thing about Opie/Charlie or Charlie/Opie, they were both smart in their way. It didn't take a brick to hit either one of them before they figured out what I was really asking.

"I would. Except for the bun in the oven part. She's still sensitive about her son. But the rest, yeah."

Then I'd tell her about everything but the baby.

"You do realize the bun in the oven part is very, very confidential."

There was that disgusted look again.

As we hit the elevators, it struck me that I should present Kenisha with Opie in a dog suit. Then, while Kenisha was still reeling from that revelation, I could tell her that I had given Maddock the rabies vaccine and oh, by the way, I was a goddess.

I don't know how much one person could take, especially a tired vampire. It hardly seemed fair to dump everything on her, but we were running out of time. Mike couldn't subsist on one transfusion after another. Sooner or later, his organs would start to fail and then we'd be too late. I might have goddess powers, but I'm not God. There's a big difference between us.

We hit the elevators and while we were descending, I talked as if I were speaking to myself, hoping that Opie would get the clue. I didn't doubt that there was surveillance equipment in the elevators and no doubt audio recordings, too. If I was talking to myself, I would be labeled eccentric. Better that than the nut job who was talking to her dog.

Or even worse: a dog that was answering her.

Once at the sub level I strode through the corridor on my way to what was essentially the intensive care wing with my shoulders back, my boobs front and center. My chin jutted out as if I were feeling pugnacious instead of terrified. I am not given to challenging authority. When I was learning how to drive, I was once stopped by a patrolman. I think my turn signal was broken, but he didn't even get to the point of telling me that before I burst into tears. He was authority and I was petrified.

But no one looking at me right now could tell that I was quaking in my sneakers. Nope, I stared each one of them down, and when I turned right into the wing where Mike was being treated, Charlie trotted along at my heels like the perfect service dog. That was my cover if anyone stopped me. He needed practice.

I didn't bother knocking on Kenisha's door. I only opened it slightly, got a glimpse of the tray, blessedly emptied of its contents, and entered. My bravado died the moment I saw her. She didn't look as drained as she had before, but there was an expression in her eyes that hit me right in the solar plexus, or wherever compassion and empathy was stored. She'd been crying. In that second everything I thought about Kenisha underwent a rapid reevaluation.

"I brought you a visitor," I said, taking a few tentative steps forward.

She glanced at Charlie. "You shouldn't bring a dog in here."

"Well, that's just it. Charlie isn't exactly just a dog."

"K girl," Opie suddenly said.

Way to ease into a situation. I was going to gradually introduce the subject of ghostly visitations, maybe even reincarnation, but Opie just stepped all over that idea.

She went up to the couch and sat in front of Kenisha.

"K girl, I've missed you."

Kenisha sat back, folded her hands in her lap and stared at the golden retriever.

"You're not losing your mind," I said. "I had the same reaction at first."

Slowly, Kenisha looked up at me. She had evidently been attending the Dan Travis School of Blank Expressions, because I didn't have a clue what she was thinking.

I guessed, however, that she thought she was going crazy.

"I know," Opie said. "It's a lot to take in, isn't it? I felt the same way when I woke up to find out I was a dog. It could be worse, I guess. I could be a snail. Then nobody would ever hear me or see me or talk to me. At least, this way, I can vary my locale. Plus, as a snail, somebody was bound to step on me."

"What would happen to you then?" I asked, curious.

"I haven't the slightest idea," she said, turning Charlie's head to look at me. "Where would you go to get that kind of information?"

I thought about Dan's archives. I doubted his grandfather had acquired anything about talking dogs or ghosts.

Kenisha shook her head, then glared at me as if I were Jeff Dunham and Charlie was just another puppet.

"I can assure you my skills don't include ventriloquism," I said. "It's Opie."

Kenisha looked at Charlie, then at me, then back at Charlie.

"Do you remember the time we wanted to know if we could get drunk as vampires?" Opie asked. "And we went through four bottles and a box of wine before we got a buzz? Marijuana worked better, but you were terrified you were going to get caught."

Kenisha's eyes widened.

"Or when you were so worried about Jake that you insisted on calling me every hour on the hour to make sure he was okay?" Opie turned to me. "Her cat got into a fight with a dog." She looked back at Kenisha. "How's he doing, by the way?"

"Opie?" Kenisha leaned forward, raised her hand as if to pet Charlie but drew it back at the last moment. "Is it really you?"

"It is. In the flesh. Canine flesh, but still..."

"How?" Kenisha asked.

I didn't mean to laugh, really, but it was such a ludicrous question from a vampire.

"Who knows?" I said. "The whole world is a little screwy right now. What's one more aberration?"

Kenisha patted the couch beside her and Charlie didn't hesitate, jumping up and putting his head on her lap. Kenisha, whom I've never seen being gracious, kind, or sweet, put her arms around Charlie and burst into tears.

There are some emotions that are a relief to feel. You cry; you get over it and you're better. What I was feeling right now wasn't the least bit refreshing, but more like an SOS pad had scrubbed my insides.

I wanted to comfort her, do something to take away her pain. The only thing I could think of doing was giving Mike a transfusion. With any luck, it would give her hope.

CHAPTER TEN

I vant to transfuse your blood

For the next fifteen minutes, the two of them were like schoolgirls, and I found myself feeling like a third wheel. I missed the friends I'd made at my apartment complex. They'd disappeared like fog after I became a vampire. I'd been promoted pretty fast at work, so I was mid-management before I had a chance to make any friends there. Once I was management, I had to make sure I didn't play favorites, which meant that friendships had to be confined to people at the same level.

Unfortunately, commercial insurance was probably one of the last bastions of male dominated industries. The two other women in management weren't my type. One was deeply into LGBT causes and the other collected cats.

I'd heard that some of Melanie's subordinates had complained of the odor and asked to be moved to different cubbies. Evidently, eau de litter box lingered on her clothes. So did cat hair. When we had pot luck lunches, I always made sure to find out what she'd brought so I could avoid it.

What was with pot luck anyway? Why was that considered a team bonding exercise? Going to the water park wasn't much better. There were certain people I didn't want to see in a swimsuit. Or, God forbid, a Speedo.

They were laughing now, and Kenisha's tears were drying up. That was the good part about Opie being "with us", if you'll pardon the very broad definition of that term.

I had gotten used to not having her body around and my mind had made the leap to accepting her in a dog suit. I think I just blanked out from time to time, especially when we were having a heart to heart talk. I wasn't used to getting advice from someone who could slobber all over me in the next minute.

I hadn't figured out how to ease into the subject of Mike, but trust Opie to take the initiative there, too.

"Tell me about Mike," she said. "He's a new guy, isn't he? Do you like him? How's it going with him? Nobody mentioned him to me." At this, Opie turned and gave me a reproachful Charlie look.

I occupied myself with studying the ceiling.

"It doesn't matter," Kenisha said listlessly. "He only has hours to live."

"About that," I began.

Charlie jumped up to catch and came to my side. I had never been herded by a dog before, but he moved behind me and shoved at my leg until I took a step forward. Finally, I sat on the end of the couch and he jumped up to occupy the space between Kenisha and me.

"When I first knew of Mike's condition," I said, "I thought we had three alternatives."

Neither Kenisha nor the dog between us said a word.

"I thought we could petition the Council to turn Mike."

"You can't petition the Council as a Fledgling," Kenisha said. Her voice had lost that dead sound to it, if you'll pardon the pun.

"How come?"

"I don't know," she said, shrugging. "All I know is it's part of the rules. You can't even address the Council as a Fledgling. You have to be a vampire for a year before requesting an audience."

See what you miss by not attending orientation?

"Well, that's out anyway. From what I understand, he's been drained too far to turn."

Charlie leaned his head on Kenisha's shoulder. The two of them giving comfort to each other was such a sweet sight.

I didn't tell them that Dan had already contacted the Council. I imagine that didn't go over very well, especially since he'd been actively trying to find his sister for ten months and suspected that vampires were responsible for her disappearance.

"The next alternative is just to let him die."

I hated to be blunt, but it was always better to face the truth of the situation and then make arrangements to mitigate them. Pretending didn't help anyone. I made a mental note to flog myself with that thought.

"But that's not really an alternative," I added. "He's Dan's best friend and you care about him a lot. Plus he's here only because he was my bodyguard and Maddock attacked him. So that only leaves one alternative. Me."

Now came the hard part. I had to trust her. I had to trust her not to take the information and go scampering over to the Council.

I looked at Opie and Charlie's brown eyes stared earnestly back at me.

"Are you sure?" I asked her.

She nodded Charlie's head at me emphatically, adding a little canine bark to the mix.

I sighed and turned to Kenisha. "Remember when you asked me if I was menstruating?"

Kenisha nodded.

"I lied."

She stared at me, unblinking.

"I'm not a normal vampire," I said. I looked away from her, staring at the tray on the table by the door. "I don't drink blood." I had to hurry up and skim over that fact before I got sick to my stomach. "I eat regular food."

"Tell her about being able to walk in the sun," Opie said.

"You can walk in the sun?" Kenisha asked.

I nodded. "I've got a lot of powers," I said. "I suspect I haven't discovered all of them. But I know that I'm different enough that I might be able to save Mike. But there's something else you need to know."

I'd wondered how much information was too much and I had a feeling that I was coming close to the edge with Kenisha. She was looking a little shell shocked.

"I gave Niccolo Maddock an injection of the rabies virus," I said, forcing myself to keep looking at her.

Only a twitch of a muscle above her eyes indicated that she had heard me or that she was surprised by my comment.

"Why?"

"Because I wanted him to die," I said.

"You can't kill a master vampire like Maddock easily."

"I know," I said. "That's why gave him the rabies virus. By the time he realized what was happening to him, it would've destroyed his brain."

Never say that Kenisha wasn't a smart cookie. She figured it out immediately.

"Mike might have rabies."

I nodded. "So, in addition to a transfusion from me, we need to treat Mike for rabies. I didn't realize until this morning that vampires can carry diseases that don't affect them."

Again, something I missed by not going to orientation.

"What the hell did Maddock do to you?"

I took a deep breath and said the words I hadn't said to anyone else. "He raped me, Kenisha. He drugged me and then he raped me."

She was still staring at me but her face had altered subtly. I wondered if it was her cop face, or the beginnings of compassion.

"Dan insisted that you had to approve the transfusion. I don't know of any alternative, do you?"

"He knows about you?" she asked.

I nodded.

"Does Mike know, too?"

"Yes."

I didn't know if that information was going to annoy her or prejudice her in some way against Mike. It might not have any effect at all. She might not care.

"Before we do anything, though," I said, coming to the nitty-gritty part. "You have to promise not to go to the Council or tell anyone what you know about me."

I couldn't afford for Kenisha to go blabbing to anyone about who I was and what I could do. It was bad enough that Maddock, Eagle Lady, the Librarian, Dan, Mike, and a talking dog knew. The fewer people in the loop, the better for me and my baby.

She remained silent for so long I was getting worried.

Before I could figure out what to do, she nodded.

"I promise. But you need to make sure the Council knows I didn't turn Mike."

"Agreed," I said.

"What do we do now?" Opie asked. "Can't you just bite Mike?"

I've never bitten anyone and I really didn't have the stomach for it now. I couldn't see having to quash my gag reflex and swallow blood. Ugh.

"No, we're going to do it the medical way. First, I need to let the grand Poobah know that Kenisha has agreed. That will start the ball rolling."

I hadn't been able to find my phone, so I had to use the intercom to let Dan know that Kenisha had agreed. One thing I can say about Dan. The man had organizational ability. I don't know if it was something that came natural to him or something he learned in the Rangers, but he could command movement.

Within a half hour I was on an exam table with my arm on a board. I was staring up at the ceiling, trying not to look at the blood in the tubing. I guess I had expected that I would be in Mike's room doing this person-to-person, but instead my blood was piped into a bag and would be transfused to him within minutes. After that, time was what we needed. Unfortunately, time was not on Mike's side.

It struck me as I was lying there that there was another advantage to giving my blood to Mike, other than saving his life. I didn't doubt he would become a vampire. But he might obtain some of my powers. Time would tell if he would be able to walk in the sun or eat food other than blood, or if he became Marcie II, in a manner of speaking. If he did, there would be two of us. The world wouldn't be looking for just me. Of course, by doubling my chances for survival I also put Mike in danger. I had to let him know everything that was facing him. That is, if he survived.

If he did obtain my abilities, it would only be a matter of time until Kenisha wanted to be like him.

That's how it started, didn't it? All revolutions started with one person, one thought pattern, one idea. It caught fire and multiplied a thousand times.

The more I tried to do the right thing, the more complicated I made my life. But humans, and humans turned vampires, are messy creatures. We don't live calm and orderly lives. After the last few months I doubted I could go back to being the person I had been. That's not necessarily a bad thing. Looking back on that Marcie, I could only pity her. She was living a life without much happiness, strung out by goals and accomplishments that, in the end, didn't really matter a whole bunch. She didn't love to the extent she could have, including herself.

Now I felt as if I were living to my full potential. Never mind that I was confused most of the time. I was feeling emotions I hadn't felt in a great many years, if ever. I was awake when I had been asleep for a very long time.

I won't say I was courageous, but I was willing to be braver. Maybe it was because I knew I couldn't die, at least not easily. Maybe some of it was because I knew I was different, not only from myself but from other people.

Dr. Fernandez's words called me back to the present.

"That'll do it," he said. "I'd like you to lay here for a little while and rest."

"You'll give Mike the rabies vaccine, too?"

He nodded, but he didn't look at me. He had been carefully avoiding my glance ever since he and Dan talked. Evidently, I'd been outed to the castle's physician.

"I wouldn't hold out much hope, Ms. Montgomery."

I turned my head and stared at his back.

"You don't think he's going to make it."

He raised his head. Since he still hadn't turned I could only guess that he was staring at the far wall. Maybe he had his eyes closed. Maybe he was looking up at the ceiling. Hell, for all I knew, he was rolling his eyes or making faces.

"I don't know all that much about vampirism, Ms. Montgomery. I do know that if he hadn't been as healthy as he was, he would have died in the first hour."

"Maybe he'll fool you," I said. Or my blood would.

He didn't answer, only left the room.

I was a good little patient for fifteen minutes. Not because of what the doctor said. I wanted to make sure that I was feeling okay for the baby's sake before I stood up. Finally, I made it to the door, but instead of heading for the elevator, I went into Mike's room.

I read this saying once, on one of those feel-good posters that are supposed to motivate you. It said: we pay attention to what we love. Frankly, I thought that was a load of crap. People pay attention to what irritates them. Sometimes, we don't even notice the people we love until it's too late.

I couldn't help but wonder if it was too late for Mike.

Kenisha was sitting at the side of the hospital bed, her feet flat on the floor, her shoulders straight, her hands clasped on her lap. She was watching Mike the way a supplicant stares at an altar, waiting for proof that God heard, that miracles were possible.

She glanced at me when I opened the door and slid inside. Vampires don't get that red eyed look from being hungry. She had been crying again.

Vampires are supposed to be hypochondriacs, but either that didn't apply to Kenisha or she was fighting it to be able to stay with Mike.

I stood there for a few minutes in the silence, watching as the blood - my blood - dripped down into his arm. I don't know if God was accustomed to getting prayers from goddesses, but I didn't think it would hurt to add one to the mix. I left after that, giving Kenisha privacy.

I made it back to my room, feeling a little wobbly. And hungry. My appetite had returned with a vengeance and I was craving anything at this point. I was going to order a tuna sandwich and some chicken noodle soup. Comfort foods again, but I needed them, both emotionally and physically.

The minute I closed the door I knew something was different. The room felt odd, but I couldn't figure out what it was.

I stood in the middle of the room, in the exact same place I'd been when the witches first called to me. I half expected a hologram to appear, but nothing did. I closed my eyes, lifted my arms slightly and turned my palms up. The pose was an automatic one and I could see how I must've looked to someone else. Strange, though, my internal vision had me glowing a little. Not the healthy glow of a pregnant woman, but more of a golden aura surrounding my entire body and joined at my feet.

I looked like a saint in an illustrated manuscript. Either that, or a shampoo commercial.

To my surprise, the aura was malleable. If I thought ahead a few feet, it stretched that way. I tried sending it left, then right, playing with it. I didn't open my eyes, but I did begin to smile, wondering if what I was seeing in my mind's eye was real or just imagination. Too bad I hadn't done this glowy thing in front of a mirror.

Well, I'd wanted to see what else I could do. Was this part of the zappy thing or totally separate from it? I didn't want to hurt anyone, I just wanted to protect myself. The golden aura was like a force field.

I sent the glow across the carpet until it pressed up against the walls, filling up the entire room. Nobody was here but me. I couldn't sense another consciousness. I couldn't feel anyone else's spirit.

But someone had been here.

Who?

One of the laundry fairies?

I opened my eyes and looked around, but I couldn't see that anything was out of place. Something was missing, though, and it took me a minute to figure out what.

I knew I'd put the Kindle on the table by the chaise, but it wasn't there now. I'd been sitting here earlier and tried to read. I walked to the other side of the room, between the window and the chaise, but it hadn't fallen to the floor. I even bent over and looked under the furniture, but it wasn't there, either. Maybe I'd put it in the bathroom. I walked in there, but no Kindle.

That was just annoying. First my phone and now my Kindle.

Who the hell steals a Kindle? A literate burglar? Was one of Dan's staff a thief? Should I say something or keep silent?

I sat on the chaise, missing Charlie. Opie had wanted to sit vigil with Kenisha and who could argue with that? Hopefully, the transfusion would work. Hopefully, Mike would live. Hopefully, Kenisha wouldn't say anything to the Council.

Lots of my future rested on hope and that wasn't a good place to be. I wanted certainties. I was a woman of spreadsheets and facts and hope was too tenuous and too uncertain.

I didn't bother making a list. I knew what I had to do. Protect my child, take the witch test, and save mankind.

Nope, hope had nothing to do with it.

CHAPTER ELEVEN

Let the tests begin

I didn't wake until ten. Nothing had changed, except that I was sick as a dog, if you'll pardon the expression, followed by a hunger so acute I thought I was starving to death. My stomach was glued to my backbone and I was nearly faint. If I didn't get a dozen pancakes or waffles inside me, I was going to die. Cereal wasn't going to do it. Neither was a donut or two and don't get me started on oatmeal. I liked oatmeal if it had enough milk, sugar, and butter in it, but if it was plain, no thanks. If you really hated me, you would give me plain cream of wheat, salted.

Just the thought of that made me run to the bathroom again.

Because I felt so awful, I thought it would have been perfectly within my rights to stay in my room, order breakfast, and have a grand old pity party. The world was against me, boo hoo. Maybe that was true, but I'd never known a circumstance that was made better by whining about it. I got over myself long enough to order tea and crackers.

Let someone in the kitchen put two and two together, I didn't care.

The intercom buzzed while I was waiting.

I pushed the button and Dan's voice filled the room.

"Why aren't you answering your phone?" he asked.

"I can't find it," I said, a little annoyed by having to admit it. I sounded like a kid who had to have her mittens pinned to her coat sleeve.

"I sent you a text. The witch test is at one in the ballroom."

Of course Arthur's Folly had a ballroom. Didn't everyone?

"I'll be there."

The young woman who brought my tray asked if I needed anything else. Answers, please, but she couldn't bring those up from the kitchen.

"No, thank you," I said, and closed the door behind her.

After I had wolfed down the crackers and sipped my herbal tea, I watched TV for a little while, finding myself entranced by a show that offered to tell a woman who had fathered her child. I imagined getting Dan's DNA would be easy enough. How would they test my unborn child, however?

I took another nap. One of the things about pregnancy: I was always tired.

A few hours later, I took a shower, went to the vanity and began to put on makeup, just enough that I felt more myself. Mascara, mineral foundation, and lipstick - nothing fancy. I opened the drawer to get my brush, but it wasn't there. Oh, come on now. I knew I hadn't moved my brush. I didn't trot through the castle with my full armament of grooming essentials. I wasn't like a friend of mine who carried around a selection of brushes, combs, a mini can of hair spray and a touchup comb in case a stray gray hair liberated itself from the masses. But Vickie also carried a toothbrush, toothpaste, floss, tweezers, and two kinds of nail files.

I wasn't Vickie.

Who the hell was stealing my stuff? Was someone trying to get my DNA? Or was someone just light fingered? The surge of irritation I felt was welcome.

I finger brushed my hair, did another inspection of me - especially of the tummy region - to make sure I wasn't looking pregnant. I knew it was much too soon, but with my goddess metabolism, who knew what was *normal* for me? I had a feeling that word should be banished from my vocabulary.

I pushed the intercom and asked for directions to the ballroom. I declined the offer of a guide. I wasn't yet infirm and I felt safe in the castle. Relatively safe, given that someone was stealing my stuff.

As I walked toward the elevators, I thought about the upcoming test. According to my grandmother, a tendency toward witchcraft was inherited. Some witch progeny had it. Some didn't. My mother didn't. Neither did Dan. Would my child, if Dan was his father, have a witchy ability? When did it begin? From the womb or later, such as when he was a toddler? Or not until the teenage years? I would have to ask someone and that posed another problem. Who? Was there a Nurse Hotline for witches? Would they be any more amenable to answering questions then the vampire nurse had been?

I doubted it.

If I were talking to my mother, I would ask her what kind of test she had to undergo. The problem was she'd escaped from custody. According to Kenisha, my mother had joined a fundamentalist sect, one of those We Hate the World groups that pop up from time to time. In this case, they weren't all that fond of vampires. Their group's name was The Militia of God. It didn't seem fair to put the God label on something that was filled with hate.

As a source of information, my mother was lost to me. I had a feeling, however, that she would pop up with The Militia of God group in tow one day. I could wait a few more years for a reunion with dear old mom.

What did the Militia think about the OTHER?

The OTHER's mission was to make sure everybody was just one happy family. That every person was alike. Sort of like political correctness taken to the nth degree. They wanted everyone to be able work spells like witches. Everyone would live for very long time like vampires. Everybody could procreate, walk in the sun, and eat burritos like human beings.

I doubt if a humans only group would go along with what the OTHER proposed. That was fine with me. The more diversity, the better. I didn't want us all to be just like each other.

The great thing about human beings was that there were so many kinds of them. I didn't think vampires were all that different. Were witches? How did someone become adept at working magic?

BF - Before Fangdom - I'd never considered that magic might be working all around me. Did I see Nonnie's house as it really was or how she wanted me to see it? For that matter, did she really look like a sweet little blue eyed grandmother or something completely different? I'd seen the power of magic with the destruction of Hermonious Brown's bookstore. I'd felt that surge of energy when the witches had come after me. I suspected that I needed to know more about magic. I was also absolutely blind when it came to the rest of the Brethren.

I needed to learn, fast.

I took the elevator to the third floor, turned right like I'd been told and followed a long corridor. As I was walking, it occurred to me that my zapping power might well be something I could have inherited. Granted, it was different from what I'd felt that first time I'd gone to Nonnie's house after being turned, but it was similar.

Was it a witchy power? Or something reserved for a Dirugu, a special Pranic vampire like I was supposed to be, so special I'd been labeled goddess. A little ludicrous, frankly, because I'm so far from a goddess it's laughable.

What if I did have witchy powers? What did that mean? What would it mean to the witches, especially?

I wanted to go check on Mike, but I'd left it too long. Maybe because I was procrastinating. Let's face it, I didn't want to attend the witch test. When I hit the ballroom entrance I almost turned around and walked away. I might be physically cautious, but I wasn't a moral coward, so I forced myself to go inside.

I shouldn't have been surprised at the size of the room, given the dimensions of the castle itself. Everything was oversized, just a bit more than it needed to be. Arthur Peterson had created his own little fiefdom here at Arthur's Folly. His millions - or billions - had made it possible for him to create what was, essentially, his own town. The inhabitants were no doubt well-paid, just as the craftsman of the ballroom probably had been.

The floor was constructed of long planks of what looked to be mahogany, beautifully waxed until I could see myself in them. The half-dozen chandeliers had five tiers, each one draped in hundreds of crystal prisms. They weren't lit right now, given that it was morning. Instead, the ballroom was bathed in sunlight from the cupola and the jeweled colors from the stained glass. I'd never seen such artistry outside of a church.

Three walls were inlaid with six floor to ceiling windows, each one bearing different scenes of what looked to be knights and ladies. Probably something from the Arthurian legends. When I had time, I was going to figure out what story they told, but right now I had to address the fact that there were a bunch of witches in white robes and hoods standing there.

Holy magic wand. Nobody told me there'd be twenty of them. Or that they would look like a contingent of the KKK.

The witches were arranged in a horseshoe shape at the end of the ballroom, each of them facing me. Nonnie was there, almost in the center, standing to the right of Janet, Dan's mother. I recognized the woman who led the Dallas covens, but that was it. The others were strangers to me, women ranging in age from their twenties to a few whose gray hair peeped out from their hoods.

Altogether, they were a scary bunch. Maybe it was the white robes. Or just the fact they seemed intensely focused on little ol' me.

I've seen a cat eyeing a bird with the same look.

I was getting vibes from some of them, and I didn't know if it was a newfound power or a corruption of the headache I used to get in the presence of witches. As I studied them, one by one, I felt that a few of them just wanted me gone, as in permanently off the planet. A few others were more curious than hostile, and one or two didn't bear any ill will toward me, but were concerned that I might bring harm to their group.

Was each witch a representative of a coven?

I didn't mind being tested. The problem was, I didn't know what was going to happen at the end of the test. Would it be a good or a bad thing if I had witch powers? Would that convince the witches to help me in my battle against the vampires and the OTHER?

That's the real reason I was here, because I needed the witches on my side. Otherwise, it was one goddess against the whole of the paranormal world and that hardly seemed fair.

I heard a whirring sound above me and the cupola began to close. The room was growing dim, the jewel toned light from the stained glass the only illumination. I was cast in green and blue, the colors almost feeling cool against my face.

I hadn't dressed for the occasion. Instead, I'd opted for comfort, wearing a dark blue sweater over a white blouse and my nearly new jeans. My pink and green sneakers almost seemed disrespectful.

They needed to take themselves less seriously, a suggestion I was not going to make to twenty witches.

They stirred, Janet stepping forward as they closed ranks behind her.

She stared straight at me while talking, as if I didn't have a clue who she was addressing. I really think she liked being head honcho of this gathering and she didn't mind me being at the point of the skewer, either.

All I had to do was keep the objective in mind: I was here because I needed their help.

"Have you come here of your own free will, Marciela Montgomery?"

We were not starting off on the right foot.

"I prefer Marcie," I said. "I don't use Marciela."

Janet didn't look as if she liked being corrected. Too bad. I wasn't going to let Dan's mother intimidate me. It was bad enough that Nonnie was giving me the gimlet eye.

I wanted to issue a blanket apology to my grandmother for anything that I may do or say in the next few minutes that might offend her. Old habits die hard, and I had been reared to respect my elders and especially Nonnie. She'd been my savior more than once, from the time she used to bring me my lunch when I'd forgotten it to the day she came to rescue me in middle school. I'd had an accident of the menstruation kind and she had been there just as I was trying to figure out how I was going to leave the school with that big stain on the back of my skirt.

It had never occurred to me back then how she'd always known when I needed her. Now I knew it had something to do with witchy ESP.

"Are you here of your own volition, Marcie Montgomery?" Janet asked.

I could be magnanimous in victory. I smiled.

"Yes," I said.

"And you have come to be tested, is that correct?"

I wondered if any of the tests I would undergo would be painful. Was it acceptable to ask?

"Yes," I said.

"Are you willing to accept our judgment?"

"There will be no judging, Mother."

Well, hell, I hadn't expected Dan. He stood at the entrance to the ballroom, about a dozen feet away from me, his gaze meeting Janet's. I had a feeling they were transmitting more information than just a question about judgment and what the hell did she mean by that?

While I was wondering, my grandmother stepped forward.

"Let the tests begin," Nonnie said.

The witches curved themselves into a circle. Nonnie motioned me to the center and I went reluctantly, all too conscious of Dan still standing at the entrance to the ballroom dressed in a dark blue suit and looking yummy. Was he going to stay there? I wasn't sure how I felt about that. Shouldn't a girl have some secrets? He was going to know everything I could do as far as witches were concerned. But perhaps any reticence or modesty was foolish at this point. His mother would probably have told him everything anyway.

At least, this way, I was guaranteed the trial would be fair.

I deliberately looked away from Dan. When I was pregnant, my hormones went wild, but I suspected they did that with every woman. I got emotional, which I expected. I also got frisky, a euphemistic term for what I felt when Dan got close. I wanted to jump his bones, do the horizontal mamba, and test out his equipment. Besides, I remembered, only too well, what he looked like naked.

I had no restraint. Opie would have called me a bitch in heat, which meant that I should probably have my dog around me at all times. If nothing else, s/he would keep me from making an ass out of myself.

It was one thing being attracted to a guy, but I felt something a little more than lust and warning bells were going off.

Dan, however, evidently felt nothing. He hadn't leered at me lately. He hadn't made a pass. He hadn't put his hands on me. He hadn't hugged me. Nor had he tried to kiss me. He certainly hadn't suggested that I return to the firing range with him. Nothing had happened and I mean nada, zip, zilch.

I might be getting a complex about it.

See, my hormones were going bananas. One minute I was telling myself to avoid him and the next I was getting annoyed because he had. I think I was in trouble, and not just from the witches.

CHAPTER TWELVE

Mea culpa times 100

Arthur Peterson hadn't been all that fond of witches. He'd banned his daughter-in-law from coming to the castle in his lifetime. I wonder if Janet was feeling all powerful now. Would Arthur's ghost make an appearance in retribution?

Speaking of ghosts, I was shocked to see someone in a white robe leading Charlie in on a leash. What the hell was he doing here?

"It has come to our attention that you have a familiar," Janet said.

I wasn't exactly sure what a familiar was, but didn't witches have cats? I guess I had a golden retriever.

The white robed figure brought Charlie to my side. I took the leash, bent to pet him, whispering in his ear, "Don't say a word, Opie."

She chuffed her agreement.

I stood and faced Janet.

What had started out as a way to get into the witches' good graces wasn't striking me as a smart decision right now.

The room was atmospheric, to say the least. The red and yellow light seemed directed purposefully on several of the witches. I was the only one standing in a puddle of blue and green.

If I knew more about witchcraft, I'd know if those colors were important to them. Or what it meant to smell ginger and something reminding me of pumpkin pie.

I began to feel a soft hum, an energy from the circle. It began at my feet, until the rubber soles of my sneakers were buzzing like they had batteries in them. The sensation crept up my legs, as if the witches were manufacturing the current with their humming.

Janet stood watching me and Nonnie seemed to be studying her, but in the shifting colors it was difficult to tell.

The humming had taken on a beat of its own. Were the witches summoning their own power or were they driving it from all the other witches out there? Could they do that? Were the witches in their covens taking a personal day in order to lend their power to this demonstration?

I was impressed. I just didn't know what was going to come next. Were they going to do a super duper zap on me?

I could feel the power build in the room. What did Janet want, an explosion? Or did she want me to respond? What would she do if I told her that I didn't know the extent of my powers? Now was not the ideal time to find out.

At least I'd discovered I had a protective aura and envisioned it surrounding both Charlie and me like a golden capsule. Charlie made a sound that was too close to a human moan, but nobody seemed to notice.

I put my hand on Charlie's head, massaging one ear. He liked that, and he tilted his head toward me as his tail rose and fell against the floor.

The capsule glowed a little more as the buzz faded, but I could still feel it pressing against the aura. It was at my waist now, circling like a candy cane stripe, trying to find a way in.

Inside the aura it was quiet, almost peaceful. I didn't hear anything but the echo of my own beating heart. The glow from the aura obscured my vision a little, but I could still see Dan standing there, his pose one of a sentry alerted to danger. Everything about him, from his widely spaced feet to the way his head was angled, spoke of a man ready to take decisive action.

I turned my head, made out Janet standing not ten feet away from me. To my surprise, she was illuminated by the golden rays of the aura. I guess I had my answer, then. It was visible to other people.

She looked surprised, but not Nonnie. She only smiled faintly, as if she expected no less from me.

Of course, my granddaughter is a goddess, you know. Oh, yes, we knew she'd be a goddess from the day she was born. Why, she changed her formula into nectar as a baby.

If anyone was suffering from shock over the events of the last few months, it should be my grandmother. First, I was human, sort of, a hybrid witch/vampire child. Then I was a vampire. Then I was a Pranic vampire who morphed into a Dirugu who was a goddess. Nonnie didn't look the worse for wear. Instead, she appeared to be having fun.

Too bad I didn't feel the same.

I tested the air by letting the aura subside a little. The humming had stopped. I guess Janet had given up that part of the test.

After another minute of silence, I let the capsule disappear completely. Charlie let out a sigh that was once again more human than canine.

"Which powers do you claim, Marcie Montgomery?" Janet asked.

"I don't know what you mean," I said, confused.

"She doesn't claim anything, Mother," Dan said. "She's never claimed to have witch powers."

She sent him a sour look. Evidently, Dan wasn't doing what she expected.

"Very well," she said. "We will just have to test each one."

She raised her right hand and suddenly a stream of fire jetted toward me.

Frankly, I didn't know if what I was seeing was real or just an advanced kind of thought control. I decided to treat it like Janet was trying to mentally manipulate my environment.

I closed my eyes and envisioned the ball of flames hitting my hand, doing a somersault and careening back toward Janet. When I opened my eyes it was to see Janet staring at me. The expression on her face indicated that she was super pissed, which didn't augur well for the rest of the test.

The tornado of air almost flattened me. Charlie whimpered at my side, and I reached out and grabbed his collar to hold him still. The air felt real and it was damn hard to control. I mentally placed it above me where it couldn't do any damage.

What else was she going to throw at me? And why? To see if I could survive? Or to see if I could control the elements? I wasn't controlling the elements; I was counteracting her thoughts. But what would the other witches think? Were they seeing what I was seeing? For that matter, was Dan? Or were the fire and the air only things I could see?

I didn't want witchy powers. I knew I couldn't be who I was, Marcie Montgomery, insurance adjuster. That ship had sailed. But I sure as hell didn't want any more abilities than I had now. I just wanted to be able to live, if that word could be used to describe a vampire turned goddess. I wanted to be able to protect my child. I wanted the other stuff, too. I wanted to be happy. I wanted to laugh. I didn't want to harm those around me. I wanted to be in love.

I didn't want to be able to do spells or harness magic. I didn't want to be a guinea pig. I didn't want to be taken advantage of, and I sure as hell didn't want to be tested.

Leave me alone.

The three words reverberated in the ballroom as if I'd screamed them into a microphone. I saw the looks on the witches' faces as they looked at one another. I felt their fear as if it were tangible, a living presence suddenly in the room with us.

I hadn't even thought of saying the words but I repeated them now in my mind.

Leave me alone.

Charlie whimpered beside me, enough of a reminder that I suddenly realized what I'd done. I'd let the witches know that I had my own brand of thought control.

Janet stepped back. The anger on her face had been wiped away to be replaced by something else, either awe or uncertainty.

She didn't know what I was and it scared her.

I needed to control my emotions or the stained glass windows were in grave danger of being destroyed.

I looked at Dan, who hadn't moved from his stance by the door. He was watching me and I wanted to know, more than at any time since I'd met him, what he was thinking. Was he afraid of me, too? Did he think I was some sort of weird and repulsive aberration?

"What do they want from me?" I asked. I wasn't sure who I addressed, either the convocation of witches or the ether. "What exactly are they trying to find out?"

"If you pose a threat to them," Nonnie said.

I turned to face Nonnie. She stepped forward until she stopped only a few feet away.

"I don't."

"They don't know that, Marcie."

"If you thought I had any witchy talents, Nonnie, why didn't you test me earlier?"

She smiled. Not her usual pleasant smile that gave you a warm feeling in the pit of your stomach, but a sad smile that made me think that she was regretting a great many things in the past. Like letting me live?

"Perhaps I should have, child. We can't change what is done, however. I am asking you to concede to the test, to let them know what you can do."

I wasn't even sure what I could do.

"Can't they just take my word for it? If they leave me alone, I'll leave them alone."

"And if they don't?"

"I'll give them back everything they send me and more."

Instinctively, I knew I could do that. In the past, all of my actions toward the witches had been in response to what they'd initiated. Now, however, I was tempted to turn aggressive and I knew I could be. Whether that would be wise was another question entirely.

Her eyes hadn't left me. She was doing the grandmother thing. The look that says you're not meeting her expectations, that you've somehow failed.

I took a deep breath, then nodded.

"Okay," I said, meeting her gaze. "Okay."

She nodded and stepped back into place, leaving me alone in the circle. I was so tempted to send another message to Janet, but I didn't. Instead, I stood there silently, waiting. What was next, a flood? Or a landslide?

Dan and Janet were looking at each other. I guessed, from their expressions, that Dan was annoyed with his mother and she wasn't all that happy with him, either. But I would bet that witch or no witch, the power was on Dan's side of the equation. That's probably the reason she turned and addressed me.

"You do not claim to be a witch of the elements?" Janet asked.

"I don't claim to be a witch at all," I said.

"Yet you have certain powers. What are they?"

She really shouldn't have asked that question.

Stretching out my hand, I sent her just a little zap, aimed at her feet. I truly didn't mean to make her dance. But the extemporaneous Flamenco and her rather colorful language almost made me smile.

"I can do that," I said. I almost wanted to ask, childishly, "Can you?" I refrained.

She glared at me. I wasn't the one who made her swear like a sailor. Even Dan looked startled.

"What else?" she asked.

All of the other witches were watching us. They had been for the last few minutes, as if our byplay was something unusual. Evidently, Janet normally made mincemeat of her opponents, and I didn't fool myself that we were anything but adversaries. I had the feeling that Janet would just as soon leave me out in the desert for the buzzards to find. Right now I wasn't feeling all that friendly about her, either.

"I guess we'll just have to find out, won't we?" she finally said.

She clapped her hands and the shutters, invisible until now, moved over the stained glass, plunging the ballroom into darkness.

I wasn't getting a good feeling about this.

As if they'd practiced, the witches began murmuring, words that sounded like a chant, a spell that made the hair on the back of my neck stand up and my lizard brain go on full alert.

I'm not sure if my reaction had anything to do with what they were saying or because my own self-defense mechanisms were being activated. I was protecting not only myself, but a baby I'd wanted for years, never mind that I didn't know if it was human or a little Vlad or Vladerella.

No witch was going to harm us.

I felt the air grow heavier, as if power were suddenly being injected into the oxygen. I took deep breaths, forcing myself to calm, even as my natural inclination was to run for the hills. Even if I hadn't agreed to stay and be tested, I wouldn't have left now. I had the feeling that if I showed fear it would be used as a weapon against me.

CHAPTER THIRTEEN

I was a wampire or a vatch

Janet shoved both her hands into the pockets of her robe, pulled out something and threw it at me. The air was instantly inundated with blue sparkles, not unlike the night Maddock had attacked Mike.

What had Dan said it was? A potion, something that the witches had developed to contain vampires.

Why the hell was she throwing the stuff at me now?

A swirling cloud hung overhead like a stationary cyclone. She was doing to the blue sparkles what I'd done with the tornado of air. I didn't know if she was performing that trick to prove that she was as powerful as I was or if the blue sparkles were supposed to affect me.

I took a step toward her and her eyes widened. Her face was tinted blue by the reflection from the sparkles. Blue was definitely not Janet's color.

She glanced around the circle and the witches, including Nonnie, raised both their hands in my direction, palms toward me. A burst of energy hit and held me, almost as if ropes were being wound around my arms, holding them tight to my body.

Charlie chose that moment to step in front of me, sit on my feet, look up at Janet and bark once. Even I was a little taken aback by the authoritarian tone of his bark. If I'd been another dog, I would've been cowed. I don't know if my familiar was supposed to be a guard dog, but that's the role Charlie had assumed.

My gaze hadn't left Janet's face, but I saw something out of the corner of my eye. Dan's stance had altered. He no longer stood there with his arms folded. Instead, he looked like he, too, was preparing to come to my defense.

Closing my eyes, I forced myself to calm down, remembering the time in my room when I had vanquished the witches simply by imagining them gone. Those moments had been close to an out of body experience, one I hadn't duplicated since.

I took a deep breath, envisioned the invisible ropes holding me dissolving, the strands falling to the floor. I created a force field between me and the witches, a space resembling an inner tube that was effectively a dead zone. They couldn't reach me. They could not touch me with their powers.

I tilted my head back, opened my eyes to find the blue cloud still swirling above me. It was beautiful as it rotated, catching the light from the stained glass around us. What a pity that most of the events held here would be at night and the participants wouldn't be able to see the majesty of the windows.

I lowered my head, looked around me first to the left and then to the right, finally settling my gaze on Janet.

If she expected me to retaliate, she was going to be disappointed. I didn't want to hurt anyone. I didn't want to prove anything. Mostly, I wanted to be left alone. It was important, however, to let her know that the witches couldn't intimidate me and that her power, drawn from this group of women, had no effect on me.

"Are we finished?" I asked. To my surprise, my voice came out louder than I intended, almost as if it were magnified.

Charlie growled as if to add his sentiments.

Janet glanced at her circle and one by one, the witches lowered their hands, looking to her for guidance.

She nodded, just once.

I thought it was over, I honestly did. That only goes to show that I still have some naïveté.

Instead of disbanding, the witches began to chant. I've never been in a room with great acoustics when twenty women were speaking in unison, but the effect was startling. I felt like a medieval sinner being drummed out of the church for being unclean.

The swell of words rose up like a brick wall being constructed by a manic mason. I could almost feel the syllables stack layer by layer, interlocking as they created a fortress.

Each witch had her eyes closed, hands loosely clasped in front of her, as if they were focusing only on the spell to the exclusion of anything else, including the possibility of my irritation.

Evidently, I didn't intimidate anyone. I wasn't sure I wanted to continue in the meek and mild Marcie Montgomery role. How did I achieve a happy medium? How did I assert myself without being dangerous? Or scary, for that matter?

Why was I even worrying about that?

I didn't know anything about being a witch, but it seemed to me that the greatest power Janet and her buddies had was intimidation. Use a person's own fear against them, turn outward emotions inward. If you're scared, you're now twice as frightened because your fear has magnified.

If you're confident, maybe the reverse was true.

I remembered the first time I stood in the sun after becoming a vampire, feeling the warmth of the sun's rays on my skin. I surrounded myself in that memory, expanded and multiplied it until I could feel it encompass me. I recalled the joy I felt when I realized I wasn't just undead but living for perhaps the first time. The perfect beauty of that moment, the smell of the honeysuckle from the nearby bushes, the soft breeze blowing the tendrils of my hair off my cheeks, the smile I could feel down to my toes - all these sensations were suddenly there in the darkened ballroom as if I'd left them and visited the past.

I heard the gasps and slowly emerged from my memory to discover that I was standing in a capsule of light, so bright that it took a moment to see beyond it to the shadows, lightened by the white shapes of the witches.

Janet was smiling, the look on her face one that I'd felt in that exact moment on my patio. I looked to the witches on either side of her and they, too, wore a rapturous expression.

I closed my eyes again, pushing down my elation, knowing that it had been transmitted to the witches. Somehow, I was recreating the emotions I'd felt and transmitting them as well. Would it work with a scary memory? That was too easily recalled: the afternoon at the doctor's office when Maddock had shut the door and smiled at me. Terror had ricocheted around in my chest like a .22 caliber bullet.

My breath grew tight; my heartbeat escalated. Fear became another entity invading my body. My stomach clenched in that moment as if my baby felt and responded to it. I placed both hands on my waist to calm him. In my memory I was running after having zapped Maddock. I knew that he was going to catch me, but I had to try to escape. In seconds, he was on Mike, his jaws open so wide it was like he had a special hinge, his teeth like stalactites in a blood red mouth.

"Marcie, stop."

I opened my eyes to find Dan standing in front of me, one hand outstretched, but hesitating before actually touching me. The first memory had been one of joy and sunlight. The second was blood and horror. I'd been bathed in light. What did I look like now? I looked down at myself cautiously, half expecting to be covered in gore.

"Marcie."

I blinked in order to focus. Only then did I realize that the witches had disbanded.

"What happened?" I asked, my lips feeling numb.

"Something you did," he said, but his tone wasn't accusatory. Instead, he'd adopted his usual non-judgmental way of speaking, as if he were reserving his opinion until more facts came to light.

"I was remembering," I said.

"Not a particularly good memory."

"No."

I bent to pet Charlie, disturbed to note that he was trembling. What had I done? I grabbed his leash, stepped away from Dan and went to where Janet was standing, looking down at my grandmother kneeling beside another white robed woman, her hands on the woman's chest.

"Is she all right?"

Nonnie glanced up at me. "She's an empath. She felt what you were doing very strongly."

I glanced around the room. Of the twenty or so witches, five had been felled. I wouldn't have done that if I'd known I could.

"Are they going to be all right?" I asked.

"Yes." Janet said, her tone icy.

"You're the one who wanted the test."

Pardon me for being snippy, but I was a little tired of learning all these new things about myself. Reliving the experience with Maddock hadn't been a piece of cake for me, either.

I advanced on Janet, stopping a few feet from her.

"I'll concede that you're a scary bunch of women. Okay? I get it. Are we really going to continue this? Wouldn't it be better to simply join forces and combine our abilities?"

The fact was, I was always drained when I exerted myself, and I wasn't feeling spiffy at the moment. I had another life to protect, one that was more important than this showdown. If she wanted me to concede, I would, gladly.

"The vampires want to get their hands on me," I said, stating the most important point. "Do you want that to happen?"

When she didn't answer me, I continued. "The OTHER want to equalize us and make everyone the same. I don't want that. I don't think you want that, either. You're going to have to choose, though. Either you consider me an enemy or an ally. Your choice. Are we done here?"

"Yes," Dan said before his mother could comment.

Charlie and I headed for the entrance to the ballroom just as the shutters were opened and light streamed into the room again. Dan was right behind me and I didn't fool myself by thinking he was going to leave me alone. He probably wanted to know what that little demonstration had meant. Who was I other than a Pranic vampire?

Hell if I knew.

The only thing I did know was that everything came down to emotion.

I could zap someone if I concentrated my emotions. Now, evidently, if I recalled those times when I was strongly moved, I could convey that as well. It was a form of zapping, but more concentrated and involving the mind and the emotions rather than the body.

Maybe everyone would be a lot better off just as long as I was kept happy and contented. I was all for trying that, myself.

When we got into the elevator, I expected him to immediately launch into a third degree, but he surprised me. Who am I kidding? Dan always surprised me.

"The consortium of witches has agreed to meet again," he said.

"Oh, goody. If that meeting goes as well as the witch test, I'm in trouble."

"The test went fine," he said.

"Which means what?"

"You're a witch."

"I am not."

The corner of his mouth curved up a little.

"My mother isn't happy either, if it makes a difference. You're a very powerful witch. She didn't expect that."

I looked at him again, "Which means what, exactly? That I've made myself an enemy? That she'll do anything to destroy me? What?"

For the first time, Dan looked uncertain. I couldn't blame him; I'd put him in a difficult position. Either he evaluated his mother objectively or he lied for her. Either one wasn't fair.

"Look, I get it," I said, deciding to cut him some slack. "Her natural instinct is to protect her own. That means both you and the other witches."

He made something go all soft inside when his eyes warmed like that, too. I really wish he wouldn't do that.

"You're very understanding."

"I'm not," I said. "I'm a little jealous." Too much honesty, Marcie. "I wish my mom had been that protective of me."

I thought about my own little bundle of joy and my mother's behavior toward me was incomprehensible. I would do anything to protect my child and he hadn't even been born yet.

"How's Mike?" I asked, desperate to change the subject.

Thinking of my baby made me a little weepy and I didn't want to break down in front of Dan. Not that he wouldn't be kind and supportive. He'd also be curious, and I wasn't ready to divulge all.

"The doctor says he's stable."

Shouldn't he be healing by now? Especially if my blood was super duper like everybody thought it was? I couldn't spare any more so all those little corpuscles needed to do their thing.

"When's the meeting with the other witches?"

"After Thanksgiving."

I blinked at him. "Thanksgiving?"

"Two days from now."

I'd let time get away from me.

"I've invited your grandmother," he said. "We always have a big dinner here at the castle."

I didn't want to do Thanksgiving dinner, but it would be rude to refuse. I was trapped by manners. I bit back my automatic, "I'm sorry, but I have other plans," and forced a smile to my face.

"It's going to be in the banquet hall."

Of course Arthur's Folly had a banquet hall. Didn't every self-respecting castle?

"If you'll be there at two," he added. "I'll take care of everything else."

When the elevator doors opened, he glanced down at Charlie. "Do you want me to take him to the kennels?"

If Charlie was as exhausted as I was, maybe a meal and a nap was called for.

I nodded and thanked him as I left the elevator. I was polite. I was gracious.

But I was not a witch.

Janet had to be wrong. Was all this stuff I could do only because I was a witch and not a goddess? How odd to have fought against that label for so long only to miss it now.

Still, I didn't think I was just a witch. I was a *wampire*. A *vatch*. A combination vampire and witch, plus I was myself. Maybe that's what Pranic really meant: confused. Whatever the hell you are, you're screwed.

I lay face down on the bed and debated having a little cry, but I fell asleep before I could decide.

CHAPTER FOURTEEN

Vagabond vampire, disconnected Dirugu

I woke four hours later, famished. My morning sickness had subsided and since I'd expended so much energy during the witch test, I needed to refuel. One thing about the vampire metabolism, however, I really didn't have to worry about weight. Neither did they, but they subsisted on blood, while my lunch of choice was two grilled cheese sandwiches, a fruit salad, and two slices of cheesecake for dessert. I wondered if being pregnant would change all that. Maybe instead of eating for two, I'd look like two people by the time I was finished.

Until then, I certainly hoped the kitchen never ran out of cheesecake.

Oh, I also had some unsweetened iced tea with lemon. As much as I loved coffee, coffee didn't love me right now. I wasn't certain about caffeine, either. I needed to hit Google or confide in Dr. Fernandez. Nope, Google it was.

The kitchen had even sent up a treat for Charlie, little sausages that smelled like liver. I set them aside for when he came back to the room.

When I was done, I almost ordered more food, but refrained because I didn't want anyone in the kitchen to think I was a glutton. If I'd been on my own – and safety wasn't an issue as it always was nowadays – I would've gotten in my car and driven to the nearest fast food place. Or two.

Yes, I was a binge eater.

I settled back on the chaise, enjoying the view of the Texas sky as day turned into night The weather was normal for November, mid-sixties and breezy. We might get down to forty at night, but rarely lower than that. Sometimes, our summers lasted until December, but this year we were experiencing in early winter. Our definition of winter, that is.

I didn't reach for the tablet on the table or the TV remote. I didn't want to hear the radio and I didn't want to read.

For a good fifteen minutes I was at complete peace, doing nothing more taxing than simply noting the sunset. My hands were interlaced over my stomach, but I didn't even think about the months to come. I didn't want any conflict in my thoughts right now.

Someone knocked on the door.

I sat up on the chaise, swung my legs over and contemplated whether not I should answer it. Few people would invade my sanctuary. One of them might be Janet and I wasn't in the mood for another confrontation with her. Nonnie might visit me. I wasn't sure I wanted to see my grandmother right now, either. It might be news about Mike. Was I feeling strong enough to hear something bad? No, not really. Or it might be Dan. It probably was Dan. He was the only one who would keep knocking.

Unfortunately, I was feeling mellow and friendly and happy, the wrong emotions to have around him.

But Dan wouldn't go away. I knew that. Or, if he did, he'd just come back later.

I went to the door and opened it. Just like I thought, Dan stood there.

It might be a function of my hormones, but he got better looking every time I saw him and he'd been handsome from the beginning. I seemed to notice his physique more than I had in the past. His shoulders seemed broader. His chin more chiseled. I even noticed his hands, and I couldn't remember noticing a man's hands before.

I wasn't short. I was an inch or two above average, but not model's height. Still, I felt almost diminutive around him. Delicate, which was a howl. I'm not sure how I felt about that intellectually. My feminist sisters would probably rise up in protest. How dare I feel cherished by a man. Didn't I know I could cherish myself?

Sure, but it didn't feel as good.

He tilted his head a little, looking at me quizzically. I realized I'd been standing there staring at him as I held the door with one hand.

I felt the warmth rise to my cheeks. He was the only man who had ever reduced me to blushing. In fact, I didn't even know I could blush before I met Dan.

"Yes," I said, in answer to nothing. "Hello."

That's me, Marcie Montgomery, world renowned conversationalist.

"Do you have a minute?"

"What for?"

I was also charming and gracious. Okay, maybe not.

"We need to talk."

Oh, no. Not one of these *we need to talk* meetings. They never turned out well.

He was going to tell me that he was engaged to someone and he loved her beyond measure. The interlude in the shooting range/target practice room - whatever he called the place - was a mistake, should never have happened, and he bitterly regretted it. Would I please not allude to it or tell anyone what happened when I met the fiancée on Thanksgiving?

Or I was being drummed out of the castle because I dared to walk away from Janet, essentially disrespecting Dan's mother.

Or he'd decided that it was just too much effort to be the protector of a Dirugu, and I was on my own. Bye-bye, so long, sayonara.

Or Mike had died because the transfusion hadn't worked.

I didn't wait for him to tell me that.

"Is Mike all right?"

"The last time I checked, yes. He's still stable, but the doctor sounds a little more hopeful than he did last night."

Thank God. If Dan kicked me out of the castle, it wouldn't be because I'd failed to save his friend.

Could I get my rent pro-rated and where would I ever find an apartment that was vampire proof, yet friendly to this particular vampire? Maybe if I begged, he'd give me a few days to look. I'd never seen a homeless vampire before, but I was kind of breaking the mold as I went.

Marcie Montgomery, Vagabond Vampire. Disconnected Dirugu.

I stepped back, opened the door reluctantly and wished I'd changed into something slinky and provocative. If the truth be told, however, I was still a little drained from the test and now I was heading straight toward anxiety.

I just hoped I had enough reserves left to handle whatever he said. I didn't want to whimper. I had my pride, if nothing else.

I walked to the window. I hadn't yet closed the drapes and my reflection revealed a tense face. I ignored myself and stared out at the lake with its gazebo framed in subdued lights. If I were anyone else other than who I was, I'd open the door and sit on one of the chairs on the wide balcony. But Maddock was still out there and although there were drones and sensors to protect me, I never underestimated Niccolo Maddock.

Turning, I faced Dan. The time had come - my mind reverted to Lewis Carroll - *the walrus said to talk of many things: of shoes and ships and sealing wax, of cabbages and kings. And why the sea is boiling hot and whether pigs have wings.*

I wasn't totally losing it, I was just freebasing mentally.

I've called this room a suite before and the area with the chaise and reading lamp a sitting room. It isn't actually a separate room as much as an alcove off the bedroom. It was designed to be a cozy retreat and it was, but one very large former Ranger made it feel smaller.

Dan retrieved the chair from the vanity and sat beside the chaise, his hands on his knees, his eyes intent.

Oh, dear. This really was going to be one of those *we have to talk* moments.

I sat on the chaise, drew my knees up and wrapped my arms around them, the better to be as small a target as possible.

I waited, but he didn't say anything, only kept regarding me in that Dan way of his.

"Well?" I finally said. "So we're just going to stare at each other?"

He might have me beat when it came to patience. I didn't know anybody else as Sphinx-like as Dan.

Even now, he wasn't in a hurry to speak. That meant this conversation was going to be really difficult.

"Look, if you want me to move out, just say it, okay? And if you're engaged to someone, that's okay, too. I won't make a scene at Thanksgiving. Will your mother be there?"

He nodded. "It won't be easy for her," he said. "Not with Nancy still missing."

I felt like a worm.

"I'll be very understanding. The interlude at the gun range didn't happen." I made a gesture with my left hand wiping the air from the right to the left. "There, it's erased from my memory. It never happened."

He sat back in the chair, folded his arms, and frowned at me.

"Why do you always do this, Marcie? I know what the hell I'm going to say, and then you open your mouth and you just blow it out of the water. You're the most confusing damn woman I've ever met, never mind that you're a vampire or whatever else you are. You're confusing enough as a woman."

I could feel my eyebrows heading toward my hairline.

"Well, thank you very much, Mr. Travis."

Maybe I was feeling just a little too emotional at the moment. I wasn't in the mood to be told how weird I was. Hell, I already knew that.

"Do you really feel that way about what happened between us?"

I was imagining things, I knew I was. Dan sounded hurt. He'd never sounded hurt before.

"Have you really forgotten it?"

"Are you engaged? Are you madly in love with some other woman?"

"What kind of guy do you think I am? Do you think I would have pinned you to the floor if I was?"

I was feeling a little uncomfortable, especially in light of his glare. There was nobody who could depict anger quite as well as Dan Travis.

I was on shaky ground here. I didn't want to reveal too much, but neither did I want to come off as the Slut of the Southwest.

"No," I said, deciding to fall back on the truth, "I haven't forgotten it. I don't act like that normally."

"Neither do I. And I'm not engaged."

"Are you madly in love with some other woman?"

"At the moment I'm not feeling all that excited about the emotion. Or about women in general, and one in particular."

"Me?" When had I started squeaking like a mouse?

"You."

"Is that what you came here to talk about, how annoyed you are with me?"

"No," he said, "but it will do to begin the conversation."

"You can be exceedingly rude," I said in my best Southern Belle impression.

"So can you."

I folded my arms, mimicking his pose. I'm sure we looked like two stubborn people to anyone else. But they wouldn't realize the dynamics percolating just beneath the surface. I might be pregnant with this man's child. I didn't want to be repudiated or rebuffed by him because my emotions were involved. What I felt for him was difficult to identify. I was grateful. I was attracted, both emotionally and sexually. I felt safe in his company. He kissed like a demon. I wanted to care for and comfort him. I wanted to ease his mind, not give him problems. Pat all that together into one big snowball and it meant that this confrontation was not as simple as it appeared on the surface.

"Why did you lie to me?" he finally said.

That question silenced me immediately. I had lied to him in the past. Maybe not lied exactly, but I'd certainly omitted the truth here and there. I was doing the same thing right now. I hadn't told him about the baby. Nor did I have any intention of doing so for a little while, at least until I was sure of the paternity.

I decided to push my luck.

"About what?"

"I talked to Kenisha this morning."

I didn't understand.

"You never told me that Maddock raped you."

Of all the things he could have said to me, that was the one comment I hadn't expected.

"I thought you knew. Or had figured it out."

"You should have told me."

I nodded. I probably should have, but I was embarrassed and humiliated. Plus, I didn't want Dan to go after Maddock. In a lot of ways, Dan was very chivalrous. Maybe it came from living at Arthur's Folly with all the knights around to remind him.

"I wouldn't have been a caveman if you'd told me," he said.

Another comment I hadn't expected.

"I do have some *savoire faire*. Not that I've demonstrated any of it to you."

"Trust me," I said. "I have no complaints."

When he just looked at me, I explained.

"I'm glad about what happened in the gun room." I hadn't had a chance to be self-conscious or to worry about sex the way I might have if he'd treated me as if I were a wounded bird.

"Are you?"

He was no longer scowling, which was a relief. However, he'd gotten that twinkle back in his eyes, the look that was decidedly dangerous for me. It warmed me from the inside out, made parts of my body tingle in anticipation.

Uh, oh.

"What happened the other night?"

I should have quit when I was ahead, marched him to the door, and bid him goodnight. Instead, he was looking at me like he was undressing me. The worst part is that I wanted him to.

"The other night?"

"When the witches were here. Who was the phone call from?"

"My gynecologist. Apologizing for Maddock."

Sometimes, the best lie is based on the truth. Dr. Stallings had called me. She had been regretful about Maddock, but she'd had more news. It was that part I wasn't going to mention.

"So the mention of Maddock made you leave? Is that what happened?"

"In a way. Does it matter now?"

"I don't know," he said. "Does it? Does he?"

I blew out a breath. "I'm no fan of his. I'd just as soon he'd turn into a mouth foaming monster, the quicker the better."

He stood, came to the chaise and held out his hand. He was going to pull me up into his arms and I had a feeling we were going to kiss. I could pretend ignorance, but I very much wanted to kiss him, be held by him, lose myself in him for a little while.

I put my hand in his and draped my legs over the side of the chaise.

"Are you sure you don't have any girlfriends coming to Thanksgiving dinner?"

"No girlfriends."

I was right. He pulled me into his arms. I was right about something else. I desperately wanted to kiss him. His mouth on mine summoned a moan almost immediately, as if I'd come home after a long time away.

I wound my arms up over his chest, linked my hands behind his neck and allowed myself to sag against him. Had I ever fit anyone the way I fit Dan?

His lips were warm, his tongue teasing. He angled his head to deepen the kiss while tendrils of sensation traveled throughout my body.

I was so grateful Opie wasn't here to witness my capitulation.

Let's face it, I surrendered. He didn't even have to crook his little finger and I caved. I didn't stand on principle. I didn't refuse him. I wanted him so much I think I led the way to my bed.

I climbed over the mattress on hands and knees, turning and grabbing him because he was too slow to accompany me. We still had our clothes on and suddenly we were clawing at each other. Buttons were pulled loose, garments were dragged over heads. At one point, my bra hooks got tangled in my hair and we both laughed as we tried to extricate me.

Finally, finally, he was naked and I could look my fill. My hands skimmed over his skin, making him swear softly. I explored his chest, fingers splaying through the soft hair, thumbs stroking over his nipples. The hair at his groin wasn't nearly as soft. His hips arched as my hands came close to his erection.

I didn't smile at my mastery. His hands were busy, too, stroking my breasts, giving extra attention to my nipples.

We tormented each other for hours, it seemed, although it was only minutes.

I didn't have to confess I wanted him. My body declared that for me. He was as hard as I was wet.

I pulled him over me as I lay back on the bed, wanting his mouth on mine. He gave into my demands with no reluctance, surprising me by slipping into me with such grace that he might have been a professional lover.

Any comment I might have made, any thought of speaking was suddenly and abruptly taken from me. He slid his hands beneath my bottom, raised me up to meet him. The orgasm startled me with its suddenness and ferocity.

I wanted to scream, but my mouth was caught again in a kiss. I bit his lip and heard his smothered chuckle.

When he erupted, it summoned another climax from me, so strong that it was like a claim. I was a country that had just been conquered. I was no longer just Marcie Montgomery. A flag had been stuck in my soil. A flag belonging to Dan Travis.

CHAPTER FIFTEEN

The man still had a marvelous butt

I woke to find myself pressed up against a warm body. At first I thought that Charlie, contrary to my rules and regulations, had jumped up onto the bed in the wee hours of the morning. But this body wasn't as hairy. Nor did he have a tail. Instead, there was this delightful long and heated object being pressed against my nether regions.

I placed my hand on his flank, not all that sure if this was a dream, one that I was experiencing with all my senses or if I'd been given a Happy Birthday, Merry Christmas present early. I let my eyes flutter shut, but I couldn't do anything about the smile. It simply refused to go away.

He inched closer. I blessed the powers that allowed me to wake in the dawn light. I'd never left the curtain opened before, or at least I can't remember when.

If I had known about this spectacular sunrise, I might never have closed them, Maddock be damned. Streaks of pink and orange stretched across the horizon like a modernist painting.

I wondered, idly, if there were angels. If so, did God give those with artistic flair a chance to color each sunrise? Tuesday was Jeremy's turn. Wednesday was Henry's. Thursday, Friday, and Saturday belonged to the triplets: Sarah, Clara, and Vera.

If there could be werewolves and shape shifters and elves and fairies, why couldn't there be angels?

I turned to face Dan.

Once again, I blessed the dawn light and my ability to be awake in it. Would the same traits be transferred to Mike? For that matter, would he survive?

It wasn't the least bit romantic, but he was on my mind.

"Will you let me know if there's a change in Mike's condition?" I said, curving my hand around the edge of Dan's face.

The man was just too good looking. He posed a danger to any red blooded American woman. Or any vampire turned goddess.

"I will," he said softly.

In the soft haze of dawn we watched each other.

I didn't try to hide what I was feeling. Sexual contentment oozed from every pore, but more than that, I was happy. Genuinely happy, as if that ounce of time had been put inside a crystal jar and saved just for me.

My thumb stroked his bottom lip, curved in a smile like my own.

Words weren't necessary and might have even been intrusive. Besides, I didn't know what to say or how to say it.

My heart was open and overflowing.

He leaned over and kissed me. I knew I would remember that kiss for a very long time and each time I did, the sweetness of the moment would nearly bring me to tears.

He rolled to his back, taking me with him. I lay my head on his chest and stretched my arm over his waist.

I should get up, invent a reason, a deadline, a necessity. I shouldn't lay here in the dawn light, as skeins bound me even tighter to Dan. One by one they wound themselves around me: peace, harmony, joy, laughter, delight, sensuality, charm, pleasure. He brought me all of these and more.

Soon, it would be impossible to leave him.

"I have a meeting this morning," he said.

I immediately sat up, but he pulled me back.

"Not right this minute," he said.

"I want to go to the archives this morning. If I'm going to meet with the Brethren, I need to know more about them."

"That's who I'm meeting with this morning."

"Oh? Last minute details or problems in paranormal paradise? Is someone objecting to attending a meeting with a goddess?"

"There is a slight problem with hierarchy. You'll find that it's a problem among the four legged shape shifters, especially. God forbid you put a jackal above a coyote or either one of them in front of a werewolf."

"That's because their alpha male is god," I said.

He raised one eyebrow, Dan speak for: *what the hell are you talking about?*

"If you don't have a higher power or a belief in a being outside of yourself, someone you call God, then who becomes God? The most powerful one in the group, the alpha male. Power becomes divinity. Divinity is power. You don't slight their god."

He stared at the ceiling for a minute or two.

"You're right. It does make sense, especially in how they treat the alpha male. They show him a marked respect."

"He's god to his people, or creatures." I glanced at him again. "I would guess that they see you as alpha male, don't they? God of Arthur's Folly."

"I sincerely hope not," he said with a small smile. "There are enough complications to my life without being considered a deity."

"You're halfway there already," I said, matching his smile. "You grant wishes effortlessly. You're the answer to a maiden's prayer. You control the environment, at least here at the castle."

He pulled me over on top of him. No fair being that effortlessly powerful. I could have added that to his godlike attributes, but I didn't want to give him a big head.

"So I'm the answer to a maiden's prayer, am I?"

"Don't ask me. I'm not exactly a maiden."

I folded my arms and rested my chin on them.

"The least you could do, however, is look surly and scruffy in the morning. Your beard only makes you look like an attractive pirate. Even the whites of your eyes are bright, not bloodshot."

"I got a good night's sleep," he said, his smile broadening. "You look all warm and cozy and I like your hair around your face like that."

He was stroking my bottom with his hands. I was almost like a cat, wanting to curl toward him. Heaven knows I wanted to purr.

The phone vibrating on the end table put an end to any thought I might have had about curling up with Dan for another hour or so.

He apologized, reached for the phone, and answered it with a curt, "Travis."

I wondered if it was news about Mike. While we had been enjoying ourselves, Mike had been fighting for his life. I shared a glance with Dan, and although I don't have ESP, I knew he was thinking the same thing.

I didn't even bother rationalizing it. Sitting alone in our separate corners wouldn't have made Mike's condition any better. I had done everything I could. So had Dan. All we needed now was time, a bit of good luck, and the answer to more than a few prayers.

If he was turned – and I don't see how Mike could survive otherwise – would the people of the castle accept him? Everyone had always been unfailingly polite to me, but I was Dan's guest when all was said and done. Any slight to me might be reported to the big guy. Would they treat Mike the same? Most people genuinely liked him, the comment I had heard from more than one person. Would being a vampire make them look at him differently?

I think it would be a case of leading from the top. The head guy transmitted a company philosophy. Sometimes it was written out in the form of a mission statement. Most mission statements, however, were a bunch of words strung together resulting in gobbledygook. Occasionally, you saw a mission statement that made sense, like the one that stated: "We manufacture products in the United States and always will. We believe in our country and our employees, in offering the fairest price and the best product we can."

Nothing ambivalent about that.

His staff would be guided by Dan's behavior. I couldn't imagine that he would turn away from Mike, regardless of how he felt about vampires in general.

He hung up the phone and turned to me.

"A complication," he said.

"Mike?"

He shook his head. "No. Something else."

He rose from the bed and started gathering up his clothes. We'd been a little wild last night and they were scattered all over the bedroom.

I was grateful for two things: Dan's great body and his comfort with himself. He didn't try to hide. He didn't gather up his clothes and hold them in front of him, like Adam with a fig leaf. He just grabbed his stuff, smiled at me, and headed for the bathroom.

The man had a marvelous butt.

CHAPTER SIXTEEN

He's an English fairy

I said goodbye to Dan at the door, kissing him lingeringly until he pulled back, swore, then pushed me away. I grinned as I watched him walk away. He turned back once and smiled at me.

Sighing, I closed the door, putting my hand on it as if to summon him back with just a thought.

That would have been witchy of me, wouldn't it? I wondered if I could.

I should have asked Dan about his mother, but the subject had never come up. There were certain times you could discuss parents, and when you're making mad passionate love was not one of them.

Still, I should have asked how Janet was reacting to the witch test. I had unfinished business with Dan's mother, things that were strictly between me and her, but it would have been helpful to know if she was seething, filled with awe, or somewhere in between.

When was the witch convocation scheduled? Had Dan told me and I'd just forgotten? I'd had enough of witches for awhile, but if I had to, I'd meet with all of them. We'd sit down and be cordial instead of throwing lightning bolts at each other.

One thing about Dan, he was determined.

Friends and enemies had to be separated into their respective categories. I'll bet he wasn't going to give the Brethren or the witches much time to choose. Either they were for me or against me.

I was handicapping him a little, because I might be pregnant with a vampire's child. If that were the case, the world as we knew it was never going to be the same.

The vampires would move heaven and earth to get to me or my child and their attempts wouldn't end with just one failure. They would keep trying until they succeeded. They were, after all, nearly immortal. The war would never end.

On that cheery thought, I dressed and prepared to go and find the archives. My attire for the day had nothing to do with the fact that I knew Diane Trenton was floating around the castle. I just felt girly, which wasn't altogether difficult to understand, given last night's activities.

I wore a navy blue pencil skirt, pale pink blouse, and blue jacket. Very conservative, very insurance industry. But my earrings were pink sparkly things that looked like roses, plus I did the whole makeup routine.

If I say so myself, I looked pretty damn good. In addition, there was an expression in my eyes that spoke of carnal knowledge and ancient wisdom. In other words, I looked like I had gotten some and enjoyed it thoroughly.

I wanted to go see Kenisha, but it was daytime, so I had to delay until this evening. Dan had said that he was going to check on Mike, so I'd wait for updates from him.

Instead of the archives, I headed for the kennels first.

Charlie was in the yard, running with the labs, his ears and tail flopping as he raced around the fence. If the castle went into lockdown, would the dogs still be able to go outside? Or would they be confined to an indoor area?

I couldn't be any more incensed at Maddock, but I just added that irritation to my long list of grievances against him.

I stood there and waited patiently, watching Charlie and the other dogs. Perhaps we humans – or almost humans – should be more like animals. Charlie lived in the now, without thoughts of the past and dreams of the future. I was talking about Charlie, not Opie. Opie had all of the baggage that normal humans have, without the body.

He noticed me and skidded to a halt, then started to run again, straight at me, tongue lolling, a smile on his doggie face. No one has ever welcomed me like Charlie. His whole body wriggled with delight. His tail was at full furl and his eyes sparkled.

I knelt and opened my arms, and he was there, licking and panting, rubbing up against me as if he hadn't seen me for weeks or months.

"I love you, too," I said, giggling and trying to avoid his tongue. "Do you want to come with me? Or do you want to stay here with your girlfriend?"

He snorted a little, and rubbed his head into my armpit.

I took that to mean he would rather come with me.

In the elevator, I pressed the button for S-2. I'd never been to this sub level. Unlike the floor above us, there was no one here. The corridor was as well lit, but it wasn't crowded with people. As for doors, there was only one, and it was marked simply: Archives. At the side of the door was a brass plaque that read: James Hattington, Archivist. Below the plaque was a large red button. I glanced down at Charlie, shrugged, then pressed it.

"Well, it didn't blow up," I said.

Charlie only sighed, sank to a recumbent position, making me frown. Opie hadn't talked to me since I picked her up at the kennels. Was she mad at me for some reason? Or had she just temporarily disappeared? She'd done that a few times since she'd started haunting Charlie, if haunting was the right word.

As I heard the footsteps coming toward me, I imagined someone like Hermonious Brown, the owner of the bookstore I suspect was blown up because of me. He would be tall with a shambling gait, stooped shoulders, and thick glasses perched on the end of a narrow nose. He would be annoyed because of the interruption and I'd have to carefully explain that I had been given permission by Dan to destroy the peace of the archives, if only for a little while.

I was so prepared for the care and feeding of an elderly man that I was shocked when the door opened.

I think I stood there for a little while with my mouth open, before I caught myself, summoned my wits back, and stuttered my name.

"Yes, Miss Montgomery. Mr. Travis said that you might be coming," he said, in an accent that sounded vaguely Scottish. His voice was almost hypnotizing. I wanted him to say something else, even recite the weather.

My hormones were working overtime.

He stepped back, opening the door.

I nodded, only because it was the only thing I could think of doing and entered the archives with Charlie at my side.

The castle had more than its share of gorgeous men and women, at least in comparison to the general population. Here I was, just barely average Marcie and there they were, Stepford people, always pleasant, always smiling, always drop dead gorgeous.

Somebody had to be average, but it wasn't this man.

I was susceptible to masculine beauty. Look at my experience with Doug. He'd swept me off my feet and I'd left my mind somewhere along the way. Thanks to Doug, I was now a vampire. But I knew enough about Maddock to know that if Doug hadn't done it someone else would have, maybe even Maddock himself.

Doug hadn't been this good looking. James Hattington was at least six foot three, which made him Dan's height. He had black hair as well, but that's where the similarities ended. Dan was handsome in a strong, virile way. This man had the face of a fallen angel, with dark green eyes like a forest pool. You wanted to stare into those eyes for as long as it took to learn his secrets. He had a dimple on either side of a mouth that looked made for kissing. The bottom lip was slightly fuller and now curved into a smile.

I was staring.

I yanked my brains back into place and tried to remember why I was there.

"You knew I was coming?"

He smiled at me, the same way you would smile at a slow person, with kindness and compassion. The back of my neck got warm.

Charlie nudged me with his shoulder. I glanced down to find him looking at me. He shook his head just once and I got the message. I was acting like a loon, so much so that even my dog picked up on it.

I looked away from Mr. Gorgeous. The anteroom of the archives looked like a normal office, complete with two desks situated on opposite sides of the room. One desk was clear of everything but an iMac and a keyboard, one of those tiny Apple things that always made me feel like a giant in a child's playground. The other desk was covered with three stacks of documents, each in a manila folder.

This desk was a little longer, the better to accommodate the two Apple computers sitting side-by-side. From what I could see on one monitor, the archives evidently ran a database file.

"Is that what you do down here? Input information day in and day out?"

"In the quiet times, yes," he said. "But I also answer research questions and that takes up most of my day."

"Do you have a staff?"

"Two part-time people, but I'll be hiring a full-time assistant in a month or two."

"I thought the archives weren't digitized."

"The data files are not available outside the castle, but they are accessible to certain staff."

"Did Dan tell you to answer all of my questions?"

He smiled again and the sun came out in this subterranean room.

"He did."

Charlie sat on my feet. I directed my attention to the wooden door on the opposite wall.

"I'm looking for information on the Brethren," I said.

"Which species?"

I glanced at him. "I don't know. I don't even know how many species there are."

"Twenty-seven," he said. "At last count, but that was last year."

Well, hell, I didn't know what to do with that information. Let's see, I had thought shape shifters, which was one broad category, werewolves, which may or may not be in the shape shifter category, fairies, elves, and that was about it.

When I said as much to Mr. Gorgeous, he smiled and gave me that village idiot look again.

"The shape shifter category contains werewolves, coyotes, and other four-legged shape shifters. Then there are the birds, which is another category within shape shifters, mainly eagles and crows. Then we have the smaller mammals, which includes dogs, cats, and rabbits."

He led me to a chair beside the crowded desk and I sat, clasped my hands in my lap, and gave him my earnest "student" look. Charlie moved with me, leaning against my right leg, his head on my knee. I was getting lots of signals from him, but I wasn't certain if they were from Charlie the dog or Opie the silent ghost.

The problems I have are not normal ones.

"A lot of the classifications have to do with nationality," he said. "For example, we have Irish elves and Scottish elves, plus Scottish Brownies who are technically elves. We also have a Norwegian strain, as well as English, Italian, and German elves. The German elves are the most productive. They have a very strong work ethic and it's because of them that people know about elves at all. I mean they show up in the literature and in children's fairy tales. But I use the word fairy only as a descriptive term. Fairies are actually completely different and don't like to be compared to elves. In fact, none of the Brethren like to mix with other species."

Oh goody, and I'd wanted a meeting with their reps. Was I bringing World War III to Arthur's Folly?

"Is there any way you could put together a primer for me? Something like Brethren for Dummies?"

He smiled blindingly at me and for a moment I lost track of my mind again. Charlie made a sound low in his throat. I dragged myself back to the present, met Charlie's eyes and nodded. I was finally understanding.

There was something very odd about Mr. Gorgeous.

"Are you a vampire?" I asked, still looking at Charlie.

"No," he said, very calmly and emphatically.

I made myself glance at him.

"Then what are you?"

When his smile began I looked away.

"I'm an English Fairy," he said.

I didn't know diddly about Fairies, but I suspected they had the ability to charm the socks off of anyone they wished.

"Does Dan know?"

Enough time elapsed between the question and the answer that I glanced at him once more.

"Does Dan know?" I asked again.

"I believe he does, yes."

"Which is why you're the Archivist," I said.

Dan had tucked him down in the subterranean level where he couldn't get into any trouble or convince any number of women to succumb to his charm. The good thing is that my hormones weren't to blame. The bad thing was that I was susceptible and that bothered me. As a resident goddess, I should have more immunity than that.

Had I ever met a Fairy before? I'd bought a car once that I had no business buying. It was much too expensive for what I needed, but I'd been desperate to buy it. Then, there was that red suit I looked awful in, yet I'd really lusted after it in the store.

"Fairies normally work in sales, don't they?"

"We do, but I don't have an affinity for it."

I'd be willing to bet his looks got him in trouble coupled with his Fairy charm. He probably had his share of sexual harassment lawsuits. Either that, or women fighting over him.

When he smiled, I exchanged a look with Charlie. There were bomb sniffing dogs and drug sniffing dogs. Was Charlie a paranormal sniffing dog? Could he be trained to be sensitive to Fairies? That would be really handy and might save me a fortune in impulse buying.

He dug around on his desk and came up with a thick folder.

"After what Mr. Travis said, I've put together some salient facts for you."

I took the file, wondering just what Dan had told him.

"Thank you," I said, standing and making my way to the door. I stopped halfway there, and made a detour to the door in the far wall. "Can I see the archives?"

He nodded and I opened the door. I half expected to see this yawning abyss of a cave carved into the South Texas Hill Country and miles and miles of metal shelves filled with acres of boxes. Instead, the Archives was a modest room with twenty or so shelves about four feet apart. Instead of boxes, each shelf was filled with manila folders with tabs, like the kind you see at a doctor's office.

"You're free to explore, if you'd like," Mr. Gorgeous said.

"I'll pass, for now," I said.

I didn't know what I was looking for, only that there was enough reading material there to occupy me for months. With any luck, the Brethren for Dummies book would give me the information I needed and I wouldn't have to visit the Archives again. I thanked him once more and got out of there as fast as I could, closing the door behind me with relief.

Did Dan really realize what the Archivist was? Why didn't he warn me? Had that just been some sort of test?

"Men," I said to Opie. Opie didn't answer me, but Charlie gave me a look, one that reminded me that he was male.

CHAPTER SEVENTEEN

Can you see me now?

Charlie came with me back to the room. Even if Opie wanted to be with Kenisha, it was still daylight. Kenisha was sleeping like the dead, if you'll pardon the pun.

He settled in on the floor beside the chaise as I got a glass of water - just about all my stomach could tolerate at the moment, darn it (I could never figure out when this nausea was going to hit me) - and began to read.

I read a few sections on the Brethren - the research about shape shifters was fascinating. According to the Archivist, werewolves were dominant among the shape shifters and were prominent in politics and sports. Just how many members of my favorite NBA team - the Spurs, of course - might go furry in a full moon? Oh, and another thing, they could go wolf at any time during the month. Or, with the anti-psychotics that were now available, they didn't have to change at all.

Modern medicine could help in a lot of ways.

One thing I didn't know was that werewolves had pelt issues. The more they transformed, the more their hair fell out. Some of them evidently looked like giant Mexican hairless dogs around the full moon. The Archivist had speculated that that's where the urban legend of the Chupacabra had originated. Several of them had been caught attacking livestock around San Antonio. Something they evidently hadn't learned. You don't mess with Texas. You absolutely don't mess with a Texas rancher.

Did werewolves go bald, then, in their human form? Lots and lots of men in Texas wore hats. Lots and lots of men in Texas wore hats to cover up the fact they were bald. Were they werewolves? And what about the flea issue? Seriously, I don't care if werewolves were hot guys when they had their pelts and their hair. We have problems with fleas in South Texas. You can't tell me that they don't have fleas in either form. That just turns me off. Sorry, it does.

I worked with a guy once who had a terrible habit of scratching himself, regardless of where he was. He always seemed to be standing, however, and not far away from a female. One hand would descend to his crotch, his thumb would flick out to adjust the offending testicle, give it a quick pat, then return to whatever he was doing before he got the urge. Or he would do the quick swerve of a hand and give the testicles a knuckle brush. It didn't matter if you were involved in something vitally important at the time, your attention was always drawn to Bob's balls.

I felt sorry for Bob's wife, especially when he retired. I knew he would be scratching himself until the day he died. Now I wondered if Bob was a flea ridden werewolf. That would explain so much.

Werewolves found it easier to form legal bonds, such as marriage, with other werewolves, but they weren't limited to mating within their species. They could, and did, mate with coyotes when in their werewolf form. That hardly seemed fair when the werewolf was so much bigger.

Their antipathy to vampires wasn't based on their form as much as historical precedence. Vampires and werewolves have each vied to be the dominant paranormal species. Knowing what I know of vampires now, however, I think they were cheating all along. They weren't actually paranormal. Oh, some of them, like Maddock, might be able to acquire some powers along the way, like the ability to move like the wind, but they were basically humans who lived with a blood disease.

The Archivist hadn't listed how the werewolves became werewolves, which disappointed me. He did state that they weren't required to remain in wolf form for twelve hours once they'd changed, although that had become the accustomed norm. Shifting too often led to the aforementioned pelt problem and also a softening of the bones resulting in severe arthritis in later years. Many senior werewolves found it less painful to take anti-psychotic drugs rather than transforming.

Werewolves weren't like vampires in that they were still in the closet and, according to the Archivist, that's exactly where they wanted to stay. The physiology of the werewolf and his transformation weren't known to science, but they suspected the minute they were outed they'd be under the microscope.

I didn't blame them for hiding.

I'd gotten to the section on elves when I decided to take a break. I stood and kneed the chaise close to the window until I had cleared an area.

Right now I wanted to see if I could expand on those powers I'd demonstrated. Not the zapping people with emotions, but the other part, the remote viewing that I hadn't practiced since the first time it happened, right here in this room.

While I was at it, I was going to try to find my phone, my Kindle, and my brush. Enough was enough. At least the thief hadn't taken my clothes. Yet.

I moved to the center of the space. Charlie, smart dog that he was, lay against the far wall, keeping a safe distance. Either he was precognitive or he had learned that when I had a certain look on my face it was better to just stay as far away as possible.

I stood there quietly, my feet spread a little. My arms were at my side, my shoulders straight, my head erect with my eyes closed.

My aura appeared in my mind, the gold glow like fiery flames. I extinguished the flames and cooled the aura. I didn't want protection now.

I visualized my belongings and raised my aura, pushing it until it hit the walls of my suite.

The items weren't here.

I extended my aura out into the corridor, something I'd never done. I saw the layout of the castle in my mind and realized that I didn't know it well enough to go room to room. Instead, I lifted my internal sight upward, like an elevator.

Higher and higher I went until I was on top of the castle. I could see the lake, the flower gardens, the outbuildings, and the drive to the gate.

I allowed my vision to go dark, then imagined I held my phone in my hand.

"Where are you?"

I heard Charlie make a noise and realized I'd spoken aloud. I concentrated on my phone and my mind reacted like a hungry cartoon character following the scent of a pie cooling on a window sill. In the next instant, I was in a small, dark place. My brush was there. My phone was tucked into a zippered pocket. My Kindle was in a flap on the outside of the purse.

I dropped down a little, locating the purse on the end of a bed in one of the castle's bedrooms. Beside the purse was a white robe. Okay, so the owner was a witch. That surprised me. I'd half expected the thief to be Diane Trenton. I hovered above the room, unable to pick out anything that would identify the occupant further.

I moved to the closet. Someone loved flowing fabric in multicolor prints.

That one dress was familiar. I remembered it from the first time I'd met Janet.

I knew she didn't like me and at first I'd thought it was simply because Dan had been kind to me. It wasn't a personal thing as much as it was a mother thing. The longer she and I knew each other, however, the more I think it had turned into a personal dislike, an antipathy that I had experienced only rarely in my life.

It's hard when somebody doesn't like you, especially when you've given them no cause. Yet it's a waste of time to try to change their minds. Opinions like that rarely change. You just have to accept it and roll on.

That's the reason I didn't bother with Facebook anymore and I rarely tweeted. First of all, before I was turned into a vampire, my life wasn't very interesting and I couldn't see boring people with what I did every day. But the real reason was the confrontation with a girl who'd attended my high school. She hadn't liked me then and her feelings hadn't mellowed over the years. She kept sending me these really rude direct messages. I kept blocking her, but she'd find a way to slip past it. The degree of participation versus the aggravation made me deactivate my Facebook profile. Maybe one day I'd go back, introduce myself as Marcie Montgomery, resident goddess, and post a few interesting tidbits.

How much you want to bet that the vampires would "Like" me all to heck and back, not to mention all the other groups who wanted to drain me of my blood?

I lifted myself, looking down at the landscape below me as if it were a Google map. I was racing upward, higher and higher until I could see the curve of the earth below my feet. The sensation of weightlessness was both exhilarating and terrifying.

Although I wasn't actually there, it felt as if I were. I had to relax and enjoy the experience. Intellectually, I knew that if I opened my eyes I would find myself in my room at Arthur's Folly. Only my mind was exploring. Otherwise, I was safe and protected and wasn't going to fall. Emotionally, I was a little spooked out by what I was doing.

I descended slowly, watching with a sense of awe as the earth grew bigger and bigger. There was Austin to the north, then San Marcos and New Braunfels, Loop 1604 circling the city. I found myself following IH-10 north past Camp Bullis and Fair Oaks Ranch.

Although I couldn't be, I felt like I was gliding through cool air, the wind buffeting me. I circled above the lake, marveling at its perfect teardrop shape. Arthur Peterson might have been a man with evil intentions, but he had created a beautiful place in the Hill Country. The story was that he'd built the castle for his wife, but knowing what I know about the man now, I frankly doubted it. In my opinion the story was good PR. I think Arthur Peterson built this place for his own purposes and I wasn't sure what those were. It had probably had pleased him, however, to be thought of as a romantic. Perhaps he wanted to be known as a legend in his own time: the man who single-handedly wiped out witchcraft and, while he was at it, vampires.

I hovered over the castle for a few minutes, then lowered myself slowly to the third floor, not far from where the powwow with the witches had been held. This long and wide space was evidently the gym. A track ran around the outside of the room while machines of all sorts and sizes occupied the center.

Only two people were there. One of them was Dan. The other was Janet, the thief.

"You don't understand," Janet was saying. "She poses a hazard to you. She can harm you."

"I don't agree."

"She has power, Dan. Power she hasn't even realized she has. Hopefully, she never will. But if she exerts one tenth of her power toward you, the cloaking will disappear completely. You know what you've been experiencing is because of her."

He was working an arm machine. Her comment made him stop and study her.

"That hasn't been proven, Mother. Besides, no one person has that power."

"That's what I'm trying to tell you, Dan. Marcie does. Find another place for her to live, Dan. Get rid of her."

"I can't do that, mother. She's a target and she needs protection."

"She doesn't. She's the most powerful creature I've ever run across and she's still in her infancy. You have to get rid of her."

Well, at least I didn't have to wonder about how Janet felt about me. Evidently, I scared the hell out of her.

Janet advanced on the machine, stood directly in front of Dan, her hands on her hips.

"I know you feel something for her, Dan, but is that wise? She's a danger to you. She will only grow more powerful. She could reveal you to the world."

Dan smiled. "Don't tell me that would make you unhappy, Mother. I know you better than that."

"You know how I felt about the cloaking. But it's done and it can't be undone."

He stood and moved to another machine. She followed him.

I was conflicted. I didn't want to eavesdrop on their conversation, but I was curious. What was a cloaking? How could I possibly exert my power over Dan, and what kind of powers did I have? What had I done to him? And, while we were at it, why had she taken my things?

The minute I got some answers, I also got more questions. The problem was that the questions became more and more difficult, life altering, and dangerous.

CHAPTER EIGHTEEN

I am goddess hear me roar

I came back to myself with a jerk at the sound of Charlie barking. He rarely barked and when he did it was because he was warning me. The sensation of returning to my body was like I'd put my mouth on a vacuum hose, the suction a thousand times more powerful.

For a moment I stood there, disoriented. Charlie barked again, staring in the direction of the dressing room. I forced myself to turn and saw a shadow standing there.

What the hell?

I'd always thought that danger would come at me from vampires or a pissed off witch.

This threat, however, was from a human.

The shadow moved, which meant he was standing in front of the opaque window in the bathroom. How had he gotten into my suite? By way of the magical door? If so, that meant he was an employee at the castle. I would have thought that Dan vetted all his staff and that they'd be loyal.

I summoned my aura, but it wasn't showing up. Only a weak pale yellow colored light appeared at my feet. I tried again, but it was like the power just wasn't there. I tried to gather up all my emotions, but the only thing I could feel was panic. In seconds, I was going to be confronted by someone who wanted to hurt me - what other reason was he in my room? Right now I had a brave dog and nothing else.

Fear froze my thoughts. I didn't go into a fight or flight response. I went into stand-there-like-an-idiot mode.

If I couldn't conquer my fear, I was a sitting duck.

I'd been afraid before, but I'd still acted. At Maddock's house, instead of waiting for him to do whatever he'd wanted to do, I'd escaped. I'd confronted the witch hologram only feet from where I was standing. When Maddock had plastered himself against my window, I'd zapped him. In my gynecologist's office, I'd been terrified, but I'd fought Maddock again.

I had protected myself, and been filled with, if not courage, then certainly outrage. I needed to remember how that felt. Taking a deep breath, I forced myself to calm. Whatever was in the bathroom, whoever was waiting to pounce on me was determined. I had to be the same. I couldn't allow fear to take over.

I raised my arms at my sides, fingers pointed to the floor. Slowly, I brought them up until my hands met over my head. The aura flowed freely with my movements, cloaking me in golden light. Charlie barked again and I stretched out my hand to encircle him until he was enclosed in the protection.

I didn't know what my aura could do. I didn't know if it acted like a force field, or simply illuminated me. Would bullets bounce off of it? Would it protect me from a knife or a rocket launcher? Or was it simply a fancy light I could generate with a thought? Could I zap someone through it?

I guess I was going to find out.

A discreet black box with a keypad and a small red eye sat on the table by the chaise. A second intercom unit was beside the bed, plus there was a keypad on the wall beside the door. I'd never pressed the panic button located on the side of the intercom, but I sidled toward it now.

When I moved, the aura moved with me, surrounding my hand as I leaned over and pushed the panic button. I didn't know what was going to happen, but I knew I'd just summoned the Army, Navy, Air Force, and probably the Coast Guard and National Guard. Hell, the Texas Rangers could be coming, too.

I wish they would get here before my confrontation with the stranger, but I knew they wouldn't. I was going to have to handle this on my own.

I bent and put my hand on Charlie's head. We hadn't practiced all that much, but I was hoping he remembered some of his training right now.

"Stay," I whispered. I didn't want Charlie involved in this. He might get hurt again. His safety was my responsibility.

I took a few steps toward the dressing room. Who said that courage was feeling fear and acting regardless? I don't know, but he was probably right. I was so afraid that I was cold inside, all the way from my neck to my knees.

"Who's there?"

It lacked a little originality, I'll grant you, but it got results.

I honest to God didn't expect the six foot six something or other guy dressed in black with a knitted cap on his head and a ski mask pulled over his face. He stepped out of my dressing room and stood there watching me.

"A messenger."

Fear became this other entity inside of me, a living force that was breathing at five times my normal rate. Fear reached up from my bowels, grabbed my heart and shook it, all the while screaming, "Do you see that? Do you see him? He's going to kill you! He's the epitome of all your childhood nightmares, plus the gory news stories you've seen about women being gutted in their beds and run! Run! Run! Run! Run!"

"You are an abomination in the eyes of God," the stranger said, his voice a low growl.

So tell me something I haven't already heard.

"You're from one of those God hates non-humans groups, right? Maybe God's not too fond of people who dress in black and trespass."

"Do you understand, Marcie Montgomery?" he asked, reaching for something on his waist.

For the first time, I noticed the belt equipped with a knife sheaf and a pistol holder. I wouldn't be surprised if he had an elephant gun strapped to his leg and maybe a grenade somewhere, all for little ol' me.

"Do you know my mother?"

Instead of answering, he started reciting, probably Bible passages or ancient Hebrew recipes for all I know.

Demi didn't like getting up to take me to church. I went with my grandmother most of the time. When I got older, I attended the eleven o'clock service along with her. I read the Bible while the rest of the congregation listened to the sermon. I wasn't that interested in the Bible, honestly, but the sermons were worse. I remembered a few of the Psalms because they sounded like poetry, and some of the first few books of the New Testament, but that's about all.

Nothing to counter the maniac pointing a gun at me.

Oh, hell.

I stretched out my hands, fingers pointing toward him, and zapped him a little in the nether region.

He screamed and fell.

Okay, maybe it wasn't a teensy tiny zap. Maybe I should have aimed for another place, like his feet. Or his mouth. He was still using the word "whore" repeatedly. I'm not all that keen about being called a whore, frankly.

I went and stood over him, kicking the gun out of the way. Watching TV does equip you with some basic skills.

"Shut up," I said. "If you don't want to get zapped again, you'll shut up."

He didn't.

I zapped him once more, this time on the rump, since he was in a fetal position.

I was going to keep him there until Dan and his men arrived. Maybe they could get something out of him other than threats that God was going to smite me from limb to limb, burn my entrails, and flail my flesh in ribbons.

His God bore no resemblance to my God. My God was shaking his head at the stupidity of some people.

Maybe if he'd started shooting before he started preaching, the outcome would have been different.

Suddenly, I was in the middle of the Oklahoma Land Rush and being overrun by a stampede. Charlie started barking and I couldn't blame him as we were surrounded by twenty paramilitary men, four of them grabbing the guy on the floor.

He was hauled to his feet, but there was every possibility he was going to find himself on the floor again if they used any of the tasers I saw.

Questions were shouted at him.

"Who are you?"

"How did you get in?"

"Identify yourself!"

The stocking cap came off, followed by the ski mask. His face was square, his nose broad, and his chin had a cleft. Hair the color of straw fell over his high forehead. I didn't know him, but he didn't seem to be the type to enter a stranger's room armed to the teeth. Instead, he looked like an attorney or an accountant.

He didn't have any identification on him and he wasn't offering any information, either.

He glared at me, his look leaving little doubt how he felt. He wasn't going to be my best friend any time soon. Had I hurt him? I allowed myself a few seconds of regret before someone grabbed me.

Adrenaline was still pouring through my body. I raised my arms before I thought about it, getting ready to zap my opponent.

When he backed away, I peeked through my arms to see Dan standing there, frowning.

He probably wanted to hug me, take me away from the confusion, comfort the scared, weak woman only to encounter, well, me.

I was in full on *I'm goddess, hear me roar, don't mess with me, buddy or I'll slice you to ribbons with the lasers from my eyes* mode and I don't think he expected it.

Hell, I didn't expect it.

"What happened, Marcie?" he asked.

I just stared at him for a minute.

"Isn't it obvious?" I asked. "I was minding my own business when the Archangel David appeared in my room."

The idiot hadn't shut up yet. He was still preaching even though one of Dan's men was threatening to pull out his tongue and wrap it around his neck.

"Who is he?"

"I don't know," I said. "But something is wrong with your security if he could get into my room as easily as he did. Did he come through the fairy door?"

Dan frowned at me. Maybe I would have been impressed by his show of irritation another time, but not now. I was still in reaction mode.

Charlie wasn't at all happy at the moment, either, because he was sitting on my feet and didn't look like he was going to move. His normally friendly face was stoic. He looked like he was giving Dan the equivalent of a doggy scowl.

I was doing the same, only mine was goddessy.

I wasn't sure, but I didn't think all this aura raising and lowering was good for me. It drained me too much. Granted, I needed to protect myself, but I had someone else other than me to think about.

Maybe that's why I said what I did next.

"I don't want to stay here. I don't feel safe."

He nodded once, which was Dan-speak for "I hear you. I agree. We'll make other arrangements."

He did the nodding thing to a few other men and before I knew it, I was paraded out of my suite and down the hall, my clothes carried by two guys, my other stuff by a few more.

Four of Dan's men took the still voluble intruder in the other direction. I assumed there was a dungeon somewhere on the castle grounds. If not a dungeon, then a state of the art prison cell. I wouldn't want to be a guest of Dan Travis and his merry men. I had to applaud the courage of the man in black. At the same time, I wanted to make him wear a gag. He was still using the whore word as they dragged him away.

Would he answer their questions?

I didn't think he would get the Miranda warning and he could kiss his civil rights goodbye. We had the Castle Doctrine in Texas. You invade my space, I have the right to shoot you. I had the feeling Dan carried it a little farther than that. If you invaded his space, he didn't necessarily turn you over to the authorities. He *was* the authority.

I hadn't meant that I wanted to sleep in Dan's room, but before I could really process it, I found myself in Dan's Arthurian bed chamber.

Charlie looked around and I could almost hear Opie's incredulity.

The walls were crimson silk, the carpet of thick gray, patterned to resemble a stone floor. The beams overhead were dark mahogany, giving the impression of a soaring cathedral. Between the two high arched mullioned windows was a suit of armor that I swore was pure silver. The view from here was magnificent, included the flower gardens, a slice of the tear shaped lake, and the approach to Arthur's Folly.

The bed sat on a dais at one side of the room. The first time I'd seen it I'd thought it was the size of a California King times two, but now it looked even larger, still covered in a collection of gray animal pelts stitched together. Was it wolf? Squirrel? I sincerely hoped it was faux fur.

The fireplace, probably from a European castle, was adorned with carvings of gamboling animals. At least Arthur Peterson hadn't mounted boar and deer heads on the walls. All those glassy eyes wouldn't make for a good night's sleep.

Charlie's presence posed a problem. I really didn't want her witnessing my love life and I had, up until now, managed to keep her out of my room when Dan was in my bed. It was one thing having your dog watch you. It was quite another when your dog had a resident ghost.

"I think Charlie has to go out," I said.

"Call the kennel. They'll send someone."

"Am I a prisoner now?" I asked, frowning at him.

"Of course not, but I'd feel better if you weren't wandering around the castle, at least not until we find out how he got in."

I buzzed the kennel from the intercom unit beside the wall. One thing about the castle, it was wired for sound. I'm sure there were lots of other things I didn't know about, just like I hadn't been aware of the drones until recently.

When the kennel attendant arrived, Dan was on the phone, no doubt giving instructions about the intruder and beefing up security.

I bent, whispered to Charlie/Opie that I would be down to the kennels to take him to see Kenisha when she woke.

Charlie answered me by licking my cheek. I smiled, stood, and watched as he was taken out of the room. The attendant had arrived with one of those loop leashes, but Charlie was so well behaved he didn't need it.

When I turned back to Dan, he pocketed his phone, and regarded me somberly.

Oh, goody. I could feel some kind of lecture coming on.

CHAPTER NINETEEN

Marcie Montgomery, resident goofus

He surprised me.

"There's a sitting room through there," Dan said. "I don't use it much, but you're welcome to. I want you to be comfortable here. If you'd like any of the furniture changed, all you have to do is punch the intercom. We've lots of spare furniture in the attic. If you need some help rearranging anything, just call. Or if you want anything."

He almost looked uncomfortable as he listed all the amenities of his suite.

"I'm sure everything is wonderful," I said. "I don't want to change anything."

"You can."

"I'm not the redecorating type. Besides, what could I possibly add to this space?" I looked around at the walls that were covered in silk, the thick carpet resembling squares of slate.

"You might want something frillier," he said.

I bit back my smile.

"I'm not the frilly type. I'm not sure I'm the squirrel pelt type, either. Maybe something in the middle."

"There's a small room across the hall. It was designed as a lady's solar. I could have it converted into a bedroom. It's not as large as the suite you had."

"So my rent check would be smaller?" I asked, allowing myself to smile.

He frowned at me. "Yes."

I doubted he'd deposited the check I'd given him, but we played this game. I paid him a trifling amount and he allowed me the illusion that I wasn't being kept.

"I think the room across the hall sounds lovely," I said.

There, a bit of self-protection.

"It won't be ready for a few days."

"The sooner the better."

"All right. I'll start the ball rolling," he said, his voice carrying an edge it hadn't had earlier. "But for a little while, I'd feel better if you were here with me," he added. "I need to know you're safe."

I was sunk. I was doomed. He'd known the perfect words to keep me silent and acquiescent. Was I so desperate for love that when the word *need* was used, I crumbled like a waterlogged cookie?

Yes.

This was Dan, and I would get to sleep beside him again tonight without feeling guilty. At least for a few night. Or until I discovered that the very worst had happened and Maddock was my child's father. Then, I'd leave the castle rather than bring the might of the vampire nation down on his head.

For a few nights, then. I'd stay for a few nights, but that was it.

"How do you think he got in?" I asked, thinking of my intruder.

"Something we need to investigate."

I studied him. He wasn't telling me something.

"You already know how he got in, don't you? Was it the laundry fairy door?"

He shook his head. "My grandfather believed in secret passages. Priest holes, that sort of thing. I think he found one."

I just stared at him, speechless. Secret passages? Wasn't it enough to have fairies working for you?

"You're serious."

"I'm serious," he said. "They were supposed to be kept locked, but I think he got in."

"How did he know about them?"

"That's what I'm going to find out," he said.

The look in his eyes made me glad I wasn't the guy in the dungeon right now.

He nodded to me in parting, and then he was gone, taking his temper with him.

Minutes after Dan left, I wanted to slap myself silly. What was I thinking? I should've protested vehemently rather than allow him to deposit me here. I should have taken a cab away from the castle. The minute I had that thought, I reversed myself. I wasn't stupid. Okay, I might be stupid when it came to Dan, but I wasn't about to put myself in jeopardy. So far I haven't found a vampire friendly place that was also impervious to master vampires. Not that I'd been looking.

Of course, I wasn't the same person I'd been when Maddock had raped me. I'd learned a lot since then, mainly about myself. I can protect myself, maybe not against bullets, but certainly against other vampires. At least I'd zapped Maddock at Dr. Stallings's office and I was doing pretty good when it came to fighting witches.

I had the zappy thing at my command. I could compel certain individuals. I had the aura, which was protective, and I'd developed the ability to float above my body. As time passed, I'd probably pick up other skills. Hopefully, protective skills that would equalize my situation.

The last thing I needed was for my hormones to trip me up.

I might be falling in love, but right now *love* looked like a giant sinkhole. I had to sidestep it as long as I could. I had to depend more on my head than my heart.

Granted, my head was telling me that I could trust Dan. It may turn out that he was the only person I could trust, but I still had a few niggling doubts. Not about him as much as the situation. What kind of investigations did he do? Why wasn't he all that open about his company? Was he more involved with the OTHER than he let on? What the hell had Janet meant about uncloaking him?

And finally, the one question every woman asked about a man, especially one about whom she was feeling mushy: what did he think about me?

He was protective and tender, but that didn't stop him from being occasionally aggravated. He wasn't a pushover, but his eyes sometimes softened when he looked at me. Plus he'd stood between me and his mother. Some husbands weren't that gallant.

Still, I couldn't be a doofus about this arrangement.

It was just safer and better if I didn't get myself too involved with Dan and sharing a bed night after night definitely classified as getting too involved. Besides, I would begin to show soon, and the longer I could keep my secret, the better.

The last time I'd stayed here, I hadn't really explored, thinking it would be rude. This time, I'd been given carte blanche, so I took advantage of the invitation. Two arched doors sat side by side on the other end of the room. I knew the one to the right led to the bathroom. I went through the door on the left.

Here was a room that struggled between Arthur Peterson's love of medieval legend and his grandson's immersion in the 21st century. The walls looked to be slate. The floors were flagstone. The mullioned windows gave a view of the lake and the sunny expanse of castle land. The sleek glass desk and computers looked discordant here. So, too, the monitors embedded in the far wall.

I moved to stand beneath them. From here Dan could see his kingdom in high definition detail. I recognized the scenes in three of the monitors. The others were places I'd never been. Did he have cameras mounted in the secret passages? If not, I didn't doubt that he would rectify that lack faster than he would have the lady's solar redecorated as a bedroom.

I went into the bathroom, grateful I was alone. Bathroom noises embarrassed me, although I doubted you could hear anything from this giant room. The toilet was located in a small closet off the main bathing area.

The tub was massive, carved from beige and brown marble, and large enough to be considered a mini-swimming pool. I hadn't bathed in it yet or in the shower with its view of the sky. Now sunlight poured into the space, illuminating the crystal blue sinks, the polished brass - or gold - fixtures, and all the plants.

I felt like I was in a jungle or an oasis. Outside, the world was a confusing place. Here was peace and tranquility.

I returned to the bedroom, took the doorway in the far wall and found myself in the sitting room. I'd never been here before and from the unused air of the room, I doubted many people had been.

Silk adorned the walls, the pattern tiny tea roses in shades of pink and coral. Bookcases lined a second wall and a desk the third. A massive window looked out over the flower garden. In spring, all the various blooms would bring the outside in and make this room feel like part of a greenhouse.

The chaise upholstered in coral silk and arranged beside a round mahogany table was the mama to the chaise in my room. This piece of furniture was twice as large, with a pillowed back and arms, and tufted cushions. A loveseat sat a few feet away, facing the window.

The lamp on the table reminded me of something I'd once seen in a Sotheby's catalog. A shepherd and shepherdess were holding hands, their gaze locked in a glance of forever love. The shade was an odd shape, conforming to the width and depth of the sculpture at its base. As I reached my hand toward it, the light went on and when I drew it back, the light went off.

Despite the fact that there wasn't a speck of dust anywhere, and the cushions had been plumped in readiness for a visitor, there was an unused feeling about the room, as if it anxiously awaited its first true occupant. I stood in the middle of the gray carpet, wondering if I was having a flight of fancy, or I was genuinely picking up something from a space that shouldn't have been sentient.

I'd never talked to anyone about ghosts and whether they were considered part of the paranormal world. I'd never told anyone about Opie. To the best of my knowledge, only Kenisha and I knew about her and maybe some labs, if they understood such things. I'd have to ask Opie if dogs had a comprehension of humans. Did they realize we were a different species? For that matter, did they know they were dogs?

Opie had been a vampire when she died. Did that mean that werewolves and other Brethren could also become ghosts? Did ghosts have to take on another form? Or were there such things as incorporeal beings that floated freeform in the ether?

Could humans become ghosts? Or was that reserved only for the paranormal?

This sitting room, however little used it felt, was a warm and comforting place, most definitely welcoming and almost grandmotherly.

I sincerely hoped it was only my imagination or because I was still drained from my confrontation with the preaching intruder. I was in no mood to meet a ghostly grandmother.

I went back to the bedroom where one of Dan's men had dumped all the paperwork he'd scooped up from the desk. All my lists were there and I hoped nobody had read them. I grabbed the Brethren for Dummies file and moved back into the sitting room, settled into the chaise, and rang for tea. While I was at it, I decided that a few slices of cheesecake were in order.

I was eating for two, remember.

CHAPTER TWENTY

You're not a zombie, are you?

The kitchen was learning my tastes. In addition to sending up two slices of New York style cheesecake, they also included small bowls of cherries, strawberries, and blueberries.

I have a new motto: if cheesecake can solve it, it's not really a problem.

By the time I finished both slices and had a pot of tea, I decided that finishing my reading could wait. I switched on the TV on the opposite wall, but the news wasn't really that interesting and I didn't want to watch any of the divorce, game, and judge shows. Maybe I needed a nap more than anything else.

I was awakened by the barest touch on my face. In my half waking state, I imagined that a grandmotherly figure bent over me. She called my name softly, adding a "dear" in a sweet and clear voice.

I blinked open my eyes to see Dan standing in the doorway.

"I'm sorry, I didn't mean to wake you."

I drew my hand over my face, looking for telltale signs of drool. Had my mouth been open? Had I been snoring?

I doubted if Dan would tell me even if I had the courage to ask. I was going to pretend that I'd been the epitome of Sleeping Beauty and he'd been overcome by my grace and poise.

"What time is it?"

The sky had darkened, leading to my brilliant conclusion that hours had passed. A conclusion that was verified when Dan told me it was nearly seven.

Maybe one of these days I would wear a watch again. My life had always been regimented by the hours. I felt like I was forever on the clock. Throwing away my watch had been a deliberate act of rebellion when I'd become a vampire.

He walked into the room, immediately warming the space. The feeling of peace and well being intensified so much I almost asked him about his grandmother.

He picked up my feet as he sat on the end of the chaise, put my feet on his lap, and began to stroke them.

"I discovered something about your intruder," he said.

"Don't make him mine," I said. "I don't know the man from Adam. Did he discover the secret passage?"

He nodded. "It was supposed to have been closed off, but the lock's been opened."

"Where is it?"

"The back wall of the closet," he said.

"How did he discover it?"

"He had a mole inside the castle."

"You know who it is," I said, and it wasn't a question.

"I know who it is," he said, massaging the ball of one foot.

Did I want to know who the mole was and what Dan had planned for him? I wasn't sure.

He was wearing black trousers and a white dress shirt with a very collegial black and red striped tie. He looked like a successful man, prominent in his field. As he looked at me, I amended that description. A handsome and successful man, powerful because of a certain indefinable air about him. You knew he was important.

He might also be dangerous, a thought I'd never had before. Yet danger was sometimes sexy and he was.

I knew, sure as God made little green frogs, that I was in deep trouble with Dan Travis.

"How many days do you think it will take before the lady's solar is ready?" I asked.

He concentrated on my other foot. I was trying very hard not to moan.

"Maybe a week or two."

I knew he was lying. He knew I knew he was lying, and he didn't give a rat's ass. He just glanced at me in that direct way of his, as if he could bore straight past my reluctance and plant himself in my brain.

I had to do something, quick. Otherwise, I would be putty in this man's hands. Just like my feet.

"What did your mother mean, that your cloaking would disappear if I used my power on you?"

Something shifted in his eyes. I wouldn't call it fear, knowing Dan, but it was close. Maybe it was wariness. Seconds later his eyes changed again to a stoic calm that hid everything he was feeling.

"What do you mean?"

"I saw you and your mother talking."

He didn't speak, just watched me. I might have been discussing the weather. Or the color of the carpet for all the reaction I got. He was good. When Dan didn't want to reveal what he was feeling, you had more luck talking to the wall.

"How?"

"Let's just say I saw you."

"You have the ability to remote view?"

The question startled me. So, too, the way Dan had asked it, in a very calm voice, as if remote viewing was all the rage. Maybe it was in his family.

"I think that's what it is."

I didn't tell him it was the first time I'd overheard a conversation. Frankly, I would have been just as happy not hearing anything, but I couldn't forget Janet's words. I didn't know what kind of power she was afraid I'd use on Dan or how.

"What did she mean, uncloaking?"

"I don't know what you're talking about."

I'd never known Dan to lie, but he was done it twice now.

I could describe the scene I'd witnessed and repeat Janet's words, but I didn't. I suspected he would deny everything I heard.

He stood, carefully replacing my feet on the chaise. I curled up, pulling away from him.

"Are you going to tell her that I can remote view?" I asked.

I didn't know how I felt about Janet knowing what I could do. She'd probably wrap herself in some sort of invisibility spell. Or cloak herself.

"What is it you don't want me to know?"

Would he tell me? Or would I have to keep guessing? My vote was for the latter.

"It doesn't matter, Marcie."

Oh, it did.

"Is it something you can do? Or something you are?"

I knew his family tree. I suspected it was something that would have really angered his grandfather. Had he and his mother arranged for a cloaking spell to hide what Dan was?

"Holy cow," I said, staring up at him. "You're a witch, aren't you?"

"No, I'm not."

His voice was flat, almost expressionless. But not so his eyes. They flashed a warning at me, but I was annoyed enough to ignore it. I'd been asking him for weeks to reveal himself and I knew I was close to finding out exactly who and what Dan was.

"Did your grandmother know?"

The question surprised him, I could tell. He just frowned at me.

"Why would you ask that?"

"You were close to her, weren't you?"

"Yes." His voice was still flat, but there was a different look in his eyes now. A softening as if he remembered his grandmother.

"Did she know what you were?"

"Yes."

That was more information than he'd ever shared. I wonder if he knew how much of a revelation it was. He'd just admitted that he wasn't a hundred percent human. He was something else.

I pressed my hand against my waist. Holy cow, part two, was he the father of my baby? If he was, exactly what kind of child was I going to have?

"Are you an animal hybrid?" I asked, envisioning scales and a forked tongue.

"What?"

A frowning Dan was very intimidating. I, however, was pushed by a biological imperative to discover as much as I could. Dan, pissed versus me, maternal? It wasn't even a fair race. I would scamper to the finish line.

"Are you part animal?"

"No."

"You promise?" I said.

"Yes, I promise."

"You're not a zombie, are you?"

"What is it with you and zombies? No, I'm not a damn zombie."

His frown had turned into a scowl. Even angry he was handsome. Was that part of the cloaking process? Was he rendered handsome because of a spell?

"Do you look the same?"

"What?"

He was losing his temper. I had to hurry up and ask what I needed to know before he stomped out of the room. It was a good thing the chaise was so comfy; I might be sleeping here tonight.

"If you took away the cloaking spell, would you look the same?"

If I wasn't imagining things, there was a glimmer of humor in his eyes.

"You're not going to stop, are you?"

Frankly, I wish I'd never eavesdropped on Dan and his mother. Not that I'd had a choice. I was trying to find my things. I knew Janet had taken them, I just didn't know why. For some kind of spell, I guessed, but I wasn't sure. Maybe she didn't want my stuff for a witchy reason. Maybe she was just trying to be annoying or wanted to piss me off.

Good news, Janet, it worked.

"No," I said. "I'm not. Do you look the same without your cloaking spell?"

"Yes, I look the same," he said. "Does that bother you?"

Hell no.

I only shook my head, however, deciding that a little maidenly reticence was called for.

He stared at me for the longest time and I swear he did something to my mind. I couldn't think of another question to ask him.

"Have you eaten?" he asked.

When I glanced at the tray, he smiled. "Not cheesecake. Dinner."

I shook my head.

He bent and grabbed my sneakers, handing them to me.

"Come on, I'll show you one of my favorite places in the castle."

Once I put on my shoes, he grabbed my hand and we left his rooms. Instead of taking the elevator to the lower floors, we walked down the corridor, turned left at the corner and continued walking until we came to a door. He opened it, revealing a set of steep steps.

"If you don't mind," he said, "I'll go first. The light switch is hard to find."

Were we going to the attic?

I've never considered myself very adventurous. Of course, that was in the pre-vampire days. I have subsequently done a lot of things I'd never considered doing. But the last week or so, I've confined myself to only a few places in the castle. Nor have I ventured out of it. Yet Arthur's Folly was so large it was like a self-contained town. I wasn't suffering from cabin fever yet, although I'm sure that I would if I had to remain here during a siege.

I hope to God Dan was wrong about that.

If we couldn't come to some kind of agreement with the Brethren and the OTHER, we might have to hunker down and prepare for the worst.

All thoughts of a siege disappeared as I followed him up the stairs, grateful I was wearing sneakers. If I'd been wearing FM heels, there's no way I could have climbed up on the roof.

Oh, dear God, was he suddenly going to take off like an eagle?

CHAPTER TWENTY-ONE

Up on the roof

I expected something fantastic when Dan opened another door. The courtyard had been spectacular, leading me to think that whatever was on the roof was a match.

Instead, he led me to a very unassuming area surrounded by potted hedges on three sides. The fourth side was open to the horizon, a wrought iron railing the only barrier keeping you from toppling over the edge of the roof.

We walked through an opening in the hedges to where two chairs sat side-by-side with a small table in between. They reminded me of Adirondack chairs, only these were made of fabric and steel, padded at the shoulders and the seat. I sat on the one to the left while Dan sat to my right, pulled out his phone, and issued instructions to the kitchen.

The black sky was pressing down on the ribbon of indigo on the horizon. Soon it would be gone and the night would swallow us. For the first time since I visited Maddock's house, I wasn't frightened. I knew the drones were around us even though I couldn't see them. I also knew that there were other devices planted in strategic positions to pick up signs of vampires.

Was I making them go bananas? Or had the tech geniuses at Arthur's Folly made allowances for my presence? Did I give off a different signature from most vampires? Since I'd become pregnant had that signature changed?

Dan leaned forward, draped his hands together between his knees.

"I've never brought anyone here," he said. "I normally come up here by myself. It's a good place to sit and watch the world."

I didn't have an answer for that. I'd chosen to hide from the world lately. It was safer. As to my being the first person he'd brought here, I was not going to read too much into that. I was trying to guard my heart, my moods, and my hormones, thanks very much.

It was a lovely place. You could almost forget you were on top of a large structure. You could almost imagine you were alone, except for the faint sounds of conversation and music from the courtyard. From here you could see the lights of San Antonio far off in the distance. If you looked to the left, you could see the foothills of the Texas Hill Country. Behind us was the lake, lit by lights that looked like fireflies from here. Hell, maybe they were fireflies, or elves with tiny little lanterns strapped to their backs.

Maybe it would be too hot up here in the summer, but tomorrow was Thanksgiving, which meant that the days were in the sixties and the nights in the forties. Still, it was pleasant, with the hedges shielding us from the wind. There must be some method of heating the space, because I didn't feel cold. Or maybe it was just being around Dan. I almost never felt cold around him.

He glanced at me. "My mother thinks you're the most powerful witch she's ever met. Did you hear that part of our conversation?"

"It was the first time I'd ever done that. I was looking for something. I didn't mean to eavesdrop."

I didn't want to touch the other part of his comment yet. Evidently, he figured that out because he nodded once, a Dan gesture I instinctively understood. He was giving me a few minutes, but probably no more than that.

"What were you looking for?"

It was one thing to not like Janet. It was another to tell Dan that his mother was a thief. Discretion being the better part of valor, I chose to soft pedal the truth.

"Something I'd misplaced," I said. "Before I knew it, I was eavesdropping."

He didn't say anything for a moment.

When he did speak, there was a tone in his voice I couldn't decipher.

"You've never done it before?"

"No," I said, then had to amend my answer. "Okay, maybe once, but it wasn't anything like that. I didn't see anyone. I didn't overhear anybody. I had this impression that I was floating on a river. I was trying to get away from the witches the first time they came to my room."

"The first time?"

I nodded.

"How many times have they been there?"

"Twice. They only did the hologram thingy once, though. That's their version of a remote viewing, isn't it?"

"Nothing like yours," he said, leaning back against the chair.

He stared out at the horizon, rapidly disappearing beneath the inky sky. The lights from San Antonio looked like the blinking eyes of a band of coyotes.

Tonight was a moonless night. Once, I used to track whether it was going to be a full moon since a great many commercial accidents seemed to happen in the two days before and after a full moon. I never could find any actuarial tables to verify that. Evidently, the higher accident rate was only anecdotal.

Now the full moon interested me because of werewolves and other shape shifters. I didn't want to be parading around in the dark because of Maddock and his buddies, but even if there were no vampires, I sure as hell wasn't going walking in a full moon.

I was sincerely trying to avoid thinking about what Dan said, but finally there was no delaying it. He didn't push, even though I felt that he was thinking it. I wasn't being "sensitive". Nor did I think I had any kind of ESP. It's just that he hadn't said anything else and sometimes, Dan's silences were very pregnant, if you'll pardon the pun.

"I'm not a witch," I finally said. "And certainly not a strong which, no matter what your mother says."

"My mother is renowned for her ability to detect witch traits," he said. She is a deputy director of the State Council. She's a very powerful witch. If she says you are one," he said, turning to look at me directly, "then I suspect she's right."

I folded my arms in front of me, not because I was suddenly cold, but because I wanted to protect myself. Not only against his words – how did I protect against those? – but against the sudden feeling I had that he might be correct. What if my Pranic abilities were a result of my maternal line? I had never given it any thought before, but surely the vampire part of me must be offset by my family's witch heritage.

My mother wasn't a witch, but the abilities could have skipped a generation.

"What does my grandmother think?"

His gaze hadn't moved from my face. Tiny lights beneath the hedges provided enough illumination that we could see each other. Shadows encircled the space, but they weren't spooky or frightening. Instead, they were strangely comforting, as if they pillowed the air around us.

"She has come to the conclusion that my mother is right."

"Say I agree," I said. "Say I agree, in principle. It doesn't change anything. If anything, it complicates the situation even further."

"No," he said. "It makes the situation easier. The witches will come to your defense because you're one of them."

I hadn't thought of that. "I don't agree with what you say, but I'll defend to the death your right to say it, that sort of thing?"

He shook his head. "No, the sort of thing that says a witch bloodline has to be protected. You're a witch. Therefore, you're an ally. The same goes for you, though. You must protect your fellow witches."

I don't care what Dan said, the situation was getting more complicated the way I looked at it.

"Even though I'm a vampire?"

"You're a witch, first and foremost."

"I don't feel like a witch, however that's supposed to feel. I don't know any spells. I don't want to affect any of the elements. I just want to be safe."

"You will be. If it's within my power to create a haven for you, Marcie, I will."

"Why me? From the very beginning, you've been my protector. Why?"

"Do you believe in destiny?"

"No. Emphatically no."

His smile annoyed me for some reason.

"When I was ten, Nonnie invited the minister to Sunday dinner. He tried to explain predestination for me. The idea that my life was charted for me before I was ever born was horrifying. He told me I had the ability to change my life within certain parameters. In other words, I could like oranges or bananas, but I must like fruit. I didn't believe that then, and I don't believe in destiny now."

"They're not the same thing," he said. "You can avoid destiny. You can sail right on by it. You don't have to answer the door when it knocks. You can avoid all signs that lead to where it's trying to point you."

I was prevented from answering by the appearance of a castle employee pushing a cart.

Dinner turned out to be surf and turf, a filet mignon with a lobster tail accompanied by broccoli with hollandaise sauce. I passed on the wine and requested herbal tea instead. That got me raised eyebrows from Dan, but almost instant service from our waiter. I did eat the cheesecake with the cherry topping, though. It would take a grievous bodily injury for me to avoid cheesecake.

When dinner was over, I expected him to start where we'd finished, but he didn't say anything about my being a witch. Instead, Dan sat back, looked up at the sky and the thousands or millions of stars creating a canopy over our heads.

"When I was five years old, I knew I was different," he said. "I couldn't tell you why, I just knew it. I also knew that it was very important to keep that knowledge to myself. If I hadn't had a mother who was a powerful witch, I wonder how long it would have taken me to understand what I was."

I didn't speak. I didn't say a word, for fear that he would stop talking. My questions about Dan were about to be answered, and I could barely draw breath. All of my attention was on him. I hoped that, whatever he said, whatever he revealed, I wouldn't be too shocked.

Dear God in heaven, what would I do if he was some kind of crocodile mutation? Or something that turned into a slug on the first and the fifteenth of the month? Maybe he became invisible. I could live with that. At least my child wouldn't have feathers or fins.

I would love him regardless, but it would be nice to know before the day he was born. I could just imagine the doctor holding up my child, putting him on my stomach and saying, "Congratulations, you have a bouncing baby boy fish!"

I just needed to quell my imagination for a little while, be patient and let Dan tell his story.

When he didn't speak, I couldn't stand it anymore.

"What are you?"

He turned his head. His smile had disappeared and there was no twinkle in his eyes. They were serious and somber as he looked at me.

"I'm a wizard."

Well, hell, what did I know about wizards? Nothing. Absolutely nothing. I knew more about crocodile hybrids that I knew about wizards.

"I remember wanting to be a policeman," he said. "If I couldn't be a policeman, then I wanted to be a soldier."

I was grasping at verbal straws here, since I didn't know what else to say. "And so you became a Ranger."

"I wanted to become a Ranger," he corrected. "But I wanted to do it on my terms. I didn't want any special favors or powers. I wanted to be treated just like any other guy."

"The cloaking," I said, understanding.

He nodded. "My mother objected, but she finally agreed. The ceremony is long and drawn out and is supposed to last a lifetime. I had to be sure that it was something I fervently wished."

"Was it?"

"Yes. But I was in my twenties. I've found that age and experience give me a different perspective."

"So now you wish you were a wizard again."

"Not necessarily," he said. "But it seems as if I have no choice in the matter. Being near you has affected the cloaking. It's wearing off, even though it's not supposed to."

"And I did that?"

"My mother thinks you have," he said. "I don't know. I don't think it matters how."

Was that why Janet had such an antipathy toward me?

"What does that mean, if the cloaking is wearing off? You'll be exposed as a wizard, or a once upon a time wizard? Will it put you in danger?"

He smiled, a curious self-deprecating smile that had the effect of annoying the hell out of me.

"My powers were never supposed to return, but it seems as if they have, even stronger than before."

There was a lot he wasn't saying, like wizards are dangerous. Wizards scared people. Wizards were probably the Tyrannosaurus Rex of the paranormal world.

He didn't explain further which didn't do a whole lot for my impatience.

"Oh come on, you're not going to leave it at that, are you? You can't tell me half the story. What is a wizard? A male witch? Are you happy or sad about your cloaking disintegrating? How many wizards are there?"

He studied me for a minute and I wanted to ask him what he saw. A woman with an insatiable curiosity? One who had a little too much interest in him? Of course I was interested and not only as a woman. Just what genetic traits had he passed on, presuming that he was my son or daughter's father?

He couldn't stop now, not after the big reveal.

I stared right back until his bottom lip curved a little and the twinkle was back in his eyes. Evidently, my stubbornness amused him. Whatever worked.

"A wizard isn't a male witch," he said. "But they are born into a witch family, primarily a powerful family with a history of practicing witches. Like yours, for example."

"Mine isn't a powerful family. My mother isn't a witch. Only my grandmother." And me, if Janet was right.

"Your great-grandmother was a witch as well as twelve prior generations in a direct line. There are more practicing witches in your family than in mine."

Two thoughts immediately occurred to me: was that another reason Janet didn't like me, because I outranked her in some way? And was my child, if he was a son, going to be a wizard?

When would the damn questions stop?

Nobody had ever told me about witches in my family. Nor had I ever asked. Until I was turned into a vampire, I didn't have a clue that my grandmother was a witch, and now I was learning that I was probably witch royalty.

Oh, goodie.

"There aren't that many of us. Only fifty currently."

"Fifty in the country?"

"Fifty in the world."

That shut me up.

"When a wizard is born, it's always in a witch family. We're imbued with the powers of the witches in our family. We also have some ingrained abilities, like mastery of the elements. Each wizard also has an affinity as well as personal talents."

"Are you always males? No female wizards?"

Again, he studied me. "No. But there are stories of an occasional witch who can match our powers."

"That isn't me," I said, before he could.

"It would take a very powerful witch to strip me of my cloaking."

"I don't even know how I could do that."

He smiled again and I wished he wouldn't do that. He had the greatest smile in the world. A little charming, a little sexy, a little mocking, it could do jumpy things to my insides.

"What are your personal talents?"

"Empathy," he said. "I seem to be able to feel people."

I didn't want to ask the next question, but I had to. He'd given me no choice.

"To feel people? Or to feel me?"

"People," he said. "But you the most. It's more powerful with you. I seem to know when you're unhappy. Or angry. But it's not limited to strong emotions. I can almost hear you chuckle sometimes. Or feel your smile."

He could open up a hole in my chest with a few words. I wanted to leap over the table and land in his lap, wind my arms around his neck and kiss him until dawn arrived.

I managed to subdue my libido - no easy task - and return to our conversation.

"There was no GPS on my phone when you followed me to the grocery store, was there?"

"I don't seem to need one where you're concerned."

"Has it been that way from the beginning?"

He didn't answer, only turned his head to look at me. I love cheesecake. I like the anticipation of eating cheesecake. I like the feeling I get when I'm eating it. Looking at Dan in that moment was like eating a thousand cheesecakes. I felt the warmth all the way down to my toes.

Was that what he meant by destiny?

Was I important to him in a way I didn't understand? I'd always felt a pull toward Dan, but I thought it was because he was kind and noble and a damn good looking guy, not to mention a great lover.

Was it more than that?

CHAPTER TWENTY-TWO

You're a what?

"And your grandmother knew what you were," I said. "Did your grandfather?"

"No. My mother was very careful to conceal the knowledge. She was afraid he'd take advantage of the situation, compel me to act against the family in some way."

Had I ever met a wizard before? Did they normally associate with humans?

As if he'd heard my question, he smiled.

"If you'd met a wizard, you would know it. You would have felt his power. I won't look different when my cloaking is gone. But anyone meeting me would know that I was."

I'd been around a few men like that. Not many, but some. They had immediately impressed me with their charm and something else, a certain magnetism. Maybe they were relatives of wizards.

"What's your affinity? Empathy?"

"I'm a warrior."

That made sense in a scary kind of way. A warrior wizard: the title alone was impressive.

I had a dozen, or a hundred, questions for Dan, but he stood at that moment and walked toward the railing on the edge of the roof. Here was where he took flight, soaring over the castle grounds. That's what I needed, to fall in love with someone who turned into a bird.

Could wizards transform themselves? What, exactly, could they do?

He didn't change, thank God. He just stood there, watching the distant light, master of probably everything he surveyed. I didn't know how many acres around the castle belonged to him, but I suspected it was a lot.

He never spoke about his wealth, which I thought was a combination of what he'd inherited and what he'd amassed through his own skills. He didn't boast about anything and he had more reason then most men I knew. He was, and the word felt odd even as I thought it, humble. Or maybe simply aware. He knew himself and his place in the world, but he didn't think himself better than other men. Yet he was.

If he had an empathetic bond with me, did that mean he knew how I felt about him? Did he know how much I wanted to go to him right now and ease him in some way? I wanted to tell him that I wouldn't harm him, that I wouldn't deliberately expose him to the world.

For the first time, I understood why Janet felt the way she did about me. I represented danger to her child and she'd already lost her daughter. She wasn't going to let anything happen to Dan.

Would his newly uncloaked abilities help him find his sister? Would they aid or hinder the meetings with the witches and the other Brethren? I imagine that the witches would welcome him, because he was born into one of their families. What about the werewolves, the shape shifters, the fairies, the elves, and all the other Brethren that I didn't know about?

And I needed to get the answer about zombies once and for all.

I was so damn grateful that he wasn't something weird - weirder than a wizard - that I wanted to burst into song. I didn't care if he had to wear a tall hat, or long robes embroidered with moons and suns. I didn't care if he set the broomstick to dancing and pails of water sloshing along the castle corridors. Who was I to quibble if he had a laboratory and shelves of small glass jars filled with potions like wing of bat and eye of newt? Was he going to grow a long gray beard? We'd have to seriously talk about that.

The good news was that he wasn't going to transform into anything furry at the first sign of the moon. He wasn't going to get scales or a tail. He was a wizard, which probably meant that he had more powers then I did. That didn't bother me in the least.

"How do you become fully uncloaked?" I asked.

He turned, far enough away from the light that he remained in shadow. Any other woman might have been a little cautious of him. After all, he had just confessed to being a powerful wizard. But I'd been in his bed and in his arms and I knew that whatever happened, he would never hurt me.

"I don't know," he said. "It's never been done. The ceremony to cloak a wizard is meant to strip him of his powers. It's permanent. To the best of my knowledge, it's never been reversed."

"How do you know you are? Do you feel different? Do you have some of your powers back?"

"It's chilly tonight," he said, walking toward me. "Are you cold?"

"No."

He smiled.

"I thought you had heaters up here," I said. "You mean it's you?"

He sat beside me again.

"As a child, I was able to make it cool when I was hot. My mother never had to worry about me playing outside in hundred degree weather."

"Can you make it rain?"

"In small patches," he said. "It's not a good idea to do it over a wide area."

"How do vampires feel about wizards?"

"I can't answer that," he said, sitting back. "There's no documentation on wizards and vampires interacting. I can't imagine Maddock would be happy about it, though."

"Your Archivist wasn't able to find anything? An odd man, Mr. Hattington," I said, which was an understatement. "You really are an equal opportunity employer, aren't you?"

"He's good at his job."

"Does he know the Librarian?"

He looked up at the night sky. "I imagine he does."

"Is she just a human or is she a fairy, too?"

He turned his head to look at me. "If she was, would it bother you?"

"No. As long as she isn't prejudiced against Pranic vampires. Or goddesses."

I didn't dislike anyone who left me alone. You only got on my blacklist when you made it clear that you wanted to wipe me off the face of the earth.

"If you were a full fledged wizard with all your powers, could you save Mike?"

"No," he said. "We can modify the natural laws, but we can't obliterate them." He reached out his hand and grabbed one of mine. "You might be the only one who can save him, Marcie."

"Why tell me now? I've been asking for ages what you were. Why now?"

146

"I had a choice. Limit my contact with you or bend to the inevitable. The longer I'm around you, the more the cloaking disintegrates."

His hand was large and warm, making me feel delicate in comparison. I was almost girly around Dan. I wanted to giggle, for the love of God. I preened. I gave him my best profile.

In other words, I was goofy.

I was also - and this would set feminism back a few decades - horny as hell. I wanted to jump his bones, invite him to my bed which was, at the moment, his bed. I wanted to purr and I've never been the type to purr around a man.

With Bill, sex had been a duty, almost a chore. It was something to check off my To Do list. I thought of sex like a heating pad. It was enough to warm me up, soothe the ache for a little while but only good for a small area. Sex was also a joining, a coming together, a sharing and it didn't matter if the earth didn't move every time. With Bill it didn't move all that much. Just a tremor here and there.

With Dan, I felt like the Saint Andreas fault.

Sex wasn't a chore with Dan. Nor was it a checkbox. It was dark chocolate and cherry cheesecake, soft rain on a winter's day, puppies and kittens, fireworks, a giant raise and an awesome title, a hefty bank balance, goals achieved, the love of friends and family - in other words, all the good and precious things we want in life.

Or, in my case, stasis.

I wanted him in a way that wasn't the least bit ladylike. I wanted to wrap myself around him, breathe in the scent of his skin, kiss him everywhere, and do things to him that might get me arrested in several states.

Most of all, I wanted to show how I felt about him without using words. I couldn't come out and tell him that I loved him. Those words were too filled with jeopardy considering my current condition. I would have to leave the castle if Maddock was the father of my child. If I didn't, I'd bring down the entire vampire population onto Arthur's Folly. I doubted that even being a wizard would be enough to protect Dan.

I stood, stretching out my hand for him. I didn't care if I was being foolish. A goddess and a wizard - we weren't a normal pair, were we? We were oddities, the two of us, but that was okay.

Together, we walked back to his suite on the third floor. At the door, he bent and kissed me softly.

"I have to check on a few things," he said. "Will you be all right?"

I nodded, feeling silly and foolish and younger than I could ever remember being.

Standing there, I watched him walk away. He didn't head for the elevators, but then I thought he probably used the stairs most of the time.

I would take a shower or maybe a bath, indulge in some of the contents of those pretty crystal containers on the shelves beside the tub. I would put my hair up, maybe dab on a little mascara and a faint trace of lipstick. I'd wear my prettiest nightgown, the sheer silk one with the pattern of Japanese flowers on a branch.

I'd wait for him in his giant bed like a lady he'd won in a Medieval tournament. I was more than willing to put aside my twenty-first century mores and values for a few hours and be his trophy.

In fact, I was anxious for the sacrifice to begin.

No one had ever anticipated being ravished as much as I had and been as bitterly disappointed.

Dan didn't return to his room for two hours. That's how long I lasted before I fell asleep.

This pregnancy business wasn't for the faint of heart. First, you lost your appetite and your sense of well-being in the mornings, not to mention your breakfast if you were foolish enough to forget to eat only crackers and tea. Then, you were tired all the time. I could sleep standing up, I swear. But the great thing about being preggers was that once past those symptoms, I felt better than I ever had. I was seriously in a wonderful mood despite my circumstances. I was also desirous of Dan's company in bed, which was a classy way to describe my current state of arousal.

I wanted to play around, but my playmate was missing.

When I woke in the morning to find the ceiling disappearing, I freaked.

I gripped the sheets and comforter with both hands, chin level, staring up as the sky was revealed in all its dawn glory, streaks of pink and pale blue greeting me. What was this, a football stadium? Evidently, the roof thing was an automatic occurrence. Did it happen when it was raining, too? Surely there was some sort of sensor operating it. Why the hell didn't he have a setting for: stranger in my bed?

A bird flew over and for a second I thought it was going to gift me with a morning wake up present, but it didn't. The sky lightened. I could hear the birds in the nearby trees calling out to each other.

Once I calmed down, I realized it was a pretty great way to start the day. You didn't remember problems or concerns. You were concentrating on the sky and the beauty of dawn.

My communion with nature lasted about fifteen minutes. Then the roof began to slowly roll back into place and I was left in the shadowy dark to contemplate why Dan hadn't returned to his room last night.

Maybe he hadn't wanted to make love.

Yeah, like that was ever going to fly as an excuse for any guy. Warm body equals opportunity. No red blooded man - wizard or not - has ever turned down an opportunity. Trust me on this.

One thing I was not going to do was to begin to list my flaws and compare them to anyone else. I was so past that. I had matured. I had grown up. I was a damn goddess. I was not going to think of Diane - aren't I a bitch? - Trenton and wonder if she offered up tea and sympathy at all hours and if she lived at the castle. Nope, not going to do it. I had evolved.

After my breakfast of tea and crackers, I made the sitting room my own little bailiwick. I wasn't going to use the intercom to find out where Dan was. If he hadn't returned to his own room I wasn't going to alert everyone in the castle. Nor was I going to let anyone know I was a roommate. I figured most people knew, but if Janet didn't, I wasn't going to volunteer that fact.

Since I wasn't expected in the banquet hall until two, I occupied myself with reading the rest of the information the Archivist had given me. I liked the way he wrote. He was occasionally droll and I found myself smiling at his comments about some of the Brethren. My knowledge was expanding by leaps and bounds.

I learned that there were creatures considered sub-elves. They were of the same genus, but they were called Nips. They had no appreciable abilities other than being small enough to be almost invisible, especially to humans. They were also, according to the Archivist, responsible for circumstances most humans called Luck or

Coincidence. They didn't blame humans for accidental harm because they were so tiny. It was deliberate malice that infuriated them. In other words, if you see something out of the corner of your eye, don't swat at it.

There was a certain type of cat, a Maine Coon cat, that introduced me to the idea that not all shape shifters turn into humans. In fact, most of them don't. The Maine Coon became an animal the size of a coyote but with feline attributes. It hunted in packs, was responsible for the decimation of sheep and chickens and was often taken for a coyote. People who had Maine Coon cats in their household were often surprised by how large the cat got and how fluffy its appearance. The fluffiness appeared after they changed, and their weight always increased after they hunted. They could eat all they killed in one night. If they were confined inside an apartment, they often became increasingly vicious when the need to change came upon them. They were one of the species ruled by the moon.

The Archivist didn't mention zombies, which made me feel marginally better. Maybe they were just a figment of Hollywood's imagination. Nor did he write about ghosts, which I thought was odd. I knew they existed, and I thought they should be consider as Brethren. Were they under a different classification? If so, what else was with them?

I lost track of the other species I read about, none of whom had been on my radar before now. I was surrounded by Brethren. I'll bet the apartment manager had been one. So, too, Charlie's owner, my hair stylist, the woman at the convenience store, and the clerk at Wal-Mart.

The question was: who was human? I stopped myself from saying normal. I wasn't sure being human was normal anymore. Was anyone human at Arthur's Folly?

How about Dan's assistant? Was she human?

I glanced at the clock, propelled by the thought of the woman to begin getting ready for the dinner. I used the little desk as a vanity and proceeded to do whatever I could to look as good as I could.

The effort was worth it. There must be something to this glowy thing you hear about pregnant women having. I had it. There was a sparkle in my eyes. My complexion was porcelain with a soft rose tint. My hair was shiny and curling just right at my shoulders.

Once I was dressed, I looked better than good. I had my war paint on and my best suit, one modeled after Chanel in a lightweight black wool with gold braid. I was wearing my small gold earrings, my gold watch, and a gold and opal ring I'd always considered lucky. I slipped on my highest heels, black with a grosgrain bow, and practiced walking across the sitting room until I was comfy in them.

I was ready for Miss Trenton. As far as Dan was concerned? Eat your heart out, buddy boy. You really should have come back to your room last night.

CHAPTER TWENTY-THREE

For this I should give thanks?

As I left the suite, it hit me.

I hadn't rescued Charlie. I hadn't taken him to see Kenisha the night before. He or she or whatever pronoun I was using at the moment was probably miffed. I had to smooth some ruffled fur.

I suspected that everybody at the castle had today off as well as tomorrow. I was surprised to find two people at the counter in the kennels. Both of them were smiling, looking happy to be there. Not like the sometimes grumpy attitude you got from humans working retail.

I think you should have to take some kind of aptitude test before you're allowed to work in a store. One of the questions should be: do you receive a great deal of pleasure from ridiculing your customers? Another question: does it give you a perverse pleasure to make people wait even when there is no need for them to do so? Do you hate your mother? Have you taken this damn job only until your: a) your ship comes in, b) you meet your sugar daddy/mommy or c) you strike it rich in the lottery? If the answer is yes to any of the above it should be an automatic disqualification for wearing an kind of orange apron or a name tag of any sort.

As a commercial insurance adjuster, I saw employees at their worst. Yet some of them were pretty damn good even in bad situations. From what I'd seen at Arthur's Folly, the employees were in the latter category.

It might be because Dan paid very well. The benefits of working at the castle might be unbelievable. Or they might all the elves and just naturally jolly. Either one was feasible.

I was greeted by name and one of the attendants turned to get Charlie before I said a word. I stopped him.

"I'm going to the banquet," I said. What else did you call a dinner being served in the banquet hall? I've been staying at Arthur's Folly too long. Pretty soon I was going to start wearing a wimple and have a long trailing handkerchief dangling from one hand, doling out my favor to the knight who struck my fancy. My thoughts went to Dan again and I shut them off.

"I can't take Charlie with me, but I'd like to see him for a few minutes. Also, do you have any treats I could give him?"

Both the male and female attendant looked at me sympathetically. Did they realize I was trying to curry favor or at least apologize for my abandonment? Not that Charlie had been neglected at the kennel. He'd been fed and watered and walked and no doubt petted and adored.

Still, he was my responsibility, and the fact that I had let my libido overwhelm everything else embarrassed me little, especially since I'd been in fifth gear, but the tires hadn't moved.

The female attendant – Jenny – reached under the counter and grabbed a wicker tray. On it were a selection of small bags of any kind of dog treat you might want. I picked out one of liver and one of cheese and thanked her.

"He's fine, you know," she said, her brown eyes warm. "He might have missed you, but he was fine."

I almost asked her if Charlie had said anything before I caught myself. I managed a weak smile and waited until David, the other attendant, fetched Charlie for me.

There was a waiting area on the other side of the counter. I sat there and opened the little packages of treats. First I heard the scrabbling of toenails on the linoleum, then Charlie's heavy panting. I looked up to find him straining at the lease, pulling David as if he were a sled dog.

David let go with the leash and Charlie bounded into my arms, as if it had been weeks since we've seen each other.

I gave a second's thought to my black wool suit before I wrapped my arms around his neck and laid my cheek against his head.

"I'm sorry," I whispered. "I didn't get you last night. Forgive me."

I pulled back to look into his sweet face. "Kenisha's asleep right now, so I can't take you to see her."

He lifted his nose to my ear as if sniffing my perfume.

"How is Mike?" Opie whispered.

I looked over at the two attendants who were smiling in my direction. Life would be a lot easier, and paradoxically more difficult, if word got out that Charlie was a talking dog. Well, not exactly a talking dog - a possessed dog.

"Still holding on," I said, ruffling the fur around Charlie's face.

I hoped I hadn't lied. Was one of Dan's errands to check on Mike? Had he been so distressed about bad news that he'd gone to grieve in private?

Ah, hell, I was some kind of messed up not to have thought of that before. The word I was searching for was selfish.

"I have to go to Thanksgiving dinner," I said, vowing to discover what I could about Mike first. "But I will come and get you afterward."

I could swear that Charlie frowned at me. I'll bet that he liked turkey. Or maybe it was Opie's reaction to being kept in the kennel on the holiday.

I reached for the snacks and nearly got my hand bit off. Never stand between a dog and liver. I managed to make him sit for the cheese treats. However, once they were gone, he turned fickle, directing his attention to David and Jenny. He was doing that on purpose to show me, without words, how annoyed he was. I grabbed the end of his leash and led him back to David.

"I'll come get him after dinner," I said.

Their comments were designed to be mollifying and I appreciated the effort.

"He'll be fine. We're having a Thanksgiving meal for the dogs, too. They're going to get just a little turkey so they don't feel left out."

I restrained myself from asking Opie if that would make up for my desertion and made my way out of the kennel before guilt overwhelmed me.

Honest, I had every intention of going to the sub-level, but a uniformed Arthur's Folly employee waylaid me outside the kennel. He wore a dark green blazer with an appliqué of the castle on his right pocket. His black hair was cut in a military style, but he was too young to have been in the service. Did Dan have an intern program here at Arthur's Folly?

"Mr. Travis asked me to take you to the banquet hall, Ms. Montgomery."

He held out his arm and I debated whether to tell him I wanted to check on Mike first. Dr. Fernandez might not be around, given that it was Thanksgiving. Or Dr. Fong might be on duty. Either way, I doubted I was going to get much information. Kenisha wouldn't be awake yet. I could probably learn more from Dan than anyone and he was, no doubt, involved in the preparations for the dinner.

So I nodded, placing one hand on his arm as he escorted me to the elevator. My other hand was occupied in brushing off Charlie's hair from my black suit.

On the third floor, my escort turned left, looking back at me with a calm, questioning glance. I followed him down the hall, away from the other rooms I was familiar with on the third floor: the ballroom, the Knights of the Round Table room where the witches had congregated, and Dan's suite of rooms.

I was led to a short staircase and descended five steps before coming to a door that looked like it had been repurposed from an old enchanted castle. When Roderick, the name of my escort, turned the latch and opened the door, I wasn't sure what to expect.

Maybe I had been thinking of something along the lines of Harry Potter. Rows and rows of long tables lit by candlelight, with bats and owls soaring overhead, the entire room presided over by Dan and his mother, a wizard and a witch.

Frankly, I was a little disappointed with what I got.

I was standing on a gallery encircling the banquet hall. A long and narrow room, it was illuminated by a wall of windows on the north side and rays of sunlight so bright my eyes watered. Only two long tables occupied the space, each covered in a snowy white tablecloth and enough silver to make the Hunt brothers proud. I had never seen so many silver goblets, for both wine and water, in one place. Even the charger plates were silver and I suspected it was sterling, not silver plate.

I guess, in keeping with my Harry Potter banquet hall expectations, I'd envisioned a gloomy room, something in dark browns and blacks, maybe with a touch of gold here and there to accentuate the medieval period.

Instead, the banquet hall resembled a monk's illuminated manuscript. The carpet was in forest green and scarlet with traces of sunshine yellow. Cobalt blue hangings on the wall revealed a crest I suspected Arthur Peterson had designed for himself. The hangings on the wall opposite the window were modern tapestries, all featuring the castle in the background. Figures were woven throughout each scene. I wondered if they represented someone who was alive when Arthur had the tapestries created. Was Dan depicted?

What about Janet? I knew of the antipathy Arthur had for Dan's mother and doubted it.

"Mr. Travis asked me to bring you to the gallery," Roderick said. "But he doesn't seem to be here."

I glanced at him. "Have you seen him today?"

He ducked his head a little before answering me. "No ma'am. I got my instructions in an email. Mr. Travis is not one to leave anything to chance."

I frowned at him. "Did he also tell you to pick me up at the kennels?"

"No ma'am. I went to your room and was told that you had gone to the kennels."

I didn't ask him who had told him, because I suspected it was a what, not a who. No one had come out and admitted it, but I thought that my movements were probably tracked throughout the castle by some kind of GPS. Maybe it was my body signature or an electrical signal that each person sends out. I didn't have a doubt that Dan could locate me at any place inside the castle in a matter of seconds whether it was his wizardly empathy or his technology. Too bad I couldn't say the same about him.

Where the hell was he?

"Well, how do I get down?" I asked.

I was feeling a little self-conscious since some of the guests had noticed me and pointed out my presence to a few of the others.

I recognized employees who'd served me in the past and gave them a smile. One of the girls who delivered my meals smiled back brightly. Had she spread the word about my penchant for cheesecake? I doubted she needed to. The whole castle probably knew everything I did. I could feel my cheeks warm. I recognized a few of the men who'd stormed into my room when Maddock had affixed himself like a suction cup to my bedroom window, and a few more from two days ago when the ski-mask guy crept into my room.

I'd forgotten to ask Dan what had happened with him. Was he one of the matters he'd had to handle? And what about the mole?

Where was Dan?

Roderick led me to the stairs. He could have just pointed, but I guess his instructions from Dan included watching over me every step of the way. I descended the steps, pasting a smile on my face despite the fact that I'd caught sight of Janet in the crowd. Let's just say that "glower" didn't quite describe the look on her face. Thundercloud. Tornado. Wrath of God. Those were all closer.

My stomach rolled or maybe that was just my child recognizing danger. Good instincts, kid. Keep 'em up. Maybe, just maybe, he was responding to his grandmother's presence. That thought was enough to knock the smile from my face.

Normally, in a situation like this, people would have dismissed me and gone back to their conversations. They didn't. The group closest to me dispersed then encircled me, almost like an amoeba absorbing another amoeba. I had the strangest feeling that I was being both protected and assimilated.

"We've heard so much about you, Miss Montgomery," one stately gentleman said.

His white hair and lined face reassured me somewhat which was stupid since I'd already learned that some of the Brethren could alter their appearance.

I extended my hand and he shook it enthusiastically before introducing himself as William, Janet's brother. Seconds later I met Sylvia, his wife. Her face was as lined as her husband's, a telltale sign of living in South Texas and not giving a flip about sunscreen. Another relative, this one a first cousin, materialized at my side. She had short blond hair and a lean, sunburned face that managed to be competitive and friendly at the same time.

"I'm Gretchen," she said. "I grew up with Dan. Ask me any question you want to know and I'll spill all." She lowered her voice. "For a price, of course." She chuckled and my imaginative mind made her laughter sound sinister.

Exactly what had Dan told his relatives about me? Where was he?

Another cousin, Connie, with auburn hair and the most beautiful blue eyes I had ever seen, began to talk about Dan as a child.

"All the neighborhood girls were mad for him, of course. Even back then he was the most charming boy, aside from his predilection for soldiering and violence. We hoped he'd grow out of that."

I wasn't touching that comment with a ten foot aura.

I had no idea Dan had so many relatives. I couldn't help but wonder what Arthur Peterson had thought about his daughter-in-law's family. Had he repudiated them also? Or had he just been overwhelmed? I could identify.

I saw Nonnie from across the room. She was wearing a dress I'd never seen before, a flowered print on a white background. It was belted at the waist but loose at the back, reminding me of something I'd seen in an old movie. Maybe Nonnie was getting into the medieval atmosphere. Her white hair was piled at the top of her head. She looked regal, important, and happy. When she caught sight of me, she began to smile. She nodded once, a gesture that caused warm feelings to wash over me. It was the first time since I'd been turned that I felt her approval.

I should have sought her out after the witch test, but I hadn't. Maybe I needed to make amends to her, too. I began to make my way across the room to her side, but before I could get there, Janet stepped in front of me.

"Where is my son?"

I blinked at her.

"I don't know," I said, trying to block out the feeling in the pit of my stomach.

I didn't like this. No one had seen Dan. As important as the Thanksgiving dinner was for him, he wouldn't have missed it.

"Did you ask his assistant?"

She looked surprised at my question.

"Maybe he had to go somewhere," I added.

He was meeting with the representatives from the Brethren, I knew that much. Maybe someone had requested to see him today. Yet wouldn't he have left word with someone?

"He would have called you," Janet said. "He would have let you know. For some reason, you're very important to my son. That's why he did all this." She spread her arms wide as if to encompass the entirety of the banquet hall.

I didn't have a damn thing to say to that. Nor was I going to pretend that I was displeased. My little heart was beating like a tom-tom and I was breathing like a real person.

Janet took a few steps toward me and, coward that I was, I backed up. She was one of those people who turn puce when she was angry and right now she was pink, bordering on crimson.

Holy crap. I was in the middle of a menopausal breakdown. Janet was losing it and her anger was directed at me and no one else. The only problem was that I had no clue where Dan was.

She threw her hands up in the air, directed her gaze to the domed ceiling, painted with cherubs, gods, goddesses and a beautiful blue sky adorned with white fluffy clouds.

"By St. Widden's Cross, I promise I will not let her live!"

Everyone in the room stopped talking.

The waiters, who were bringing in trays of food, halted in their tracks. The ushers, who were directing people to their seats, turned to stare at her. Uncles, aunts, cousins, business partners, employees looked wide-eyed at the two of us.

Embarrassment swamped every other feeling until I was drenched in the flop sweat of the truly humiliated. Seriously, was I supposed to stand there and take this?

"I don't know where your son is," I said, irritated beyond measure. "I do know that wherever he is, he is not expecting you to trash Thanksgiving."

My voice was rising with each word. I could feel my emotions increase until power was pulsing in me. I stretched out my hands but kept my palms toward the floor to prevent my aura from rising and to stop me from pointing my fingers at Janet and zapping the hell out of her.

That would be one for the reunions, wouldn't it? *Can you remember when Marcie laid out Janet? God, that was funny.*

I doubted that Dan would see it quite that way.

"Instead of venting your spleen at me," I said, "why don't you put your not inconsiderable energy to use finding Dan? You're a witch. Don't you have some kind of directional finder in your bag of tricks?"

I don't know if the gasps I heard behind me were because people didn't know that Janet was a witch or if they just weren't expecting someone to be super pissed at her.

Not only had I been stood up last night, but now I was being accused of doing something with the guy who had stood me up. I don't get all dressed up for bed for just anybody. Not that I was going to make that comment to Janet. Sometimes, I had enough sense to keep my mouth shut.

"By the way, I want all my stuff back. I can understand why you stole my brush, but my Kindle? And I need my phone."

I had the pleasure of seeing Janet's mouth open. Not a word came out. The blood drained from her face.

I didn't say another word to her. All I did was turn and head for the door, thinking that this Thanksgiving was even worse than some of the ones I had at home and that was saying something. But at least I could leave and thanks to my goddess powers, nobody tried to stop me.

CHAPTER TWENTY-FOUR

We were flying blind here

No one followed me, thank God. I could barely control my emotions. I didn't want to accidentally hurt someone. I made it out of the banquet hall and to the stairs without being stopped by anyone. At the top step, I looked around, grateful that no one else was on the roof.

Maybe this place was off limits to everyone. Maybe it was Dan's place to come and survey his domain. Whatever it was, I was glad to be alone.

I walked in between the hedges to stand where Dan had stood last night. I wrapped my arms around my waist, looking at the same view he'd studied, only bright now with the noon sun. Although late in the season, the cicadas were still going strong. The temperature was probably going to get to seventy today, the memory of hundred plus days not that distant. The earth seemed to cling to the heat as if afraid of the chilly days to come.

Daring myself, I walked closer to the edge. From here I could see the cars filling the road leading to the gate. Each vehicle represented a guest or two in the banquet hall. Dan had opened his home up to his employees, his relatives, his friends, and his business associates, eager to share what he had with others. I'd always known he was generous. Look how he'd treated me from the beginning.

When I first met him, I thought he was a vampire, but he'd only been working for Maddock and assigned to me as a bodyguard. Now I knew why he'd gone to work for the master vampire: to learn what he could about his sister's disappearance.

I suspected, from the beginning, that he was different. I never guessed that he was a wizard, but then my knowledge of wizards was somewhat lacking. I was going to have to learn more and quickly.

If I hadn't shown up, if I hadn't begun to dissolve the cloaking somehow, would he have ever changed? Would he have wanted to become a wizard again?

I wanted to do it on my terms. I didn't want any special favors or special powers. And now? Now he didn't have a choice, did he, because I'd done something.

What the hell had I done? How had I done it?

Where was he?

This morning when I'd awakened to the dawn being revealed above me, I'd known. I'd felt it. Something warned me. Something felt wrong and now I knew what it was. I was suddenly so sad I could barely stand. Emotions flooded over me. I knew, but I couldn't tell you how I knew, that something terrible had happened. A corner of my world was crumbling. Some safe place had disappeared and would never return.

Dan.

I couldn't feel him, and until this moment I hadn't realized that I always had. There wasn't a warm spot, a feeling of protection, a safe zone in my heart or maybe my soul. Something elemental was missing and I needed it to live. I needed him and I'd never been the type of person to need someone else so desperately it felt as if air had been stripped from my lungs.

Come back. Wherever you are, come back.

I was getting a sick feeling, like having morning sickness but not localized to my stomach. This involved the whole of me, heart, soul, body, and mind. I'd never been as terrified, not even when Maddock had drugged me. Then, I could anticipate what was going to happen and be afraid. This was worse. This was like standing at the edge of the abyss and seeing into the darkness, but having no idea what would come next. Nor how I would be able to face it.

He said he didn't need GPS to find me. Maybe I didn't need it to find him, either.

After I closed my eyes, an act that took its share of courage, I stretched out my hands on either side of me, palms up. In seconds, my aura was surrounding me like a capsule or a balloon of light. I stretched out my hands, my fingers splayed, and extended the aura outward until it was the size of Arthur's Folly. I sent my thoughts to every room, known or unknown, every corner, every wall, every ceiling, every floor, every cubic inch of the massive castle. I thrust the aura into the sub-floors, feeling for Dan's presence, his essence, his warmth.

I saw his smile in my mind's eye. I felt the touch of his hand on my arm, his kiss on my lips. I breathed in his air and stroked the bristly curve of his cheek. I whispered his name into his ear, recalled those moments when he effortlessly brought me bliss.

Come back to me. Dan.

Only emptiness met me.

Slowly, I allowed my aura to expand, over the lake, the gazebo, the flower gardens, and the invisible fence near the access road. Even farther, over the cars, the gate, the mesquite trees with their twisted trunks and branches spotted with mistletoe. Over the earth, scaring a family of armadillos, startling jackrabbits, and a few tortoises sunning themselves on a flat rock. When my aura threatened to dissipate into nothing but gold tinted air, I fueled it with my fear, with wishes, hopes, and the memory of our passion. I sent it flying, strengthened, over the bison of today, the whining eighteen wheelers speeding down IH-10 on their way to San Antonio.

He wasn't there, either.

The world was empty, black, and joyless.

I opened my eyes and let my aura creep back to me, exhausted and weakened. I had failed at the one time I couldn't fail.

I wanted to weep. No, I wanted to scream.

Turning, I saw Janet standing there. At that moment she wasn't a powerful witch, but a woman in the depths of grief. She had already lost one child. Losing a second would destroy her.

"How did you know?" she said. "How did you know I'd taken your belongings?"

Oh, hell, I didn't want to have that conversation, but it looked as if it were inevitable.

"The same way I know that Dan's a wizard," I said, watching her carefully.

I didn't tell her that Dan had told me in this exact spot. For some reason, I felt like the revelation would hurt her feelings. I may not like Janet, but I didn't want to be the one to cause her any more pain. I wasn't a mother yet, but I was already protective of the child in my womb. I couldn't imagine the anguish the loss of her daughter caused her.

The fact that I couldn't feel Dan, that I couldn't locate him, scared me. That no one else had seen or talked to him was adding to my fear. I didn't know where the hell he was.

"I saw you," I said. "Talking to Dan."

"What do you mean?"

For a powerful witch, she was being a little obtuse.

"Dan called it remote viewing."

She stared at me. "You have the ability to transport?"

That term didn't seem quite right, either.

"I guess," I said.

She looked away, her gaze on the horizon.

Why couldn't we just be honest with one another? We were both afraid. We were both worried about Dan. Why couldn't we share what we were feeling?

I decided to go first.

"I can't sense him," I said. "It's as if there's a wall between him and me."

I didn't tell her that, until a little while ago, I hadn't realized that he was always in my consciousness. Just a little to the side, standing back as if tucked into a corner just for him. The feeling of warmth was missing now, as if the world were newly cold and strange.

She turned her head. I avoided looking in her eyes. I couldn't see her pain at the moment. I was trying too hard to contain my own.

"Would you try again?"

"I don't think it would help," I said.

"Please."

I've run into people who are so sure of their own opinion that there's no room for anything else. I ran into that problem a lot with older men in the insurance industry. They thought they'd seen it all, could anticipate anything I asked and consequently never answered the question the first time. They didn't even wait for me to finish asking in their rush to answer. I would have to bite back my irritation, then circle back around to the real question once more.

I had a feeling that Janet was just like those older men, not accepting my word for anything. I knew nothing would come of trying again, but I also knew I couldn't refuse her.

Without a word, I turned and walked back into the middle of the hedges. I replicated my movements, spreading out my arms. This time I added a prayer to my aura, sending it spinning over the landscape, stretching out farther than I had before until I was nearly sick with the effort.

I don't know how long I stood there. I sent thoughts of Dan over the twisted trees, sparse grass still not recovered from a dry summer, trickling streams, and the last of the horny toads in this area. Time itself meant nothing as I called out to him in words only he could hear.

Dan, answer me. Where are you? Send me a message. Give me a word. Let me know where you are. If you're safe. Please.

I only heard the echo of my own voice.

My stomach suddenly cramped, shocking me. A moment later I doubled over in pain.

Janet led me to one of the chairs as I collapsed. I wrapped my arms around myself, holding on, terrified and trying not to remember the two miscarriages I'd had in the past.

No. It was the only word I could think. No. It was a command, a prayer, an entreaty. No. I couldn't lose this child, even if his father was gone.

Pain squeezed me until I felt cut in two. I closed my eyes, forcing my panic down. I breathed in deeply like I had before I'd been turned, letting the air out slowly. Again, and then again, until I was calmer. I wasn't going to think the worst. I couldn't. I wasn't going to twist myself into knots. I was going to get through the pain until it eased.

"Are you all right?" Janet asked.

I nodded, forcing a smile to my face in response to the genuine concern in her voice.

She sat beside me, pressing her hand on my arm.

"What's wrong?"

"Just a cramp," I said, close enough to the truth.

"Shall I say a spell?"

The last thing I needed was to have to protect myself from a powerful witch's spell.

"No," I said. "I'll be fine in a moment."

To my surprise, she withdrew her hand, sitting quietly beside me. The pain wasn't as bad as it had been just a few minutes earlier. I tried to remember those other occasions, memories I'd avoided until now. This had been a sharp pain, not what I'd experienced before. After the first miscarriage, I hadn't read any books about pregnancy. I hadn't wanted to predict or discover anything before it happened. A good thing, as it turned out. Now, however, I wished my ignorance wasn't quite so deep or pervasive.

Or maybe no book could answer questions about this pregnancy.

Maybe I'd been stabbed by a fang.

I closed my eyes, said another prayer, hoping that God wasn't too annoyed at me. Not a fang, God, please. Let it be a little wizard hat that had poked me in the uterus.

"It's the cloaking," Janet said. "It prevents you from feeling him."

I pushed back my anxiety and looked over at her. She was feeling her own panic, and in that moment it united us.

"Dan said it was fading."

She didn't look surprised at my words. "Perhaps if we removed it completely, you could sense where he is."

"Can you do that?" I asked. "I thought once he was cloaked, it couldn't be removed."

She waved her hand in my direction. "That might have been true once, but since you appeared in my son's life, Marcie Montgomery, a great many things have changed."

What the hell did I say to that? Nothing that wouldn't have raised her hackles once more. I wasn't in the mood to fight with Janet.

"How does an uncloaking happen?" I finally asked.

At that, she stared off into the distance.

"I will have to consult with some of our elders." She stood and glanced down at me. "Will you lend your power to our coven?"

At the moment, I wasn't feeling the least bit powerful, but I nodded.

"Is it safe?" I asked. "If someone has restrained him or taken him, is it safe to uncloak him now?"

She frowned at me. "What do you think will happen once his power is revealed?"

"I don't know," I said. "I've never met a wizard."

"You might have," she said. "And never known. After all, you lived among witches all your life."

She was right about that, but that was a recent revelation. I was hesitant to tell her that. Or to admit how limited my knowledge of witchcraft was. I was flying blind.

Janet left me, no doubt to go and talk to the elders. Was she going to summon them to a holographic meeting? Was she just going to send them text messages? How technologically advanced were the witches? I know that whenever my grandmother texted me, which wasn't often, it startled me.

Or were they all here in the castle, come to celebrate Thanksgiving? Do witches acknowledge holidays? See how much I don't know?

I sat there until the pain subsided completely, probably a quarter hour. Finally, I stood, taking inventory. I no longer hurt. There weren't any pains anywhere, only a hollow emptiness that seem tied to my sadness. It didn't take a rocket scientist to figure out I was missing Dan.

The strangest feeling came over me then. I knew things were going to be all right. Not everything. For example, I didn't know where Dan was or if he was safe and well. I didn't know about the man who had come into my room or the organization he represented. I didn't know about Mike or my mother or my relationship with Kenisha or what would happen to Ophelia if anything happened to Charlie – both events I avoided thinking about. I didn't know what was going to happen with my relationship with Nonnie.

One thing I did know, the one thing that had worried me down deep, was that my child was going to be fine. I didn't know who his father was, but I knew my son would live. He might have fangs or he might have wizardly powers or he might have fangs and powers. That was not yet decided. Or perhaps it was decided long ago and I just hadn't figured it out yet.

CHAPTER TWENTY-FIVE

Not a combination to warm the cockles of my heart

I wasn't going to return to the banquet hall, even though Janet and I had made a sort of peace between us. I was a little hungry. If someone showed up in front of me with a few tacos, I could eat. But I didn't want to sit in a room filled with people who were watching me surreptitiously. I didn't want to pretend to be pleasant, not with Dan missing. I wasn't that good an actress.

I didn't want to return to Dan's suite of rooms, either.

There were a great many places I could go at Arthur's Folly – the library on the first floor, the Great Hall, the courtyard. The chances are, each one of them would be occupied and I didn't want to be around anyone right now.

I found myself standing in front of the door to my old suite. It felt like home, even though it had been invaded by a stranger. I placed my hand on the plate to the left of the lock, heard the click as it identified me. I opened the door, smelled my perfume, and walked inside, closing the door behind me. Daring myself, I walked into the dressing area. I couldn't see the secret panel and I wasn't going to try to find it right now. All I wanted was to make sure I was alone.

There wasn't anyone here but me.

I sat on the end of the chaise, wrapped my arms around me and let the tears fall soundlessly. I felt as if I were melting inside. Something was dissolving. Maybe my optimism or my belief in happy endings. Or maybe the last trace of my innocence.

I'd had an eventful few days. All I needed now was to be confronted with Maddock or one of his minions to make my stress complete. Just kidding, God.

The emotionality was normal, something I'd experienced before. I cried at everything. I cried because I was happy, sad, hungry, cold, hot - you name it, there were dozens and dozens of reasons why I cried.

When I was done, I grabbed a tissue, dried my eyes, blew my nose and fought back the urge to take a nap. I didn't feel all that comfy sleeping here. I didn't know if someone was going to come out of the closet attired in a ski mask again.

Would it be really rude and insulting to order room service, especially when the whole of the castle was catering Thanksgiving dinner? I could always order turkey with a cheesecake chaser. I decided to wait a little while, so my absence wasn't that blatant.

The knock on the door made me wonder if there were such things as mind reading fairies at Arthur's Folly. Please let them have interpreted the part about the cheesecake right. Oh, hell, who was I kidding? I'd take a taco or two. Or even turkey, if push came to shove. Maybe a little dressing, some rolls, mashed potatoes and gravy?

Bring on the carbs, please.

I opened the door, my smile already in place. It took a lot of effort to keep it there once I saw who it was.

Diane Trenton had a body made for fooling around. The emerald sheath she wore left no doubt of it. I would bet, however, that her boobs were courtesy of one of the best plastic surgeons in San Antonio.

We eyed each other for a moment. The seconds ticked past without anyone to witness our mutual antipathy. I knew why I didn't like her. I was jealous. There was no way to pretty it up or make it sound more noble. She worked closely with Dan every single day. She was gorgeous. She was probably smart, too. Not a combination to warm the cockles of my heart.

The question was: why did she dislike me?

"Is this yours?" she asked.

She shoved something at me, and I automatically reached out to take it. As I did, I felt the corridor drop about forty degrees. No, that was me.

I stared down at the evening bag. I hadn't seen it since the night Niccolo Maddock had raped me. Call it what you will, a chemically induced seduction was rape and I would never forgive him.

My hands began to shake, the sequins on the bag's surface seeming to pick up the vibration.

"Where did you get this?" Something was wrong with my voice. It sounded thin and reedy, as if I rarely spoke.

I forced myself to look at her rather than the bag.

"It was on Dan's desk. I went to the office to see if he'd left any kind of note or message."

She didn't know it, but the bag was a message. It was a clue as big as China and one that had stripped all the warmth from me.

"I looked inside," she said.

I only nodded. I didn't give a flying flip if she'd used my lipstick or run my debit card. That wasn't the important thing about the bag. Its presence indicated where Dan was. The vampires had him.

Maddock had him.

I nodded again, forcing the words from my lips. "Thank you."

She didn't say anything, just frowned at me. A moment later she turned and walked away, leaving me still standing in the doorway, holding onto the damn evening bag.

Maddock had him. I knew what that meant, even as my stomach did a somersault. Maddock wanted a trade for me and if it didn't happen, Dan would never come home.

Like hell.

I closed the door, went to the intercom and asked the person who answered to convey a message to Mrs. Travis. I wanted her to meet me in the Knights of the Round Table room as soon as possible.

Call me Buffy; I was going vampire hunting and the witches were going to help me.

CHAPTER TWENTY-SIX

Smite, smote, smitten

I locked my suite and returned to Dan's set of rooms. I hadn't been back since learning that he was missing. The rooms felt empty. Not the empty feeling you get when a house in temporarily unoccupied. This was the hollowness of a home vacated by its owner. A cave whose bear had awakened and left until next season. The den of a fox who'd been hunted and killed.

My skin crawled. I felt like something was watching me and wondered if any of the witches visiting Arthur's Folly had remote viewing abilities. For that matter, did Janet? Had she turned the tables on me?

I looked up and around, checking for cameras, wondering if Dan would have allowed them in his rooms. I doubted it.

I tried to dismiss the feeling as I walked into the sitting room.

The suit I was wearing was my armor. I felt comfortable in it and I knew I looked good. I wondered if that's how most women considered their clothes. I didn't change, even though I did slip off the heels and replace them with sneakers.

I dared someone to say something to me. In the mood I was in, it wouldn't be a good idea.

I'd smite them, a word that sounded right and one I intended to use again. It beat the heck out of zapping someone. *I shall smite them*. Didn't that sound all goddessy?

I checked my makeup, another form of armor, and got rid of the mascara that had melted when I'd had my crying jag. Had Trenton seen me looking this ragged? Damn it. I reapplied my mascara, added some lipstick, then grabbed my evening bag, and made my way to the Knights of the Round Table room.

On my way there, I investigated the contents of the bag. My old phone was still there. It wasn't as fancy as the one Dan had gotten for me, but at least I had a way to communicate now. I tucked it into my bra since my suit didn't have pockets.

I entered the Knight's room. The last time I'd been here, the witches had convened to hear Dan's idea of them supporting me. That ship had sailed. They better damn well support me or I would zap them - oops, smite them - into kingdom come. Or whatever the witchy equivalent was. We were talking life and death here.

Could Dan be made a vampire? Did the vampires know he was a wizard? Could he fight them off?

Okay, enough with the questions. In the next hour, I was damn well going to get some answers. I'd just about had it with being ignorant and left out of the loop.

Nobody was there when I entered.

When I'd first seen the room, I'd been startled by the fourteen suits of shiny silver armor placed along the circular wall, each of them positioned behind a throne-like chair. Now I hardly noticed them, being so used to Arthur Peterson's love of all things medieval and Arthurian.

Above me was a chandelier equal in circumference to the polished table. On my last visit the candles had been lit. No doubt to lend atmosphere to the room. The sun had set in the last few minutes, but there was enough light still coming through the mullioned windows.

I sat in the chair Dan had occupied last time. When the door opened a few minutes later and Janet entered, I didn't spend any time on pleasantries.

"The vampires have him," I said.

She didn't say a word. That was left to Nonnie, who followed her into the room.

"How do you know, Marcie?"

I held up the evening bag. "I left this at Maddock's house when I escaped. It was on Dan's desk. Either he had a visitor, or someone sent it as a lure. I doubt if he would have opened the doors to a vampire willingly."

"My daughter," Janet said, pulling out one of the chairs and sitting heavily. "He would have if they promised news of Nancy."

I had already come to that conclusion, so I only nodded.

"We can't wait," she said. "We must do the ceremony now. As a wizard, Dan can defeat them. Cloaked, he's only as strong as a human."

Even human, Dan was pretty damn awe-inspiring. I wouldn't count him out in whatever guise he was in, but I agreed with her. Although I didn't know everything a wizard could do, I was all for giving him every asset he could handle.

"I'll gather up the people who are here," Janet said.

"Do you want me to call my sisters of the faith?" Nonnie asked.

"Can they be here in less than an hour?" Janet stood and walked back to the door.

"Yes."

I swear, my grandmother could read minds. She turned to me and smiled.

"No, Marcie, they won't be using brooms, either."

"She really doesn't know very much about witchcraft, does she?" Janet asked.

"It was thought that keeping her in ignorance would be safer for all of us," Nonnie said, her voice sounding strong and commanding.

To my surprise, Janet looked rebuked.

Of the two of them, who was the more powerful?

I agreed to meet them in yet another large room at the castle. I hadn't seen this one, either. The sparring room was evidently off the gym - another room I hadn't visited - and its main claim to fame was that it didn't have windows.

"We don't want to put anyone in danger," Janet said cryptically before disappearing down the corridor with my grandmother.

What the hell were we going to do that might blow out the windows?

I guess I was going to find out.

I didn't know what to do with the evening bag. Neither Nonnie nor Janet had seemed very interested in using it. I'd thought they could do a directional spell or some kind of who-used-this-last potion. I really did have a lot to learn about witches. I decided to drop it off in Dan's room so I headed in that direction.

I put the bag on the chaise and made my way to the surveillance room. I wasn't all that technologically adept, but one thing I had in my favor right now was that I wasn't timid. I needed to know everything I could and if that meant screwing up along the way, that was okay with me.

I fiddled with some of the settings until other scenes appeared on the screens in front of me. I saw the kitchen, a massive expanse of stainless steel counters, shelves, and equipment, suitable for preparing meals for an institution. Right now they were bustling. I lost count of the number of turkey carcasses being put into a large vat for boiling. Waste not, want not, a comment my grandmother had often made in my childhood. Evidently, we were going to have gallons of turkey soup and other turkey based leftovers.

Hopefully, there'd be some stuffing left.

I tuned into the garage next, then the Great Hall. People were milling about. Had they finished their meal and were hoping for some entertainment? Had Dan planned for any? I felt inept and wishing I'd known the schedule for the day, but I am not now - nor have I ever been - the world's greatest hostess. If the situation had been different, I would have offered to lead a team in charades or something, but I was more intent on saving Dan than rescuing his party.

No matter what I did, I couldn't figure out how to rewind the surveillance footage to the night before. What I did see didn't strike me as odd. All I was left with was a better idea of how big Arthur's Folly was and how well it was run. What I needed to do was touch base with the center of video operations and this wasn't it.

Dan, being a military man, would have set up a chain of command. With Mike ill, who was next in charge? Whoever it was, I needed to find him, get into the real nerve center of the castle, and see if Dan had been taken from the castle or left of his own accord. I had a feeling it was the latter, but until I actually saw with my own eyes, I couldn't be sure.

Janet had given us an hour to do everything we needed to do to prepare for the ceremony. I didn't know where to start, so I began with the intercom. My question seemed to stump the young thing on the other end of the line. I finally thanked her and hung up, realizing that there was one person in the castle who would know, damn it, and I had to talk to her.

I used the intercom again, got Diane Trenton's phone number and dialed her. She was probably looking at the phone as it went into voice mail.

I left her a message, trying to imbue my tone with some warmth. If I never had to talk to the woman again, I'd be happy, but this task was more important than my feelings.

"I need to know who has access to the surveillance video from last night. The nearest I can figure is that Dan disappeared after nine. Did he leave the castle on his own? Or was he helped?"

I decided to throw myself on Diane's mercy. Besides, I was going to go into an uncloaking ceremony and it might drain me down to the bone. Let her feel important. Let her *be* important, for that matter.

"Look, I need help. We need to find Dan. Can you look through the footage?"

I just couldn't wrap my mind around the idea that Dan would have disappeared without alerting someone to his whereabouts. Unless that was part of the deal. Come with us and we'll lead you to your sister, but tell no one. No, it still didn't compute. Dan would have found a way to let someone know where he was going. Unless he was so independent that he thought he could handle the situation on his own. No, he wasn't that foolhardy. Besides, he had all those paramilitary guys at his command.

"I'll be with Dan's mother," I said. "I'll check in with you later."

I didn't know how much later. Hopefully, I'd given Diane enough information to start working on the problem. I knew the woman was competitive. I'd seen it in her eyes. She would move heaven and earth to get the information I needed, and that was fine with me. I'd give her all the credit she desired.

My ego wasn't important right now. All I cared about was finding Dan.

On my way to the gym, I decided to make a side trip to the kennels and pick up Charlie. The witches had considered him my familiar, and it might be helpful to get Opie's take on everything. Besides, it would be a good idea to mend fences there. All the liver treats in the world wouldn't make a difference if Opie was really mad.

Jen wasn't there, but David was, and so was a whole pumpkin pie. My stomach growled and I lectured it sternly. I didn't know what I was going to have to face in the uncloaking ceremony. It was probably better that I wasn't going into the situation with a full stomach.

"Back for Charlie?" he asked, looking up from his slice of pie.

I nodded.

"How was the banquet?"

"Very nice," I said, not mentioning that I hadn't stayed for the food. The decorations were beautiful and the guests were all well dressed and attractive. The banquet hall was equally impressive. What was there not to like?

The fact that Dan was missing was one.

I paced in the waiting area until Charlie arrived. When he approached me, a little less enthusiastically than before, I understood. Opie was in charge, which meant that she was pissed. I doubted she wanted to attend the banquet for the food as much as the human interaction. Being a woman trapped in a dog must be a little brain draining. Not that Charlie wasn't a very smart dog.

I took the end of the leash from David, thanked him and wished him Happy Thanksgiving again. I was going to wait until I hit the elevator to talk to Opie and then only surreptitiously. I needed to warn her about where we were going.

I didn't get the chance. Outside the kennel I was bodily assaulted by Kenisha. She grabbed me and hugged me, so tight that I thought I'd lose what breath I had. She was crying so hard my heart sank.

Please, no.

I dropped the leash and hugged Kenisha back.

"K-girl, what's wrong?"

I was vaguely aware that Opie was talking. We hadn't moved far from the kennel door and there was a camera mounted on the ceiling nearby. I knew her voice was more mental than audible. In other words, people overhearing our conversation might hear me, see Charlie's mouth open, but I'm not sure they would hear Opie's voice like I did.

Still, when Kenisha pulled away and looked at her, I was worried. I wasn't really keen about someone watching either one of us talk to a dog. Either we'd be labeled for the loony bin or they might suspect there was something to our conversation. Neither one was a good option.

"There's a camera up there," I whispered to Kenisha, who understood immediately.

Opie, however, was a little slow on the uptake. Either that, or she didn't give a flying flea.

"What's wrong, K-girl?"

I had to shut her up.

I bent, scratched her behind the ears, smiling as I whispered, "Camera, Opie. Stop talking."

I'd given Trenton a job to do. I didn't have any doubt that she would be monitoring my movements as well as trying to find Dan. It's what I would do. Confession might be good for the soul, but it made me feel a little like a weasel. I needed to advance beyond my lesser nature.

I straightened and faced Kenisha.

"Is Mike worse?" I asked.

"No, he's better. So much better."

"Mike's okay?" I asked, hope buoying my words and my mood.

She nodded, still smiling, even as she brushed away her tears.

"He's better than okay. He's going to live, the doctor says."

Now was not the time to ask *how* he was going to live, as a human or a vampire or something more. I'd leave that for later.

"Dr. Fernandez did give him the rabies vaccine, right?"

She nodded again. "He said he didn't think it was necessary, but he listened to Dan."

Fernandez and I were going to have to have a heart to heart one of these days. The man was a throwback to an era when the little woman read magazines all day, worried only about what was for dinner and if she looked good enough for her husband. Not that life was ever that way, but men like Fernandez thought it had been and fervently wished it replicated.

Good luck with that.

Charlie parked himself on Kenisha's feet. I knew that was Opie again.

"I need you," I said, hoping the camera thought I was talking to Kenisha. "We have an uncloaking ceremony to attend." I'd tell her about the participation part later.

She looked between me and Kenisha. Great. I was odd man out again. I wouldn't have minded all that much but I was already feeling a little vulnerable, scared, and nearly sick with worry.

"You don't have to come," I said. "You can go with Kenisha."

It was Kenisha's turn to do the tennis look from one of us to the other.

"I think you should go with Marcie. I'll be fine."

Call me contrary. Call me bitchy. I was hungry and I tend to get snarky when I'm hungry. But because Opie had delayed, now I didn't want her with me.

"Never mind," I said. "Go on with Kenisha."

Me, the non-hugger, reached over and hugged Kenisha again.

"I'm so glad he's going to be okay."

"Only because of you."

"I doubt it was all me," I said. "Maybe some, maybe some prayers, and some of Dr. Fernandez's care, along with just plain luck."

We'd see how much was credited to my blood when Mike recovered and became whatever he was going to become.

Before Kenisha could argue with me or Opie change her mind and come, I turned and headed for the elevators.

I have my pride. I wasn't going to beg anyone to be my friend. But had she forgotten the liver and the cheese treats, the belly rubs, the praise and appreciation? Had she forgotten all the times I'd asked the kitchen to send up doggy treats?

I was confusing Charlie and Opie. Charlie was loyal. Opie had conflicting loyalties. I needed to remember that and not blame one entity for the other's behavior.

I was tired, a little bit weepy, and out of sorts. I needed to eat something and take a nap. Instead, I was headed for yet another ceremony and this one scared me. Even Janet didn't know if it could be done. Was there a "should" in there? What would happen if we screwed up? What would happen if we didn't? By uncloaking Dan would we put him in danger? Would he start to glow or something? Would anyone suddenly realize that he was different? What if I couldn't "feel" him after the uncloaking?

Nope, I wasn't getting a good feeling about this, but I didn't know what else to do.

If in doubt, do nothing. Some wise person had once told me that. Unfortunately, doing nothing wasn't an option.

The elevator door opened and I had a choice: continue on or run like hell.

I headed for the gym.

CHAPTER TWENTY-SEVEN

I had been pushed to the edge

The sparring room turned out to be a room off the gym where they'd installed a boxing ring. As I entered, the last of the foundation was being removed and stored along the wall, along with the ropes. The space, about fifty feet by seventy feet, was unlike the rest of Arthur's Folly. It was ugly. The walls were gray, as was the floor. Although nothing was made of cinderblock, that was the impression I got. Industrial concrete, a man's place, not one centimeter of it feminine, girly, or - God forbid - attractive. There wasn't one window or a skylight, only strips of florescent lights overhead.

To my surprise, William and his wife, Sylvia, entered the room and nodded to me, but halted several feet away. Gretchen, Dan's cousin, joined them a minute later. Evidently, I was to be seen and not gotten near. Susan, Terry, and Barb from my grandmother's coven - or sisters of the faith, as she called them - entered next. Other people I'd seen in the banquet hall but hadn't met followed.

I could feel the energy in the sparring room. I didn't know if it was just from the presence of powerful witches or if they were afraid like I was. I couldn't help but wonder what they felt from me. Did I give off vibes? I knew I did when I tried. When I my off button was engaged, could they sense anything from me?

My grandmother had changed clothes. Now she was wearing a dark blue dress with a plain white collar and cuffs. It took me a minute to realize that Susan, Terry, and Barb were all attired alike. Did their uniform, for lack of a better word, help to unite them? I'd never attended one of Nonnie's coven meetings so I didn't know.

A low drone of conversation was building in the room. It, too, had an energy. I tried to block out the voices and I succeeded, for the most part. From time to time, however, I would hear Dan's name and mine. The former was always spoken in loving tones. The latter not so much. I couldn't blame these people, a great many of whom might be related to Dan. They didn't know me. Of course they would suspect me. I might feel the same way. Or maybe I'd cut me some slack, wait until I got more information and then judge me.

My hunger was turning me bitchy.

"Are you well, child?"

My grandmother had approached me and I hadn't been paying attention.

"Yes, Nonnie. I'm well."

I'm scared to death and I'm starving, but other than that, I'm fine.

"Did you know that Janet's son is reputed to be one of the most powerful wizards ever born?"

Surprised, I looked at my grandmother. I'd rarely heard fear in her voice, but it was there now. A stranger might look at her and see, not a powerful witch, as much as a frightened woman in her eighties.

"If it is known he exists," Nonnie continued, "the vampires will stop at nothing to eliminate him. He poses too great a threat." Her gaze was direct and difficult to avoid. "They will also destroy anyone close to him, Marcie."

"They already have reason to want me," I said. "You don't need to warn me about vampires."

I wasn't really happy with God at the moment. After all, it was God's fault for allowing all these divergent creatures to exist on earth. What was He thinking? So far, there hadn't been an internecine war with one winner, unless that had been the human race and now everyone else wanted a shot at the brass ring.

God should have seen this coming. A sentiment I wasn't going to voice to my grandmother.

"I worry for you, my child."

I was worried enough for me already. I put my arms around her, feeling her frail shoulders. When had she gotten old? Had my actions and those of my mother caused her to age more rapidly than she would have otherwise?

I had a lot to answer for, too.

"You don't have to do this," I said, concerned about her. "Janet shouldn't have asked you."

"Nonsense," she said. "I'm looking forward to it. I don't doubt that books will be written about this night, Marcie. No one else has ever attempted an uncloaking ritual. We shall all be famous."

I didn't care about being famous. I just wanted to be alive when it was over. If I could feel the pulse of power in this room already and nothing had happened, what was it going to be like with fifty witches all chanting spells and doing their thing?

We were about to find out.

The witches began to form a circle and Nonnie went to join them. Janet entered the room, made her way to the center of the circle and addressed them all, turning slowly as she did so. I stood to the left and rear, waiting to be summoned.

Her voice carried easily and I wondered if it was the acoustics in the room or if she was simply used to speaking to a crowd and adjusted the volume of her voice accordingly.

"In the cloaking ritual," Janet said, "the subject's power is used to create the cloak. The stronger the abilities, the greater the cloaking."

If Dan was as powerful as my grandmother said, then no wonder his cloak had lasted all these years. Did that mean that I was Dan's match in power? My presence, according to him, was sufficient to erase the cloaking. Or maybe I was just some kind of magical backspace.

"You are all here by virtue of your abilities and your love and affection for my son. We suspect he is in danger and needs his powers to escape."

At least she didn't mention me.

"Some of you have never taken part in a cloaking ceremony. None of us have ever done what we are about to do."

To their credit, none of the witches looked perturbed by that comment. Nor did anyone look at another witch with a glance that said, "Let's get out of here." They all looked fixed and purposeful and, like my grandmother, downright eager.

"The ritual will have two parts," Janet was saying. "The first will be to build up our power." She glanced at me once. That's where I came in. "In the second part, we will have to reverse the spell we did ten years ago."

Now some of the witches looked worried. Since I didn't know diddly about spells, I wondered if reversing a spell had some inherent danger built into it. Maybe a spell carried with it a failsafe device: whosoever shall mess with this will be in danger of hellfire, or at least draw back a bloody stub.

Janet waved me into position at her side. That was new. Maybe she just didn't want me standing behind her. I couldn't blame her. I was a loose cannon as far as she was concerned, the woman who single-handedly screwed up her son's cloaking.

Amazing what passion can do.

I pressed my palm against my waist. My prayer was simple. *Please, God, don't let anything happen to my child.* The second prayer was layered atop the first. *Please, God, don't let anything happen to Dan.*

Did God hear the prayers of humans turned vampires turned Dirugu, Pranic and heaven knows what else I was? Or was God super pissed because I'd called myself a goddess once or twice? Take it out on me, God, and no one else, but not until my child is safely born.

Would God accept ultimatums?

In a world overflowing with creatures of all shapes, sizes, and abilities, were there such things as angels? Were angels truly what they were billed to be, messengers who interceded between humans and God? Did they ever lobby for vampires? If so, I needed to locate my guardian angel and have the dude do something.

I needed all the help I could get.

Janet made a gesture with both hands. The witches started chanting what sounded like Psalms from the Bible. The florescent lights suddenly dimmed. I hadn't seen a dimmer on the wall switch, so I figured it was something the witches were doing. They weren't attired in robes like they'd been at the witch test. There weren't any candles. But even without the trappings, there was so much atmosphere in this room that it was almost like another entity.

I felt something rolling around my feet, then rising slightly to my knees. It didn't hurt; it wasn't warm or cold. It was just there, like Charlie sat on my feet sometimes. Just to let me know he was near in case I was tempted to forget. What I was feeling was the active, sustained, and directed consciousness of fifty witches. They were anchoring me in place. I was the wick to their lighter, but they held the fuel.

I've never been more terrified in my life.

I was alone as I've never been alone. Dan wasn't here to protect me. Mike wasn't my bodyguard. I didn't have anyone - not even Nonnie - to ensure I was whole and safe after all this.

Marcie was going to have to look after Marcie.

One of the funny things about terror. It can ice your stomach, give you a taste of bile on your tongue, seemingly freeze your bodily functions, slow your heart and keep you rooted to the spot.

Yet it was powerless in the face of anger.

I turned my head to look at Janet. I don't know if she was stirring up my emotions somehow or if I'd just had enough of everything. I had been pushed to the edge of my patience, understanding, and tolerance.

Anger had changed since I'd become a vampire. It was a being, one that I now let occupy my body. I felt the redness of it, the fire-like heat enter me. All the slights and irritations I'd absorbed over the months merged and solidified.

I allowed myself to think of Doug, who'd seduced me on cue and Maddock who'd taken advantage. There was my mother who'd killed another creature trying to eliminate me and Nonnie who'd never told me the truth in my entire life. There was Kenisha who'd blamed me for Opie's death and Opie who hadn't told me she was possessing my dog until it suited her. Meng and Dr. Stallings had both betrayed me. The Librarian had lied and deceived me. Even the man I'd always thought of as my father had lied. He couldn't be bothered to say, "Hey, kid, no same-o DNA." Janet had hated me on sight, but hadn't bothered to explain why. While I was at it, I was going to throw in Diane Trenton to the mix just to prove that I could be a shallow bitch at times.

The only person who hadn't betrayed me, lied to me, or tried to harm me was Dan. Okay, maybe he hadn't told me about being a wizard, but I was willing to forgive him for the sin of omission.

I loved him. I hadn't wanted to. It was inconvenient, painful, and it was probably going to be messy. I'm sure it was going to hurt down the road, but I didn't care.

If anger was a force to fight terror, then love had to be worth something, too.

I turned away from Janet, surveying all the witches in the room. By the faint light I could see they were all watching me. Did they think I was going to explode like a roman candle?

Look witches, watch and learn. See what one angry Pranic goddess can do.

CHAPTER TWENTY-EIGHT

I was wind, fire, earth,
water, spirit, and life

My mouth curved in a half smile as I closed my eyes. Slowly, I lifted my arms and turned in a circle, taking my time, feeling the power from each one of them. They fed me and I took their fuel and expanded it, multiplying it by a thousand percent.

I heard Janet speak beside me. I couldn't understand the words she spoke, but I thought they were Latin. If she was reciting the spell, then I needed to pump up my effort.

I thought of Dan, the way he had of smiling that made his eyes crinkle at the corners. I thought of the morning when the dawn sky had been revealed to me and the sense of goodness and joy I'd experienced. I remembered the sound of my own laughter, the rumble of it in my chest, the sting of tears when I cried despite my resolve.

I felt the wonder of the moment when I was told I would bear a child. I thought of all the scenes I'd envisioned since, of holding him in my arms, of watching him learn about his fingers and toes and the world beyond.

As the power grew, I began to understand the magic the witches commanded.

None of it was founded on base emotions. Only love and joy were invited into their meetings and their spells. Hatred, fear, anger, envy - none of these emotions were welcome.

I recalled those times with Nonnie when I stood at her side by the stove, waiting until that magical moment when our concoction turned into jam. Or when I sat at the table impatiently waiting for the first bite of peanut butter cookies we'd baked. Later, we had remarkable conversations about men and love and life and disappointment and achievement and ambition. Through it all, I'd felt the thread of love so strong that I was ashamed I hadn't always acknowledged it. She might have lied, but as she told Janet earlier, it was to protect all of them.

My aura began to rise even though I hadn't commanded it. That wasn't the only change, either. It wasn't gold. It was red, a pure crimson so bright that it made me blink when I opened my eyes.

I wasn't the only one to see it, either.

Janet's voice faltered a little before she carried on with the spell. Nonnie came forward and stood in front of me, her eyes steady as she regarded me. I nodded to her, just once, and she nodded back. We hadn't spoken the words, but we'd said them, regardless.

"Are you all right?"

"Yes, I am, Nonnie."

The other witches kept up with their prayers, their eyes widening. William put his arm around Sylvia. The gesture made me like him more. If all hell broke loose, his arm wasn't going to do anything to help Sylvia, but he'd declared himself her protector anyway.

I dropped to my knees, the sudden fall jarring and scaring me. At the same time, I felt a heaviness, like a cloud of lead, drop on top of me. I had a feeling that the spell had taken on a form and it had decided to pick on me.

Sitting, I crossed my legs and put my hands on my knees. I closed my eyes again and envisioned a cannon. A second later I changed my mind. A cannon is a gun and guns were used in warfare and there are a lot of emotions swirling around during warfare, but few of them were filled with love or joy.

If I was going to give power to the spell, then I was going to have to think differently.

I remembered the night I spent in Dan's arms in my bed. The warmth of his skin against mine. The curve of his smile as he kissed me. I felt his skin beneath my palms even now, could sculpt his muscles in clay. I liked the bulb of his shoulders, the way his arms flexed as he lowered himself over me. I even liked his feet and I don't think I'd ever noticed a man's feet before.

This was the most dangerous part. I knew that instinctively. I turned my hands over until my palms were exposed. I sat up straight, my eyes still closed, and opened my heart. I released everything I was feeling, every secret thought, every hidden wish or prayer.

I allowed myself to reveal my vulnerability. All the times I'd messed up and hidden my flaws, all the secrets I held, all the insecurities I had about my character, my personality, my body. With the revelation, I discovered something curious. I wasn't weaker by admitting everything. Instead, I was stronger.

The space where I'd stored everything that embarrassed or shamed me was cavernous, but nature does indeed abhor a vacuum.

In the next minutes I felt myself being filled by a crimson light. A light the same color as Valentine's Day hearts and Christmas wreaths, lipstick painted lips and strong emotion. The color of love and romance and words like till death us do part.

I understood in that moment. I began to smile as the knowledge flooded into every pore, every nerve.

Love would save Dan. Love would strip him of the cloak he'd worn and restore him to himself.

What he'd wanted was to be himself, to achieve and win as Dan Travis without powers. He'd not understood that he would never simply be Dan Travis and that the world needed him to be his most authentic self. Wizard and warrior.

Perhaps a father, certainly a lover. A protector and friend. An employer and example.

I couldn't see him, but I could feel him. His goodness and his exasperation at the roadblocks he had to occasionally navigate. I knew of his impatience and his kindness, his diligence and his impulsivity. I knew the whole of him and respected the man, his mission, his determination to be better than his limitations.

As a wizard he would have few restraints but many temptations, and having been mortal, human, and frail had prepared him for the role he must assume. He knew that already.

The witches' power was making the air in the room hum.

I concentrated once more on Dan, envisioned a gray woolen cloak covering his body. In my mind I erased it, one section at a time. The cape was the first to disappear. The arms the next part. Around his neck was a drawstring and hood. Like a drawing program, I slowly went over it until it, too, vanished.

He stood before me in my imagination without the cloak, looking as he always had, strong, virile, a man of courage and conviction.

I stood, moving closer to Janet. I didn't get the chance to tell her that I thought her spell had worked. The air suddenly changed, the power grew, and I was nearly knocked on my keister again when I stood.

I felt the vortex, the sensation of the room spinning, before I saw the clouds of blue and green. At first they looked like ribbons a gymnast twirled before they blended together, forming a bluish green funnel. The air inside the vortex grew darker as the funnel spun faster and faster.

Closing my eyes didn't seem to help my disorientation so I opened them again, blinking rapidly in order to keep my balance. I could feel the air on my face from the rotation, but it wasn't making a sound. The silence was eerie and complete, even blocking out the chants from the witches along with Janet's voice.

The darkness was blacker than anything I'd ever seen, so deep that it was a mirror, reflecting my own image back to me.

I folded my hands at my waist, tucking in my elbows so I wouldn't touch the funnel swirling around me. Maybe another person would have been courageous standing there, but little ol' me was scared. I'd never heard of a personal tornado. Nor had I ever expected to experience one, but I knew it was because of the power we'd amassed.

Now what the hell did we do with it?

I closed my eyes again, this time to concentrate. I remembered Dan from the last time I'd seen him, standing at the edge of the roof, turning his head to smile at me, his face relaxed, charm and sex appeal oozing from every pore.

And I saw him.

Not as he had been only a day ago, but now.

He was wearing black trousers and a shirt that had once been snowy white but was now dotted with blood. My heartbeat, normally slow, escalated as I tried to figure out if what I was seeing was real or was only a desperate wish fulfilled. If I was imagining Dan, I sure as hell wouldn't have him looking so damn white.

Nor would I have envisioned his neck looking bloody and raw.

I nearly fell again.

I can be damn stubborn sometimes. Ask my previous bosses. Hell, ask Dan. Now I refused to cave, surrender, fall down, or do the Victorian thing and succumb to the vapors.

The vampires weren't going to win this battle. They weren't going to take Dan. Okay, I was a vampire, but I never felt like one and I'll be damned if they turned Dan into one.

I hoped like hell that my grandmother was right and Dan was a super powerful wizard. I hoped that being uncloaked was enough to fight off the blood suckers.

If they won, then I'd just have to transfuse him, too. That would royally piss off Maddock, wouldn't it?

I had remained perfectly still while the vortex had spun around me. Now I decided to try to control it. Not to slow it down but to increase its power. The vortex was a channel, a paranormal coaxial cable that had opened between me and Dan. I wasn't going to send him a signal. I was going to send him power.

Slowly, I raised my hands, inch by inch, feeling the rotation escalate. I kept my eyes on his image, noting everything around him. He was in a small room with one door. The background was hard to separate from the mist surrounding Dan, but I finally realized it was nearly the same color. A steel counter was behind him, empty except for odd containers that were silver as well.

He was bound at his ankles and wrists to a wooden chair that resembled an electric chair without the components. The arms were wide as was the back. His head was free, but there was a metal band hanging on a hook near the chair that made me wonder if they'd had to restrain him when they bit him the first time.

I hated bullies. I hated people who took advantage of others. Vampires were manipulators. They never played fair. They didn't know what the word meant. Instead, they were underhanded, grasping, and greedy. There was no need to turn Dan. Or to do what Maddock had done to Mike.

I was going to infuse Dan with strength. All he had to do was hang on until we found him.

My hands were almost at my waist now. I stretched out my arms, made the vortex wider, and heard, for the first time, the whine of the wind. My hair stood out from my head as if I'd been shocked by static electricity. I could feel the tiny hairs on my arms and a charge run over my body as if I were being electrocuted. I spoke to the vortex as if it were sentient, cautioned it not to think itself more powerful than me.

I am wind. I am fire. I am earth. I am spirit and life.

I raised my arms still higher, commanding, still seeing Dan.

He lifted his head, his eyes intent on mine. Could he see me? Did he know I was here, watching him? This time I spoke to him.

I'm here.

Not exactly an impassioned promise to save him, but it seemed to be enough. His smile was soft and sweet. The sparkle in his eyes made my heart stutter.

I'm here!

Stronger this time, prompting a larger smile from him.

I knew he could hear me. He might even be able to see me.

This next part was tricky, since I'd never done it. Nor had I ever heard of it done. But I knew I could. In a far off place I'd never identified as mine, I was aware of a great many things I could do and had never before done. Now was the time to claim some of those abilities, to save the man I loved.

I threw the vortex to him.

I extended my arms as far as I could, catching the vortex with them. In the next instant, before the power could drop, before it could wrap me into the funnel, I tossed it to Dan. I sent it racing through the channel to him.

For a moment, I couldn't see him, only the blue green mass of air and light and power.

His head was thrown back as the vortex hit him. I heard someone scream, but the sound was female, high pitched, and screeching.

Something hit my face, the pain rocking me back on my heels. My nose hurt, and my lip was bleeding. The next series of blows kept me from understanding. I could only react.

The sudden noise was deafening, the strident sounds ricocheting around the room, magnified by hysteria.

"Stop it!" Janet screamed as she hit me. "Stop it. You'll kill him!"

I pushed her away, aided in my efforts by Nonnie and a few of the other witches. William finally managed to subdue her, holding her shoulders, pinning her arms to her sides. That still didn't shut her up. My grandmother managed to do that with a spell she uttered, something that allowed Janet to keep talking. Blessedly, whatever she said was muted.

Of all the spells witches used, I wanted to learn that one.

I pressed one hand to my nose and wondered if Janet had broken it. I'd always liked my nose just as it was, damn it.

"Is she right?" William asked. "Is it dangerous for Dan?"

"If we managed to remove the cloak, no," Nonnie said. "If he was just plain Dan, I don't know."

"We removed it," I said.

Nonnie was talking to William and wasn't paying any attention to me. Janet was still yelling, thankfully soundlessly.

If Janet hadn't interfered, I would have been able to see how the vortex affected him. My vision of Dan had disappeared along with the vortex. I didn't have any hope of getting it back, but that wasn't going to stop me.

I was going to find Dan and if that meant going alone, that was fine with me.

CHAPTER TWENTY-NINE

*The witches, the goddess, and
the dog go vampire hunting*

I left the sparring room without saying another word to anyone. My last glimpse of the witches was a strange one. I've never seen them milling around with a look of fear on their faces. Was it because Janet was still being restrained by William? Or because Nonnie was giving them all "the look"?

I'd gotten that look as a child when I'd done something wrong. Not just wrong, but something about which I'd already been warned. It was one thing to be naughty, another to ignore Nonnie's cautions.

She hated to be ignored.

It was only about nine o'clock although it felt like midnight. I was exhausted to the point my hands were trembling and I didn't feel all that steady on my feet. But time was of the essence. I knew we'd removed the cloaking, but Dan was still at the mercy of the vampires. As much as I hated to go out into the night, I would hate to lose Dan even more.

I did have one ace up my sleeve, however.

I hit the elevators and punched in the sub-level button. The descent had never felt so slow. I nearly raced through the empty corridor, almost slamming into the corner as my shoes squeaked on the linoleum. I knocked on Kenisha's door, opened it, and found Charlie curled up on the sofa.

"She's with Mike," Opie said before I closed the door.

I opened the door fully again. "Is he really okay?"

"Better than okay," she said. "How about you? You look like hell."

"I think my nose is broken," I said, fingering it gently.

"Your lip doesn't look good either. Who hit you?"

"Janet."

"Want me to bite her?"

"I may," I said. "Later."

I turned and walked across the hall, surprised when Charlie followed me.

The door was open a little, so I just pushed it in at the sound of laughter.

Kenisha was sitting on the end of Mike's bed. He was sitting up, holding one of her hands. Both of them looked flushed, healthy, and happy.

Color me stunned, because that's exactly how I felt. I'd expected Mike to be wan, barely able to hold his head up, but not this manly specimen, with all of his tubes and bags removed. Even the machines and monitors beside his bed had been turned off.

I was immediately suspicious about that. Was it because he was technically dead and didn't register anything? Was he a vampire? For that matter, was he more than a vampire?

A tray was on the end table beside the hospital bed. I wasn't sure, but it looked like the remains of turkey and dressing. If that were the case, then Mike was a vampire with Thanksgiving tendencies.

Welcome to the world of gods and goddesses, Mikey boy.

I was really going to have to ask. Later, when there wasn't a more pressing matter on my mind.

"The vampires have Dan," I said.

Mike immediately threw one leg over the side of the bed. What is it with guys? Do they think they're immortal? Okay, maybe he was, but he'd just been saved from the jaws of death. Mike wasn't in any shape to be a hero. Kenisha felt the same way, because she dragged his leg back onto the bed.

I turned to her.

"Do you know where they might have taken him?"

She shook her head.

"Is there any way you could find out?"

She shook her head again, inciting my irritation.

"I'm not exactly on good terms with the Council," she said, before I could get really angry.

"Why?"

"Because I'm here. Because I've been staying here."

"Did they tell you not to?"

She looked away. "Maddock did."

Well, hell.

Mike grabbed her hand again.

"Did you know Dan was a wizard?" I asked.

Kenisha's eyes widened.

"Yeah, I knew," he said. "Dan didn't want anyone else to know, though."

"That was then," I said. "This is now. He should be a full fledged wizard again."

"Should?" Mike asked.

"If everything went according to plan." Seriously, when had anything gone the way it was supposed to have gone in my life lately?

"What are you going to do?"

"Find Dan."

I was going to send my aura on a field trip.

"Take Felipe," Mike said. "And Paul."

I smiled at him. Smart man, to know that it would have been a waste of time to argue against me trying to find Dan.

"Dan trusts them. They were part of our team."

I took that to mean they were in the service together. Before I left, I had one more question.

"Did you ever investigate any of Maddock's labs?" I asked. "When you were looking for Nancy?"

"Yeah, why? Is that where you think he is?"

When I'd seen Dan, there was something in the background that had finally registered. The flat silver dishes on the counter were weighing boats, disposable containers for industrial or laboratory applications. I'd seen them before when one of the labs my company insured had been damaged by a fire.

"Let's just say we're going to start there," I said.

"I'd start with the ones on the north side. The locations on the south side are smaller, used for storage. They only have a security guard on duty."

I nodded. Before I left, I turned to Kenisha.

"If Maddock gives you any trouble," I said, "you're always welcome here."

Mike smiled at me. Evidently, I'd done something right.

I slipped out of the room, heading back toward the elevators.

I didn't realize Charlie was beside me until I stepped inside.

"I'm coming with you," Opie said. "If you don't let me, let's just say I'm going to be talking and not just to the labs."

I eyed her. "You're kidding."

"Not kidding," she said. "I'll start with David. He might freak out a little at first, though. Jen seems like she'd accept it right away. She has cousins who are shape shifters."

"You would, wouldn't you?" I asked.

Opie had always been her own person, if you'll pardon the word. What the hell did you call a ghost vet possessing a dog anyway?

"I'm coming," she said.

Who was I to argue?

I realized fifteen minutes later that Opie wasn't the only stubborn one in the group. I'd wanted to slip away from the castle and start heading east on my own. Instead, I had two SUVs filled with people who were determined to accompany me.

Nonnie refused to stay behind, as did Janet. The former did a healing spell on my nose, for which I was grateful. The latter wouldn't look at me, which was just as well. I didn't want to have to punch her in the nose in retaliation.

Paul turned out to be a behemoth of a man I'd met before when he'd stormed into my room the night Maddock played spaghetti against the window. Felipe was less muscular, armed with a charming grin, brown hair longer than most of Dan's guys, and a look in his eyes that warned me danger could come in small packages.

William had left Sylvia in the care of Gretchen and insisted on driving the second SUV. Since the man was a witch and probably had hidden powers, I was willing to have him tag along. Besides, Nonnie and Janet felt comfortable with William. Right at the moment, they were sitting in the back seat, eyes closed, their lips moving in unison as they recited a spell.

I absolutely refused, however, to allow the Archivist to accompany us. I opened the back door of the SUV Paul was going to drive, and motioned him out.

"I need to be able to record this event for posterity," the Archivist said. "You should have invited me to the uncloaking."

"What powers do you have?" I asked, being a little forceful about it. "What powers, as a Fairy, do you have?"

"I can manipulate locks," he said. "I can be invisible. I can summon the wind."

"Not good enough."

He frowned at me. "What do you mean, not good enough? I'm a very old, venerated Fairy."

"Stay here and talk to some of the witches. They'll tell you all about the uncloaking. If you don't, the details will be lost to posterity."

He looked torn.

"I promise to disclose everything once we return," I said.

"Cross your heart?"

"Hope to die," I said. "Stick a needle in my eye and all that."

He finally got out of the SUV and Charlie jumped in beside Felipe. I just shook my head and opened the passenger door and sat beside Paul.

"Where to?" he asked.

"Toward San Antonio," I said.

Beyond that, I didn't know at the moment. I was hoping to get a signal or a sign from Dan. Barring that, we'd head for the first of Maddock's labs.

This area of South Texas wasn't very developed. Other than the castle and a few houses plopped on hills between here and San Antonio, that was about it. The lack of lights meant that the sky looked as if it were only an arm's length away, the sparkling stars so bright they could almost illuminate the way. On the way east, we passed Fair Oaks Ranch and Camp Bullis, landmarks that meant civilization wasn't far.

My stomach quivered and I put my hand over it protectively. I closed my eyes and concentrated on feeling Dan. The lemon air freshener kept distracting me. I opened my eyes and looked for it, prepared to tuck it away in the glove compartment. When I couldn't find it, I realized that it was Paul. His aftershave must be pure lemon extract.

"Why didn't you want the witches with you?" he asked, glancing at me. "We could have all gotten in one car."

Smart guy, to figure that out.

"I think they're casting spells," I said. "I don't like to be around witches when they're casting spells."

That was the truth, but not the whole truth, so help me God.

It was one thing for them to think Charlie was my familiar, quite another to be cheek to jowl next to him, so to speak. In such close quarters, they'd figure out that Charlie wasn't just a dog.

Besides, I think I scared Janet. She was looking all bug eyed around me since the vortex incident. I thought Nonnie might calm her down. There was another reason, one I was trying to convince myself I hadn't seen. Before she got into the SUV, Nonnie had given me the head to toe look, the equivalent of a grandmotherly MRI. I could swear she knew I was pregnant. A little distance would be a good thing.

As we hit the outskirts of San Antonio, I wasn't getting anything. We were inside Loop 1604 and nothing was making my little antennae quiver. I closed my eyes again, wondering if I could send my aura ahead of the SUV, searching out Dan.

There was no time like the present to try.

I envisioned the golden light surrounding me, then sent it out as fast as I could, which was pretty damn fast considering Paul wasn't exactly obeying the speed limit. I couldn't help but wonder if Dan's organization had special dispensation or if the black SUVs were just ignored. I never once saw a patrol car and that was unusual.

The aura sprang back to me when I called it, like a border collie puppy aiming to please. It hadn't caught anything, not a vibration, a feeling, or a hint of Dan.

"Where to?" Paul asked.

"Where's the closest MEDOC lab?" I asked, referring to the company Maddock owned.

"Near Stone Oak."

"Let's go there."

He nodded, but I caught the twitch of his lip.

Paul didn't have any faith in my ability to find Dan. I couldn't blame him. At the moment, I didn't have any faith either.

I sent my aura out again, but just like the last time, I didn't feel anything.

Was my ability to find Dan being blocked in some way?

Charlie stuck his head between the seats and nosed me on the arm.

Paul glanced at him and smiled. "He wants to be up front where all the action is."

Some action.

Charlie rolled his eyes, then looked back to where the second SUV was following us. The SUV with the witches. The SUV with Nonnie and Janet chanting a spell.

What the hell?

Were they preventing me from finding Dan? Could Charlie/Opie somehow sense that? Or had my imagination flipped into overtime and was making everything more sinister than it was?

"Could you keep your eyes on the road, please?" I asked, then dug into my bra for my phone. It was nice and warm.

I dialed Nonnie's number, half expecting her not to answer. When she did, I let out the breath I was holding.

"Nonnie, whatever spell you two are using is screwing up my reception."

"It's a simple location spell, Marcie."

"I don't care what it is. Please stop. And tell Janet I want my stuff back."

I hung up after saying thank you and goodbye. I couldn't hang up on my grandmother without the niceties.

I sat back against the seat, sent out my aura on another Olly, olly in come free journey. My stomach clenched when we neared the Stone Oak area, but I lost the sensation when we pulled into the parking lot of one of the MEDOC labs.

I wanted to say that he wasn't there, but I wasn't sure I was right. I'd been through a lot in the last two days. The event tonight in the sparring room was enough to confuse my senses for weeks. Maybe I couldn't feel Dan anymore. Maybe I hadn't seen him.

Yes, damn it, I had.

"Stay here," Paul said, leaving the car. Felipe followed him, leaving Charlie and I alone.

"Studs," Opie said. "They're studly."

I looked back at her. "Are you kidding? Your mind's on sex?"

"Your mind would be on sex if you were trapped inside a dog who humps everything in sight."

I stared at Charlie. "He doesn't."

"He does. When he doesn't, he thinks about it."

I just shook my head and turned to face the windshield.

The SUV with Nonnie and Janet inside pulled up next to us in the nearly empty parking lot. The only other car was a red Ford, model unknown. I'm not good at cars, but I don't think it mattered right at the moment.

William rolled down the window, which meant I did the same.

"Where did they go?"

"On a reconnoitering mission," I said.

"Do you think Dan's here?" he asked, staring at the one story brick building.

"No, I don't."

He looked like he wanted to ask: then why the hell are we here, but didn't. Thankfully, I couldn't see through the tinted windows to the back of the car. I didn't know if Nonnie and Janet were glaring at me or not. I assumed they were, so I rolled my window back up.

Just then, something pinged. It was the strangest sensation, like a sonobuoy making a connection.

"Did you hear that?" I asked Opie.

"Hear what?"

Maybe I hadn't heard anything. Maybe I'd felt it, instead. I closed my eyes, put my hands over my ears, and concentrated. It wasn't a ping. It was a scream, not one of pain as much as rage.

Every sense I had was abruptly on alert.

I sat up, staring at the building in front of us.

"Is he in there?" Opie asked, picking up on my body language.

"No. But I think I know where he is."

I was about to leave the car when I saw Paul's hulking shadow. He and Felipe were creeping around the side of the building.

I reached over and hit the horn. At another time, I would think of how they jumped and laughed. Right now, however, I just wanted them to get in the car.

A minute later, Paul jerked open the car door so hard I expected it to be pulled off the hinges. He greeted me with a colorful Anglo-Saxon word I've used on occasion. I let him vent for about ten seconds before I interrupted him.

"I know where Dan is. I think I know," I amended. "MEDOC has a warehouse on Blanco," I said. "He's there."

"A warehouse? Are you sure?"

"About where it is? No. I've never been there."

I remembered reading about the warehouse opening when I was doing research on Maddock. The warehouse was one of those completely automated ones where they employed robotics instead of people. The mayor and a few other dignitaries had been present for the ground breaking. I still recalled the picture with all of them - taken at night, naturally - with Maddock smiling proudly and the others looking enraptured to be in his presence.

Paul did some checking on his phone, got the address and left the car to talk to William. I could just imagine the words he was using. He returned two minutes later, got behind the wheel and pulled out of the parking lot.

The pinging got louder. I was thinking of it as pinging because I couldn't bear to hear Dan scream. I hadn't mentioned the screaming to Paul and I wasn't going to now. The only thing I did say as we crossed 1604 again was that we needed to hurry.

He glanced over at me.

"Really," I said.

Fear was a blanket coming down over me. I was beginning to smother under it. I'd never been afraid like this. Maddock had terrorized me, but I'd always had hope. I'd always believed I could win. What I was feeling now was different. Hope had disappeared along with any positive thinking. I knew that if we failed, the ramifications would be long lasting. No, not long lasting.

I'd feel them forever.

CHAPTER THIRTY

Holy crap, you're a werewolf!

The closer we came to the warehouse, the stronger I felt the connection. I could feel Dan's breathing as if he were beside me. His pain, pushed down and not vocalized was in the lower octaves. They'd hurt him, but they'd also pissed him off, and his rage was a high C.

I didn't hear it as a sound as much as a vibration of that sound. His power touched me, making me wonder why they didn't feel it. Why it hadn't shattered them.

The warehouse was one story, with six bays in the rear and an office in the front. Like the lab, there weren't any lights, but Maddock and his fellow vampires didn't need any. They functioned quite well in the dark, like mutant cats.

Paul parked the car on the edge of the parking lot, close to a veterinarian clinic. The second SUV pulled in alongside. I didn't lose any time leaving the car. Charlie bounded to the front seat and followed me.

Paul grabbed my arm. "Wait a minute," he said. "What the hell are you going to do?"

"Save him," I said.

"We need a plan."

"My plan is to save him."

"You can't just go in there."

I stared up at him, annoyed and too damn close to tears to want to argue the point.

"We don't have time, Paul. Trust me on this."

I jerked free of his grip and started running toward the building. I didn't hit the office, but rounded the corner to the door beside the first of the bays. They'd just moved Dan to the third bay.

A cloud moved over the stars, blanketing them from sight. Concentric rings formed in the air, each shaded a little differently. I immediately felt the power, knew that what I saw wasn't really there, that it was merely an allegory for what was happening inside the building. The air vibrated with the rings moving outward from the warehouse. Another image I wasn't sure anyone else could see.

"What the hell?" Paul said from a few feet behind me.

I guess I wasn't the only one who could see and feel the rings of air. They were almost like an atomic explosion, the waves of air blasting a few seconds later.

Charlie let out a howl. I'd heard him bark, but never that sound.

Paul immediately joined in, followed by Felipe.

Maybe I was a little slow on the uptake, but I didn't expect the tearing of shirts and trousers or both men to fall to their hands and knees.

Nonnie and Janet were rounding the building as the two men's backs arched, their hands and feet elongating and growing claws. Their noses became snouts, their ears pointy and moving to the tops of their heads. Felipe's skin was filled with silver fur while Paul's was as black as the night surrounding us.

"Holy crap, you're a werewolf!" I said.

In all the books I've read, mainly about female werewolves, bras are left hanging around their necks after they transformed. Or they had some decorum and kept their panties on. Um, not with male werewolves. Evidently, the act of transformation also brings about prurient thoughts, because both Paul and Felipe were, shall we say, excited.

"Good grief," Nonnie said, staring at Paul. "What a boner."

I turned to my grandmother, open mouthed, as Charlie began to make a choking noise. I knew it was canine laughter, just as I knew that both Charlie, the dog and Opie, the resident ghost, were amused.

"Get a grip," I said, striding to the door.

We had more important things to do than admire a man's/werewolf's attributes. The door was locked, but it didn't matter, because Paul the werewolf, erect penis and all, just pulled it off its hinges.

I rushed in - where angels feared to tread - and headed for the area where I felt Dan. A door in the wall was my target and just like before, Paul merely pulled the door off its hinges. Handy to have a werewolf around when you needed him.

I stood in the doorway, my aura in full glowy mode when I saw him. Dan had ripped off the leather restraints on the chair and was standing there in a nimbus of yellow light. Who knew a wizard could glow? He was also roaring, the same sound I'd expect from an aggrieved lion.

His eyes were bright green, beautiful and scary. I was more impressed than frightened. He had to be the most glorious creature I'd ever seen, angry and capable of handling any number of vampires.

Maddock stood facing him.

I knew Maddock. He wouldn't have come here alone, not with just one Fledgling.

Um, I hate being right.

The far door opened and a dozen white faced children of the night flooded into the room. One of them was Meng, the guy who'd betrayed me.

"Hello, Marcie."

I turned, hearing that voice and knowing who it was before I saw her.

She was dressed in black. Very atmospheric, plus my mother had always looked good in black, kind of like a menopausal Snow White. Not that she looked menopausal, either.

I would have liked to tell her she was going to be a grandmother just to see her blanch, but I don't think her skin could have gotten any whiter. Her lips were blood red, though, and I knew she'd been the one to bite Dan. Not simply because she could, but a way to slap me in the face.

My mother had thrown in with the vampires, specifically Maddock.

Had she gone after him or had he sent her feelers?

Now was a sucky time to be feeling vulnerable and childlike. There wasn't a shred of maternal love in my mother's eyes, not one gleam of motherly affection. I wasn't exactly surprised, but I was sad. I knew this encounter wasn't going to end well. She was either going to be hurt or I was. At the end of it, she was going to be hauled off to jail.

"It's my mother," I said to Opie.

Charlie growled. I couldn't blame him/her. Opie had a right to be pissed. My mother had killed her. I had a right to be angry because she was my mother and had tried to kill me.

What sort of mother does something like that?

Not the mother of the year kind. Did Child Protective Services have a rogues' gallery of really bad mothers? Pictures of women in the last stages of drug abuse, prostitution, or alcoholism?

Demi hadn't had any of those problems. She just didn't care. Shouldn't there be a classification of apathy?

My mother had liked Bill, but then my mother liked men. Any man was better than any woman in my mother's estimation. We once had a block party and I remember, even as a little girl, watching my mother interact with other people. She dismissed the women almost with a wave of her hand, smiling and flirting with the men so outrageously she was almost a parody of herself. More than one wife frowned at her, but it never made any impression on Demi. She was a social butterfly, batting her eyelashes like Scarlet O'Hara in an attempt to bring every man under her control.

Most of them were instantly charmed. The few who weren't she dismissed as either being gay or beneath her contempt. More than once she'd gone after someone who initially spurned her, charming him until he was under her spell. The minute it happened, she dropped him. The ultimate aim wasn't to acquire his affection as much as it was to prove that she could.

I knew, in a way that wasn't precognitive as it was based on years of observational experience, that my mother had been intimate with Maddock.

I wonder how Maddock stacked up in the lover department? I seriously needed to take a bath after asking myself that question. Or disinfect myself with bleach. I'll bet Maddock didn't need to give Demi Spanish fly or whatever he'd given me.

She took another step toward me.

Her eyes didn't look quite right, having a glassy sheen. Her lips were formed in an odd smile, one I'd seen her practice in the mirror. A half-smile guaranteed to eliminate those brackets on either side of her mouth. But what stopped me in my tracks was the wound on the side of her neck, signs of where she'd been bitten.

Had it been consensual? Had she wanted to be made a vampire? Or had Maddock just done what he had to my mother as a form of revenge?

I couldn't help but think she'd be happy as a vampire.

One of the Fledgings crept closer to Dan.

Leave him alone!

My voice thundered through the space, so loud that the walls reverberated. Several people, creatures, and vampires, turned to look at me, their eyes wide.

Leave him alone!

One by one, the vampires crept closer to Maddock and away from me. Big, bad Maddock was not going to save them.

"Daughter."

Nonnie stood in the doorway. One hand reached out and flipped on the light switch. All of us blinked for a minute or two.

We formed a strange tableau. Dan was facing Maddock while I didn't let my mother out of my sight. The two werewolves stood on all four legs just inside the door. Nonnie was in the doorway with Janet behind her.

I didn't know who was responsible for the power I felt all around me, but I thought it was mostly Dan with a little from my grandmother.

Nonnie wasn't happy at the moment.

"So, you finally gave in," she said, addressing Demi.

My mother had a thing for vampires all her life, but she'd handled the addiction in the last several years by attending an Al-Anon group specifically for vampire lovers.

Charlie growled when my mother took another step toward me. I rested my hand on his head, uncertain if I could stop him if he suddenly lunged.

Silence stretched between my mother and me, but then we've never been conversationalists. Most of our talks in the last few years had consisted of my listening to her complaints about the world. I'd never volunteered anything about my own life simply because it would've been a wasted effort.

Why the hell didn't revelations come at quiet times? Why didn't you suddenly understand something in the dead of night, when you were trying to fall asleep? Or when you were contemplating your navel in the bathtub? Why did you suddenly realize things in the middle of a crisis (and this was definitely in the middle of a crisis)?

I realized I didn't hate my mother in that second. I didn't grieve for the loss of her affection. I was no longer the little girl who wanted her mommy to love her. I didn't feel anything for her. Not one ounce of any kind of discernible emotion.

It was like this giant vice had been unscrewed and dropped from around my chest. The sudden freedom was euphoric.

Charlie growled again.

My mother glanced behind me and smiled. I knew better than to look over my shoulder. If I did she would pounce. An old gambit I'd learned from cartoons.

Besides, I already knew who was there. Maddock had moved in the last few seconds. He'd been too fast to see, but my Pranic senses knew where he was.

"Marcie, I knew you would come."

I didn't turn to face Maddock because that would have left my mother at my back.

"That's why you grabbed Dan," I said. "He was bait."

"He didn't have to be involved, Marcie, if you'd only shown a little sense."

"What, like falling into your arms? Are you nuts?"

I sidled a few feet toward Dan and only then glanced at the master vampire.

He was fully fanged. I wondered why he had never gotten his fangs gold tipped. Some of the older vampires had done that, a gilding of the lily that made them look like pimps. Not a bad description, considering how they treated Fledgings.

Maddock's lips were blood red and there was blood on his teeth, which made my stomach roll. His eyes warned me that this encounter would not be merciful. He was going to do to Dan what he'd done to Mike and he was going to make me watch.

No, he was going to try.

The look my mother was giving Maddock bordered on worshipful. How sick was that?

Both Paul and Felipe moved closer to me, each of them flanking my mother. She didn't look worried, but she should have. She smiled as she approached me, the expression making my stomach rebel again.

Dan raised his right arm and I swear, lightning traveled from his forefinger to land at my mother's feet.

"Get away from her!"

I heard that and I didn't have any doubt about people a couple of miles away hearing it, either.

Maddock's face was transformed, not by fear but something more like amazement. I guess he hadn't expected Dan to be a wizard.

My mother, though, has always been stubborn. A bit of the oak from whence this acorn fell. Or maybe it was just stupidity. She merely smiled at the hole in the floor and lunged at me.

Wouldn't you know that the first kiss I got from dear old mom in years was the kiss of death?

Charlie charged, grabbed my mother's thigh and hung on like a piranha. She screamed, turned to strike him and Dan threw another lightning bolt at her.

Gotta admire the guy's theatrics. The only bad thing was that I was temporarily blinded. I saw a cloud of black, assumed it was Maddock and raised my hand to zap him. I didn't have any trouble collecting power to throw. I wasn't sure if it was because I was angry or if Dan was sending me some of his emotions.

Maddock lay on the floor where he'd fallen. I watched him out of the corner of my eye as I stepped over my mother's fallen body being guarded by Charlie. The Fledglings flew at me. I took great delight in zapping Meng so hard he flew up to the ceiling and knocked his widdle head on the rafters. Oops.

I didn't recognize the other Fledglings I zapped. I thought they were Fledglings because they had that "oh shit" look when they encountered either Dan or me. Maybe a better person would have spared a little sympathy for them. After all, I'd been manipulated by Maddock, too. But this was survival and everyone I cared about was going to walk out of here on their own two feet.

I don't know a lot about werewolves, and I think I've been honest on this point from the beginning. I wasn't expecting them to savage the vampires that Dan and I felled. I wasn't looking closely, but from all the growls and guttural sounds, I got the distinct impression that they were eating them. Vampires don't regenerate, so if one lost an arm or a leg, it would stay missing.

Janet was still reciting a spell while Nonnie was watching my mother with a strange look in her eyes. Was she the reason Demi hadn't moved?

I learned something very important about witches tonight. They might be very effective in certain situations, but they weren't very fast. If you needed someone to really get the job done, make sure you have a wizard or a goddess on hand.

I was getting closer to Dan which was exciting since he was electrical. He was throwing lightning bolts everywhere and with such ease it looked like he was having fun. He raised both arms so I could get closer. Well, hell, I decided to press myself against his chest. He lowered his arms and got another vampire right in the chin. The poor thing screamed as he was hurled across the room.

"I had no idea you could be Thor," I said.

"You ain't seen nothin' yet, babe."

He'd never called me babe. I wasn't sure how I felt about that.

"Okay, babe," I said.

He grinned down at me.

"How are you feeling?" I asked.

"Pretty damn good," he said. "How about you?"

I did a quick inventory. My mood had definitely improved. I wasn't afraid. I had some fences to mend, but nothing that wouldn't keep for a few hours.

"Pretty damn good," I said, repeating his words. "Are you ready to go back to the castle? Or do you want to stay here and keep zapping the vampires?"

He actually gave it some thought.

"I think it's time to leave, don't you?" he finally asked.

I nodded.

"We need to call the police," I said. "About my mother."

She was still out on the floor. Nonnie was still standing over her, now making a sign in the air that looked remotely like the sign of the cross. Since my grandmother was firmly Presbyterian, it was probably a witchy sign.

"Or should we call the Council now that she's a vampire?"

"She killed someone as a human," he said. "That takes precedence. I think it would be better if I called from the car. Otherwise, there are a few questions I don't particularly want to answer right now."

I nodded and turned in his arms. Paul and Felipe were still gnawing. I made sure not to look in their direction.

"They won't turn back anytime soon, will they?"

"Not for a little while."

"Will they get in the car?"

"Oh, yeah. I'll grab an arm for the road."

I glanced over my shoulder at him.

"Just kidding," he said, still grinning at me.

He called the two of them and I got Charlie. Together, we convinced Janet to stop chanting. William, I discovered, had decided to stay with the SUVs. I couldn't fault him for his decision.

Paul and Felipe jumped up in the back of the SUV as if they'd done it before. Charlie, however, wouldn't go anywhere near them and I totally understood why. They looked at my dog as if Charlie might be a good dessert after their vampire entree. I held him on my lap in the passenger seat while Dan drove.

His white dress shirt was torn in two places and the cuffs were rolled up, showing the marks on his wrists. I could feel my temper rise again. My mother and Maddock had a great deal to answer for.

"How did they get you out of the castle?" I asked.

He glanced over at me, then back at the road. I had the curious thought that he was embarrassed. Okay, I once walked right into Maddock's trap. I'd screwed up royally. I wasn't about to condemn Dan for doing the same.

"What?" I asked when he still didn't say anything. "Was it my purse? Diane found it on your desk."

"In a way," he said. "Your mother brought it to me."

"My mother came to the castle?"

I sat there waiting, but his explanation wasn't all that forthcoming.

"I wanted to talk to her," he said. "In private."

No, I hadn't imagined it. He was definitely embarrassed.

"What about?"

"Later," he said. "We'll discuss it later."

I just stared at him over Charlie's head.

"How did they get the drop on you?" I asked.

"It was almost a cliché," he said. "I walked out the door and someone hit me over the head."

Dr. Fernandez was going to look him over the minute we got to the castle. And before Dr. Meng treated anyone else, I wanted to make sure she wasn't related to the guy I'd catapulted to the ceiling tonight.

Dan and I needed to talk about a great many things. The time for secrets was up. I looked down at Charlie. Now was as good a time as any.

"Go ahead, Opie," I said. "It's time to let Dan know."

Dan glanced over at me, then at Charlie before concentrating on the road again.

Opie didn't say a damn thing.

"Really. It's okay. He needs to know."

"Opie?" Dan asked.

I nodded. It was easier to show him rather than telling him, but Opie had other ideas.

"He needs to know, Opie, come on."

Charlie turned his head and licked my nose. Ouch. I needed a renewal on the healing spell.

"Okay, fine."

"What's that about?" Dan asked.

"Nothing," I said.

The minute we were alone, I was going to let Opie know what I thought about letting me look like an idiot. If she was still miffed at me, that was a hell of a way to show it.

Dan shrugged. The two werewolves whined in the back. I turned and gave them a look and they shut up.

As we drove, the tips of Dan's fingers occasionally gave off a little light along with a faint buzzing sound. Every time it happened he laughed.

Evidently, it's good to be wizard.

CHAPTER THIRTY-ONE

I'm mad at you...really

We pulled into the garage and got out of the cars.

Dan went up to his mother. For a moment, neither of them spoke. Then he opened his arms and she began to cry, throwing herself at him. I'd done the same thing earlier. He held her gently, patting her on the back.

"It's okay, Mom," he said. "It's all right."

It took me a minute to realize why he was saying that. He hadn't wanted the uncloaking ritual to take place.

"You're nuts," I said.

"My child." Nonnie put her hand on my arm as if to stop me.

No, not after everything I'd endured tonight. Didn't he realize how much crap I'd gone through for him? I've been worried, scared, more scared, terrified - and more worried. Didn't he have a clue?

Dan turned his head and looked at me. Wizard or no wizard, he was going to get it with both barrels.

"What's so damn wrong about being a wizard?" I asked.

He frowned at me.

"You're a wizard. That's what you are. Stop wishing you weren't and be yourself. Hell, if I can learn that lesson, so can you."

I turned and stomped away. Unfortunately, my grandmother was keeping pace.

"You really have to stop expending that much energy," she said. "Especially the emotional kind. You have no idea how that might be affecting your child."

We'd reached the elevators. I stopped an inch away from pushing the button and stared at her.

"What?"

"Do you deny you're with child, Marcie?" she asked softly.

She had the sweetest smile on her face and there wasn't the disapproval in her eyes that I'd seen before, the look that said she wished I'd been married first.

"Um."

That's me, queen of the quip, diva of dialogue.

"How do you know?" I finally managed to say.

"The witch test. I suspected then, but when you were able to command a vortex, I knew. A pregnant witch has incredible power. Does Dan know?"

Hell's bells, what did I say now?

The truth was going to have to suffice.

"I don't know if he's the father."

"Of course he is," she said easily, as if there was no doubt.

I think I needed to explain the birds and the bees to my grandmother. Or maybe she was trying to explain something to me.

"Can you sense that Dan's the father?" I asked.

"You need to go rest now," she said, and pushed the elevator button to the third floor.

Well, she evidently knew I was staying in Dan's room. What else did she know?

"Nonnie," I said, keeping my voice low as the elevator traveled upward, "this is really important. Is there a way to find out for sure?"

She drew back a little, studied me in the way she had when I was a child. I'd learned, early on, never to lie to Nonnie. She had a way of finding it out, seeing it on my face. Evidently, that's what she was doing right now.

I didn't look away or try to hide anything from her all-seeing eyes.

"No, Marcie, there isn't. I know of no spells or incantations that would serve your purpose. Nature will as nature will."

Okay, then.

At Dan's door, she pulled me down to kiss my cheek.

"You will be fine, my dear girl."

"I'm sorry," I said.

Her brow furled with her frown. "About what?"

"My mother."

She smiled, a little sadly, I thought. "She was always going to go her own way, that one. I'm not all that surprised she became a vampire. You were the one who surprised me. But you're not one anymore, are you?"

"I'm not sure what I am," I said.

"You're a worthy mate for a wizard." She patted my cheek. "A very powerful wizard. What a pair you'll make."

I stared at her, surprised.

She patted my cheek once more, smiled enigmatically, and turned and left me.

I entered the room, veered into the sitting room and flopped down on the chaise. Within seconds, I was asleep.

I dreamed that I was being carried across the land to a soothing, far off place perfumed with sandalwood and spices. In my dream, I thought it must be a sheik who bore me along on his camel. We rode over the sands, until it became so hot that my sheik stripped me of my clothes one by one, then tucked me up into his bed.

Turning to him, I murmured a question I always wanted to know about a sheik. How did he stop all that sand from getting into uncomfortable places?

His chuckle made me smile and wiggle down into my dream, holding his hand between my breasts.

Despite everything that had happened today or for the past week, I was suddenly happier than I'd ever been.

Until I woke up.

I was being seduced, expertly, sweetly, softly. I was awakened with Dan's mouth on mine, his kiss curling my toes.

"I'm mad at you," I whispered against his lips.

"I'm not mad at you."

"That's very obvious."

He pressed against me, showing just how mad he wasn't.

I'd never had a conversation while I was being seduced, but I found it strangely arousing.

"Why are you mad at me?"

"That's a ridiculous question," I said rather breathlessly, because he was doing very interesting things with his fingers.

"I never assume. If I assumed, I might be wrong. What have I done?"

Really, he was making it almost impossible to talk.

"You didn't want to be made a wizard again."

Speaking of being a wizard, I could swear there was a charge coming off his fingers. At least it felt that way.

"No. I just wanted a choice in the matter."

"We didn't have the luxury of waiting," I said. I had to say it twice because I lost my thoughts in the middle of the sentence. "The vampires had you."

He lowered himself over me and for several minutes we didn't say anything but one syllable words.

"You were worried about me," he said, some time later, kissing my neck.

"Perhaps a little," I admitted.

"I was a little worried about myself," he said. "Until I saw you in the vortex."

I framed his face with my hands.

"You saw me?"

He nodded and bent to kiss me again. "Marry me."

"What?"

Of all the things he might have said, that was totally unexpected.

"You saved me. In some cultures that means you own my life."

"Is that the only reason?" I asked.

He'd just made love to me, sweetly and deliciously, but I wanted hearts and flowers and romance.

"I like being around you," he said, moving to my side and pulling me to face him. "I like who I am when I'm with you."

"A manly man," I said, smiling at him.

"Better than I am without you." He wasn't smiling.

He brushed the hair away from my cheek.

Something occurred to me and I stared at him.

"Is that why you wanted to talk to my mother?" I asked. It was something he would do, something a little old fashioned and very Dan-like. "You wanted to ask her permission?"

He looked up at the ceiling, anywhere but at me. A good thing, too, because it gave me a chance to brush away that silly tear.

A moment later he kissed the corner of my eye.

"I want to share my life with you, Marcie Montgomery. I want to share my dreams. I want to laugh, fight, confide in you."

"I'm too sweet to fight with," I lied. "I know a number of men who would tell you."

He kissed me on the nose. Thanks to my grandmother it no longer hurt and the swelling had gone down.

"Marry me, Marcie. I have a castle I'll give you."

"I don't want your castle," I said.

"Then what do you want?"

I smiled at the corniness of what I was about to say. Sometimes, the best emotions are contained in the most clichéd expressions.

"Your heart," I said. "If I'm in love with you, it seems to me it's only fair for you to feel the same."

"You love me?"

I sighed heavily. "Yes, you idiot wizard, I love you."

"Good. I love you, too."

I couldn't say anything for a few minutes because I was being kissed into submission.

When he was done and I lay there quivering, he smiled down at me.

The room was colored in rose light. Masses of roses and honeysuckle and lilacs were clustered around the room. He made a gesture with one arm and the massive bed levitated, rocking back and forth gently in the air.

Living with a wizard might prove to be very, very interesting.

CHAPTER THIRTY-TWO

I have a secret and one I have to tell you

I was due to be married in an hour, but I was one pissed puppy. Hardly the image of a smiling bride. Only a week had passed between being asked and the ceremony, but that's not why I was irritated.

First of all, there was the red haired witch who wasn't a real witch. I was not going to hint to Dan that I would be a happier bride if he got rid of Diane Trenton. I was not that petty. I would rise above. I would not indulge in small minded pursuits. I would ignore her. If she decided to take another job, or hook someone into matrimony, I would be the happiest of creatures for her. I'd even arrange to give her a humongous going away gift.

Anything but have to deal with the woman again.

She was angry at me because I hadn't acted on her intel. Her word, not mine.

Yes, I'd set her to watching the surveillance footage in the castle. Yes, she was to be congratulated for catching the woman entering Dan's office Wednesday night. Yes, she was also to be praised for using Dan's facial recognition program and correctly identifying the mystery woman as my mother.

I truly appreciated the fact that Diane had texted me what she found, then followed up with a voice mail. She didn't know that Janet hadn't given me back my stuff and I was using my old pre-castle phone. Nor did I bother pointing out to her that I'd called her. All she had to do was use that number, but she hadn't.

Janet had finally returned my phone, my Kindle, and my brush. Well, not exactly. She'd had one of the castle employees deliver them in a box. No note of apology. I swallowed my irritation and kept saying, "Ohmmmmm," until it worked, a little.

Trenton and Janet weren't the only source of my annoyance. Opie still wasn't talking. She hadn't said a word since the night at the MEDOC warehouse. I don't know what I did to irritate her, but she was also giving Kenisha the silent treatment. Not that Kenisha noticed. She was so involved with Mike that she didn't see anything or anyone else.

Dan had given her an apartment next to Mike's. I had the idea that we were probably going to have to tear down the common wall in a few weeks and just make it one big apartment for the two of them.

The phone rang, and I pulled it out of my pocket. Please don't let it be Nonnie saying she couldn't attend. But it wasn't Nonnie. I listened to the recording from the jail, pushed the button to accept the collect call, and waited for my mother to say something.

Demi was in a special unit since she'd been turned. She was allowed exercise after midnight and kept in a shielded cell during the day. I couldn't wait to hear what she had to say. Would it be along the lines of: sorry I tried to kill you - again? I doubted it.

"Marcie! It's your wedding day! I'm so happy for you!"

I was a little taken aback. My mother had never been happy for me. In fact, I don't think she'd ever said those words to me, even when I graduated from college.

"Are you?"

"I am. You deserve someone hunky like Dan."

"I do?"

"Yes, yes, you do. Besides, he's the baby daddy, I just know it."

I didn't say anything for a minute, maybe two. I had to clear my throat before I did.

"Opie?" I asked, very carefully.

"Yes! You're so smart. It's me."

"You're haunting my mother?" I asked.

"I seem to be. It took me a day or two to work it out. This is really rude, Marcie, but I have to say, your mother is not a happy woman. I let her out from time to time, but the woman is a pill. Of course, it's a paradox, don't you think? I mean, she killed me, and here I am, haunting her. Maybe it's divine justice."

I swear, I couldn't think of a damn thing to say.

"Otherwise, I'm in seventh heaven, Marcie. You can't imagine what it's like after being on all fours for weeks and weeks. But I miss you. And K-girl."

"I've been worried about you," I said, which was the truth.

"Just think of the ramifications! I've been mulling it over. I realized I don't have to be a vampire to be immortal. In fact, I'm giving some thought to transferring to a different body now that I know I can. Who wants to spend years in jail? I need to talk to your grandmother because I think that's how it happened this time."

The night at the warehouse had been chaotic. Maybe Nonnie had been saying a spell that overlapped with Janet's. What had William been doing in the parking lot? Had he been throwing spells, too?

Just when I think the world had stabilized a little, another layer of weird was added.

"How did you know?" I asked. "About my wedding day?"

"It's all over the news. Evidently, Dan is quite a catch."

Oh, goody. Maddock would know. The beep on the phone was a signal that the collect call time had run out.

"Can I call you back?" Opie asked.

"Yes," I said. "And I'll come and visit, if you like." Although I wasn't all that eager to tell Kenisha that her best bud was in jail.

"Would you? Oh, that would be wonderful. Happy wedding day!"

I hung up the phone, staring out at the horizon as night bullied day into vanishing. The wedding was timed so that Kenisha could be in attendance with Mike as her escort. Soon I would have to go and put on the wedding gown Janet insisted I wear, a frothy garment specially blessed by a couple of covens with health, wealth, and happiness spells. I didn't need spells, but in the interest of family accord, I'd shut up and accepted the dress.

The internecine war that so worried Dan looked as if it might be in abeyance at least for a while. The Brethren that we'd met with had agreed to support us, plus we had the witches on our side. It turned out that Maddock wasn't as popular as Maddock thought he was. He'd burned a lot of bridges over the years. But the one thing that might save us was Mike. Or what had happened to Mike.

Mike was eating regular food, which was an answer to what he was. In fact, I teased him from time to time about being a goddess. He just frowned at me in that intimidating way of his and didn't say a word. He kept vampire hours which was fine with Dan since he needed someone he could trust on the graveyard shift, if you'll pardon the expression.

Mike and I might take turns giving a pint of blood away in a lottery scheme, but I hadn't had a chance to talk about the idea with either Mike or Dan. It would keep all the various entities off our backs and give them an incentive to keep us healthy and happy.

What we needed was a human volunteer, to see if he or she could become a Dirugu. The idea made me feel weird. I tabled it mentally for more thought and discussion.

Dan had turned the burglar over to the police, but he made a point of contacting the head of The Militia of God to let him know that he wouldn't welcome any further "visitors". Or, if they insisted on coming to the castle, they would be met with prejudice, Dan-speak for guns, cannons, knives, or medieval weapons of torture. Dan didn't say anything about the burglar having developed a severe case of *I can't remember diddly-itis*, to the extent the poor guy couldn't even recall his middle name. Whatever he'd learned on his expedition here had been lost. It was handy having a wizard around who could just point his finger and make something happen.

In a week we would meet with the second contingent of Brethren, Paul's relatives who were representatives for the werewolves. I wondered if Dan would use his power during that meeting. He'd already used his wizardly abilities to send out feelers for Nancy. She hadn't yet been found, but I think it was only a matter of time.

My stomach hadn't been upset for days and days, as if my child were content with everything. I wondered if it was also because he knew Dan was his father.

I still hadn't told Dan about the baby, but I couldn't go into marriage without saying something. Maybe a part of me was afraid that Maddock still was the father. Maybe I worried that Dan didn't want to be saddled with a child right away. Whatever the reason, I had to be honest with him.

I felt him as he walked down the corridor and up the stairs to the roof.

"You wanted to see me, Marcie?" he asked, coming to my side. "Isn't that considered unlucky on our wedding day?"

"I think we make our own luck," I said, smiling at him.

He stepped in front of me and extended his arms around my waist. Heat flashed through me. His smile did something to my heart. I looked into his eyes and felt myself tumbling head first into love again. He did that to me.

I wasn't prescient. I didn't think I could foretell the future and now was a weird time to suddenly know what I knew. This was our land. This was our kingdom. Dan would reign, not as the chicken king like his grandfather, but as the wizard who kept all the factions of the Brethren in their own bailiwick. No one segment, including the vampires, would rule over another. Neither the OTHER nor the human only organizations would gain a foothold. Instead, they would be kept in check by his wisdom and power.

Our children, as powerful as any ever born, would grow to adulthood in grace and peace.

I fervently hoped that what I felt was the future and not my own wishes.

"You haven't changed your mind, have you?" he asked, sliding his hands down my arms. I was instantly warm. Not because he was a wizard, but because he was Dan.

I shook my head. "No," I said.

The next few minutes would be critical. How would he take the news? Would he be happy? Excited? Stressed?

I reached up and put my hand on his cheek.

"I have a secret, Dan," I said. "A very important secret and one I need to tell you before we're married."

EPILOGUE

I'd been learning Were, a language I hadn't even known werewolves had, separate and apart from whatever they spoke in their human form. Gladys, a new resident of the castle, was my teacher and she'd impatiently informed me that most werewolves, unless they're very old or very talented, could not enunciate in their animal form. They'd devised a series of grunts, whistles, and back of the throat sounds to communicate.

Right at the moment, I was telling Dr. Fernandez what I thought of him in Were. He would have been insulted, but it made me feel better.

"Push, Marcie!"

"I am pushing," I said, the words accompanied by a few more Were oaths. "Trust me, I'm bloody well pushing!"

My son wasn't all that eager to emerge from his safe and warm home for the last nine months. I, on the other hand, was looking forward to being able to sleep without being pummeled from the inside, and walking more than four feet without having to go to the bathroom - again. Not to mention I was tired of being examined by Dr. Fernandez, who had taken an interest in vampire physiology and was determined to usher this first child of a vampire mother successfully into the world.

Dan was being a pain as well. Dan had been a pain since an hour before our wedding when I told him about the existence of our child. He hadn't stopped staring at me for hours, doing the sweep from my face to my nether regions and back. I could tell that he was mentally comparing my boob size now to what he remembered in the gun range. Let's talk luscious peach versus cantaloupe, shall we?

He had been overprotective to the point I'd finally gone to Janet and enlisted her help in convincing him that I was better than fine. I was gloriously healthy and ecstatic about being in love, being married, and being pregnant. Janet, who had decided that I was the gift who kept on giving, would have done anything for me at that point, and lectured Dan sternly. He'd relented a little by not following me around everywhere.

I surprised everyone by refusing to have him in the delivery room with me. Our sex life, up until a few months ago, was glorious.

I didn't want to freak him out by introducing him to the miracle of birth. He was with me up until the moment our son was imminent, and then I banished him to an outer room where Mike and his buddies promised to try to get him drunk.

Good luck with that. Being a wizard affected Dan's metabolism in a lot of odd ways. Neither of us were cheap dates anymore. It took gallons of bubbly to make me frisky. That's okay, I really didn't need an incentive around Dan.

Nonnie and Janet were in the next room as well. I could feel the power they exuded with their good fortune and perfect health spells.

Only Dr. Fernandez and I were in the delivery room and that was fine with me. I wanted to make sure my son wasn't fangy before anyone saw him.

"Just a few more pushes, Marcie."

Five minutes and several hundred Were swear words later, my darling son was plopped onto my stomach where he opened his beautiful green eyes and stared straight into mine.

Correction, please. Not a son, but a daughter.

How the hell had that happened?

When I'd had an ultrasound, I wanted to know about fangs more than appendages. Dr. Fernandez hadn't been all that familiar with where things were supposed to be, evidently. I told him our child was a boy and he hadn't quibbled with my diagnosis.

My daughter squinted up at me, then at the humming and glaring florescent lights. They sputtered and went out. I was one savvy goddess. I didn't need a brick to fall on me.

"Stop that," I said gently. "You're too young to do stuff like that."

She smiled at me.

We'd chosen the name for our son. Gordon, a family name and one that had no negative connotations. As I stared at my incredible daughter, her name occurred to me. Frankly, I didn't know if I'd come up with it, or she somehow sent the name to me mentally.

Antonia.

When I whispered it, she smiled again.

"You don't have fangs, do you, Antonia?"

She giggled, a sound that prompted Dr. Fernandez to pop up from between my legs and stare at her.

I had a feeling he was going to do a lot of that in the next few years. The staring, not the popping up from between my legs part.

I exchanged a smile with my daughter and couldn't wait to introduce Antonia to her father, the second most powerful wizard at Arthur's Folly.

Other books by Karen Ranney

For current information about new books: http://karenranney.com/

THE FURRY CHRONICLES
The Lottery - Furry

THE MACIAIN SERIES
In Your Wildest Scottish Dreams
Scotsman of My Dreams
An American in Scotland

THE MONTGOMERY CHRONICLES
The Fertile Vampire – Book 1
The Reluctant Goddess – Book 2
Pranic, Pregnant, and Petrified - Book 3

THE CLAN SINCLAIR SERIES
The Devil of Clan Sinclair
The Witch of Clan Sinclair
The Virgin of Clan Sinclair
Return to Clan Sinclair

THE SCOTTISH SISTERS
A Scandalous Scot
The Lass Wore Black

THE LOVED SERIES
My Beloved
My True Love

THE HIGHLAND LORDS
One Man's Love
When the Laird Returns
The Irresistible MacRae
To Love a Scottish Lord
So in Love

THE TULLOCH SGATHAN SERIES
Sold to a Laird
A Highland Duchess
A Borrowed Scot

STAND ALONE NOVELS (HISTORICAL)

NOVELS SET IN ENGLAND
Tapestry
Above All Others
My Wicked Fantasy
Upon a Wicked Time
After the Kiss

NOVELS SET IN SCOTLAND
A Promise of Love
Heaven Forbids
Till Next We Meet
An Unlikely Governess
Autumn in Scotland
The Scottish Companion
The Devil Wears Tartan
A Scotsman in Love
A Scottish Love

STAND ALONE CONTEMPORARY NOVELS
Murder by Mortgage
The Eyes of Love

What About Alice?

NOVELLAS AND SHORT STORIES
The Greatest Gift
A Dance in the Dark
Scottish Brides
Flash Fables
The Unmentionables

34667097R00126

Made in the USA
Middletown, DE
30 August 2016